# About Last Night

By

Mia Faye

# TABLE OF CONTENTS

# Copyright

# I. THE NIGHT

# Chapter 1

PENNY

"So, here's the plan," my sister said, teasing her hair under a layer of her bun to give it some more volume, "we go out, dance, and drink until you forget he-who-shall-not-be-named, and then you help get my ass to the train tomorrow when we're both hungover and hating life."

I sniffled, shoving my fork deeper into my plate of spaghetti. It had turned out wonderfully, despite being made over a riverbed of heartbroken tears and cheap red wine. Grandma would have been proud, and part of me was glad to be in a place of such comfort going through the awful events of this afternoon.

"I don't know if I'm up for it tonight," I said, slurping down another noodle. "There's barely anywhere to go in Abilene, anyway; there's only, like, two bars. I think only one has music, and it's line dancing. I'm definitely not up for line-dancing."

"You said two, right?" Grace grinned. "Sounds like there's a bar waiting just for us. Is it the old place on Decatur?"

I groaned, setting the plate down before walking over to my room to find something to wear in the massive piles of clothes I'd yet to put away. "Don't you want to just stay in and wallow with me?"

"No!" Grace said, following me in to help. "That jerk kept you off the market for three years, and I'm going to make sure he didn't ruin you on it."

I gave her an exasperated sigh, knowing when my sister got her mind set on something, there would be no getting out of it. "Fine, fine, I'll go," I huffed, digging in the piles and yanking out an orange maxi dress with some frills at the bottom where it met my ankle. It was a comfortable choice, and I always thought I looked cute in it. I forced myself to put out of my mind that Marcus found it cute on me too.

"I'll help you," my sister exclaimed, following me to keep digging. She tossed a few shirts and jeans aside and then found a dark blue mini-dress that came up to my mid-thigh. It had ruching on the torso, and the last time I wore it, I was twenty pounds lighter. "This one."

"Are you out of your mind?" I asked, picking up the dress and holding it up to myself in the mirror. "My tits spill out of it."

"That's exactly why you *should* wear it." Grace's hands went out to grab my boobs and push them up toward my chin, making me laugh. "Penny, no one's seen you since you were in high school. Why not greet them properly?" she said with a grin.

"As a slut?" I scoffed. "There's no way I can pull this dress off. I haven't worn it since college, and I haven't been to the gym in a year to keep my ass in shape."

"This dress will help with that." Grace smiled, and she shoved it into my chest. "Put it on. I promise you won't regret it."

I furrowed my brow and resigned to her request. The least I could do was try it on and see if it still fit.

And it did, albeit like a sausage casing. Granted, that was how it was designed, but it still didn't make me feel very comfortable.

When I stepped out to walk in front of the mirror, Grace's hand went to her gaping mouth. "That's the one; you're wearing that." She wrapped her arms around me in a raucous celebration and almost made my boobs pop out of the bodice. "Perfect."

7

My sister went with a pair of skinny jeans and a revealing tank top, which she paired with a huge and dramatic sweater with the lining covered in faux fur. Normally, as my younger sister, she would get the most attention. But now, the playing field might be a bit more even, and that terrified me.

As we got ready and left the house for the car we'd called, I felt anxious about the upcoming evening. My stomach began to twirl slightly, and my knee repeatedly bounced, annoying my sister.

"Calm down; you're going to do fine," she reassured me, and I took a deep breath to make it sink in.

"I know; I'm just nervous. I haven't been single in three years, Grace."

"Yeah, and you're going to do fine. It's like riding a bike, and sometimes, you get to ride other things in the process!" She gleamed.

The car pulled up to a quaint little bar with a lantern outside the door. It didn't look like there were more than ten people in there, so my anxiety dropped at the thought of fewer people to deal with than in a massive club. I remembered walking by this place every so often as a teenager, yearning for the day that I could get into a bar and drink as if that would make me feel like the adult I wanted to be. Back then, it seemed like all my problems would be fixed by being older than I was.

If only it were that easy.

"Let's get a drink in you, first of all," Grace said, leading the way for the two of us entering the bar. It was quieter than I thought it'd be, with just as few patrons as I'd thought. It was a Wednesday night, after all—not the most active of nights for bargoers. An older gentleman who looked like a regular perched at the back of the bar, two or three guys parked along it nursing various beers and cocktails. A couple sat at a booth in the back, clearly in the middle of much more than heavy petting. It was a dive, and I much preferred that to a party.

It didn't stop Grace from wanting to get me absolutely plastered, though, and I didn't mind the distraction with the state my heart had been in.

"What's this one, a rum and coke?" I asked, sipping it from the red straw and tasting the alcohol heavily layered at the bottom.

"No, the last one was a rum and coke. This is a Cuba Libre. It took me three tries to explain the difference to the bartender, though, even with just the lime and bitters. The first one was supposed to be a Cuba Libre too."

I didn't question it and took a big slurp, hearing the ice swirl at the bottom when it was through.

"Damn, sis, I forgot how easily you can put it away," Grace said as she took the empty glass and set it back down on the bar.

"Easily isn't the word," I said with a cough, struggling to fight the alcohol taste, as delicious as the drink was.

"Seems like you might need a refill," a voice from behind me said, and I saw one of the men from down the bar approach. Facing both of us, my sister gave me the subtlest "holy shit" expression she could manage and turned around to give me and the stranger space.

I reached out to grab her arm and keep her next to me; my brows raised and eyes wide, but she slipped out of my fingers. Without her to distract me, I turned, unable to avoid my new friend.

"I guess I might. I'm in need of strong drinks tonight," I said, and only then did I bring my eyes up to look at the man I was talking to.

I had never seen someone so strikingly attractive in my life.

He had a light beard that came up into dark brown hair slicked back a little, but not enough to appear firm. He was older than me, maybe in his thirties, and he was wearing a thick black peacoat and a deep blue scarf that brought out the blue in his eyes. They twinkled when they looked at me, and I suddenly felt like I was standing naked in front of him.

In this dress, that was half-true.

"What are you drinking?" he asked. "My treat." He was confident in a way that drew me in, but not so much that he appeared egotistical.

"Can I get your name if you're buying me drinks?" I asked.

He smiled. "It's Owen. And you are?"

"Blair," I said too fast as I took a sip, going much slower in drinking this time. I used to have a fantasy of a strange man approaching me in the bar, and in all those fantasies, I'd used my middle name. Granted, it came from a place of wanting to protect myself from strangers, but now it just added to the excitement, and I couldn't take it back once it was out. "Are you from around here?"

"That I am. I don't think I remember seeing you around," he said, sipping his cocktail.

"I grew up here, but I haven't been back in a while. My sister's helping me move back in."

"That would make sense. I've been here about four years, so we probably missed each other."

"I'm glad we didn't miss each other this time," I said, and I had no idea where the confidence for it had bubbled up.

He asked about where I was from, and when I mentioned New York, we traded stories back and forth about the life there. He'd visited a few times, and it was nice talking to someone who knew the area and would understand references.

Once I finished that drink, I went to order my own fourth one, and my head started feeling the fuzziness I was yearning for in a night of emotional numbing. I hadn't thought about Marcus all night, and I wasn't about to start now. After another drink, bought by Owen, I couldn't remember Marcus's name at all. My sister came by to check in once, but she seemed to have found her rhythm with a guy of her own down the bar, so once she saw I wasn't being coerced and actually had leaned into meeting someone new, she slipped off again.

"Your friend seems to be having a fun night," Owen said, nodding over to Grace, whose hand was currently resting on the ass of a guy she was talking to along the bar.

"My little sister. She's always been good at the bar scene. She's only twenty-one, so I try not to think about how she's managed to practice." I laughed. "It was her idea to get me to come out tonight," I said, and my words ended in more of a drunken slur than I thought they would upon letting them fall from my mouth.

"Well, I'm glad she did. I've had such a great time talking with you." His words came out a bit fumbled too. I was glad we were at the same level of drunk.

"Me too," I said, and as I smiled, my phone buzzed. My hands slipped a little when I pulled it from my pocket, and when I saw Marcus's face light up on the screen, I almost threw the phone out the window.

"You sound like a big fan of whoever that is," Owen said with a laugh, and he slipped his hand behind me on the bar, drawing me in closer as he leaned in.

"He's the reason I wanted to come out tonight. I need to forget about him," I said, exasperated and trying not to let the call ruin my buzz. I turned and took my drink, either my sixth or seventh and sipped it down forcefully.

Before I knew what hit me, Owen's lips came down to meet my ear as his hand caressed the small of my back under the bar table.

"Let me help you."

The many drinks mixed with the allowance of knowing he was okay being a numbing agent for me was the only green light I needed. I stared at him for a moment, considering my options, then pressed my lips to his.

He was surprised but immediately went with my actions and kissed me back, taking a second to suck on my bottom lip before squeezing my waist and lightly pressing me against the bar. I felt so small in his hands, and I wanted those hands all over me.

Without a second to think about the consequences, I looked over his shoulder to the bathroom. "Come with me," I said and slipped out of his grip before he knew what I was doing.

I didn't look back as I strode off, but I knew he was following me out when I felt fingers on the lip of my dress where it rode up under my ass. It made me shiver, and I made sure the coast was clear in the women's bathroom before I pulled him in with me. He seemed shocked at my brazen behavior, but I wasn't about to look a gift horse in the mouth and stop.

I locked the door behind him to ensure us a moment of privacy, then wrapped my arms around his neck and pulled him down to kiss me again, deeper. My mouth opened, and our tongues swirled against one another's, needing to feel closer with every touch. His hands found my waist and squeezed firmly at my love handles as I backed up toward the sink. My skirt rode up my thighs when he pressed his knee between them, then he placed his palms under my legs and hoisted me against his groin, sitting me up on the counter.

My panties were made of a thin fabric that hugged my cheeks, but I knew they were already soaking through at the unexpected and adventurous turn of events. I'd never done anything like this before, but if there was any night to live on the edge, it was tonight.

To my shock, a small tray of condoms sat in the far corner of the sink counter, and I chortled as I reached for one. "Really?" I asked, shaking my head. Now I was glad I'd never tried to sneak in here when I was younger.

Owen laughed, taking the condom from my fingers. "Dave knows who his customers are."

"I feel less bad about this then." I grinned, nodding as he looked down at the condom I'd handed him. "Is this okay?"

Owen nodded firmly, looking more boyish and innocent under bathroom fluorescents than he had in the dim bar lighting. "God, yes. I just ... this isn't something ... I've never—" he muttered, but I cut him off.

"I'm not normally like this either, but ..." I looked down at him once he'd unzipped his pants and revealed the bulge in his briefs. "I want this. I want you right now."

He loved that, and he pushed his underwear down the rest of the way to roll the condom on. He did it mostly with one hand by some miracle, once he had it on the tip. With the other, his fingers found the line of my panties under my dress, and he teased my lips beneath them.

I was surprised he didn't just jump to shoving himself inside me, but I loved the feeling of his hands so much that I didn't protest. He noticed my squirming and held me down with one side once the condom was on. I watched him grin as he pulled the panties to the side

13

and slid a finger past my entrance, lightly painting me with a layer of my own wetness.

Then he pulled out his finger and licked it.

"Fuck," I whispered, and he was inside me without another word.

He was bigger than Marcus had been, and it took a second to adjust. He felt me tense up and went slower until I wrapped my legs around his waist as he thrust into me again, making us both moan in delight.

His fingers slid down to my behind, and he pulled me closer to him, spreading me wide. He rocked back and forth, and I met the rhythm as I felt the churning of ecstasy burning in my stomach. My eyes closed in delight, but when he started teasing my clit with his thumb as he fucked me, it was only another few minutes before I started unraveling.

I howled as I came around him, squeezing tight as the orgasm rifled through me. The feeling of me tightening and twitching around him made him thrust faster until he, too, was climbing his edge. I was still floating from pleasure when he shot through me, surely filling the condom deeply as he came.

"God," he huffed, holding me tight to ensure we wouldn't fall from our precarious position.

"That was—" I started, lowering my legs from his waist to sit back on the counter. "Oh my God," was all I could get out.

"Yeah," he agreed, panting as he reached down to pull up his briefs and slacks. His hands fumbled with the buckle of his belt, and a part of me was prided knowing sex with me made this incredible man unable to fasten a belt.

His eyes found mine once he was fixed up, and he pressed a palm to my face, kissing me again. Despite being in total silence, it was a small moment of deep intimacy, and I relished it.

Breaking the silence, someone slammed their fist on the door, yelling from the other side. "Can whoever is in there get a room or an alley or something? I have to pee, and the guy's room smells like bourbon and vomit!"

I immediately recognized Grace's voice, and I slammed back down into reality. "Shit, that's my sister. Hold on." I left Owen standing there, still in the post-sex haze, and unlocked the door just a peek to greet my stunned sister. I also saw a hickey on her neck, so I knew the night had treated her well too.

"Oh my God?" Her drunk and pink face went from furious about needing the bathroom to prideful delight for me. "Holy shit, you little minx! Good for you!" she said with a squeal. "I still have to pee, so y'all better skedaddle, but hell yes! I'll give you a second; then I need this place clear." She winked, slipping away to give us some space.

"Coast is clear," I said back to Owen, nodding toward the bar with a smile.

He followed me out, shuffling his feet like a kid who had been caught peeking at presents by Santa. "Can I get you another drink or something," he asked, and I knew he had no context for how this kind of thing was supposed to go.

It was kind of adorable, and it made me grin.

"No, but I'll give you my number, and you can buy us a car home if you really want to."

He seemed surprised by my brash request but took it, nonetheless, pulling up an Uber. It was amazing how much you could get away with corrupting an innocent stranger in a bar.

15

"Move it!" Grace said, shoving her body through us and to the bathroom. "John Doe got handsy, so I'm peeing, and we're out!"

Owen and I stood, looking at each other after hearing my sister's shouting, and we laughed. "You heard the woman," I said, nodding to his phone. I grabbed a napkin and pen from the bar, scribbling down my number. "Get on it, Casanova."

# II. THE DAY BEFORE

# Chapter 2

OWEN

"Dad, we're gonna be late!"

Lilly raced down the hallway leading to their kitchen; her backpack was already slung over one shoulder. She was munching on a Pop-Tart, and she had a few sprinkles hanging from the side of her lip.

"Did you brush your teeth?" I asked, pulling my coat on and slinging my business bag over my shoulder. Bringing my wrist up, I checked the time and saw it was already nine, meaning we'd be lucky to get Lilly into class before sitting down for warm-ups. "Never mind, we don't have time. Just go get in the car."

"Okay, I'm putting on Hannah Montana!" she hollered as she ran out the door, leaving it swinging open behind her.

I followed her out, pulling the door behind me and checking to make sure the lock engaged. Once I made it out to the car, she was already buckled in, keys in the ignition, and bopping her head to some song she'd played a hundred times. After a while, it drove me insane, but I just didn't have the capacity to worry about it this morning.

"When did you grab my keys, you little weasel?" I asked with a chuckle, buckling up and ensuring she was too.

"I left the door open for you; what's the big deal?"

Her tone was sassier than I was used to, and it made me double back to her when I pulled out of the driveway. "Watch it; you're not going to talk to me like you're in high school just yet."

Lilly snorted, shoving her head back and rolling her eyes as far as they would go. She was lucky I didn't have time to deal with her attitude today.

When we arrived at her music class, we could see through the window that all the students were already in their assigned seats and tuning their instruments. One chair in front of a keyboard remained empty, and Lilly yanked open the door the minute we pulled up and dashed inside.

"Lil!" I shout-whispered, not wanting her to disrupt the beginning of class. But with Lilly, there was no holding back.

I stood in the doorway as all the other students peered over at her, the girl late to class again. I chided myself for not getting us out the door faster, but I was finishing some last-minute paperwork for Lorenzo last night and ended up awake well past three in the morning. It nearly took a bulldozer to wake me up, but instead, Lilly's music blasting at full volume did the trick.

Once she was inside and I'd taken the slightly dirty look from her instructor, I moved out to the waiting room to sit with the other parents and do some work on my phone. The minutes ticked by, and I swiped through file after file, annotating where the wording in contracts could be adjusted to avoid loopholes and signing on dotted lines where required.

On the chairs around me sat about five or six mothers from around town. Some of the moms—because no other dads brought their children to class—knew me, but they'd stopped trying to talk to me a few sessions back. Something about being a single dad made them think I had time for socializing, but when my eyes stayed glued to my phone, they kept their hands to themselves. A few did, however, look over more than once while crossing their legs seductively. I didn't look up, but they didn't go unnoticed.

Approximately seventeen emails later, I looked up at the kids piling out of the music class. They all dashed to their mothers, hugging them around the waists and telling them how much they enjoyed the class. I kept a lookout as I stood, and Lilly came stomping out, her head never lifting once. She didn't say a word to me before going out to the car.

"Lilly?" I asked, going after her for a moment. I stopped and turned back to the classroom, catching the door as the last student exited. "Did something happen with my daughter today?" I asked her teacher, who was collecting sheet music from all the stands around the room. She was a tall and lanky woman, so she met my eye line, leaving me surprisingly intimidated.

"You're Lilly's father, right?" she asked, clapping the papers together and setting them on her desk. "Yes, I wanted to speak to you about some of her behavior in class."

"Behavior?"

"Yes," she started with a sigh. "Lilly is constantly ignoring instructions, playing on her own while we're supposed to be working on assigned pieces."

"Sounds like she's talented and creative on her piano," I said, defending her.

Her teacher furrowed her brows and pursed her lips. "Perhaps. But she lacks the discipline needed to play classical piano, which is what I train in this class. She also is constantly talking back to the point that it's disruptive for the other students. Today other students complained about her balling up the paper and throwing it at them. I think it might be a decent idea to find another class for her, or maybe a private tutor."

I was somewhat shocked, though I'd heard this story before. "Another class? Ms. Garnum—"

"It's Mrs. Garnum," she corrected, her voice curt as her glance turned to a slight glare.

"Mrs. Garnum," I said, "please. This is the third class she will have been removed from. She's just ... she struggles to focus sometimes, but that's no reason to kick her out."

"It sounds like she has a pattern then. Maybe you ought to look at how you discipline your child to ensure she won't have this problem in the future." She turned from me, returning to sorting the papers on her desk as if she couldn't be bothered to finish the conversation.

I scoffed. "Oh, really?" I shook my head, walking over to Lilly's spot in class to collect her piano and chair. "I think I know how to raise my daughter. I'll be sure to let everyone know about the kind of class you're teaching here, *Miss.*" I nearly hissed her incorrect prefix, making her burn eyes through my back when I left the room.

The other moms must have heard the altercation because what was once a light chatter out in the hall and waiting room became total silence. Their eyes watched me as I fumbled to get Lilly's keyboard out the door without running it into the doorjamb.

Once out at the car, I opened the trunk and put her keyboard in. She didn't even turn her head in the back seat. Instead of the normal Hannah Montana or Frozen soundtrack, the car was practically echoing with quiet tension instead.

"So," I asked, getting in and buckling up before putting the car in reverse. "I talked to your teacher."

21

"I know." Still, no looking up.

"She says you can't come back to class because you're being disruptive. Is that true?"

From where I watched her in the mirror as we drove off, Lilly's face turned cold. "I just didn't want to play her music. It's boring, and the other kids in class don't like me."

I sighed. "There's always going to be other people who don't like you, Lil. But that doesn't give you a justification to disrupt the class. And she's teaching you that music so you can build a foundation in your piano."

"Well, it's stupid, and I don't want to do it anymore!" Lilly yelled and crossed her arms over her chest.

"Don't shout at me like that, young lady!"

"Why not? You shouted at me!" she retorted just as loudly.

I pulled the car over onto a small mall parking lot and sighed, turning around in my seat to face her. "I'm sorry for yelling at you, kiddo."

She didn't say anything in response, so I let my stare dig into her until I took her little hand in mine.

"I'm sorry," I said, giving her hand a light squeeze. "Anything you want to say too?"

Lilly was quiet for a moment, and then she brought her head up to me again. "I'm sorry." She squeezed my fingers back.

"Now, how about we go get some lunch, and then we can see about getting you over to Darlene's house." I turned back around, putting the car in drive.

Lilly grumbled and squirmed in her seat. "Darlene's house always smells like cat pee."

"That's because her cats pee everywhere," I said, making my daughter laugh. "How about some McDonald's, huh?"

"And an ice cream cone?" she asked, her eyes wide and hopeful.

"You bet."

# Chapter 3

PENNY

"What does this even mean?" I asked, shoving my phone in my sister's face.

Her head raised from the cardboard box it was currently shoved in, now slightly covered in dust, and she looked at the text my boyfriend of three years had sent. "What the hell?"

"I know; all I asked is what he's doing right now because I'm curious, and he accuses me of being paranoid and helicoptering?" I scoffed, rereading it multiple times before shoving my phone in my back pocket. An unfortunate downfall of the fashion industry has been the depth of phone pockets decreasing in women's jeans.

"Sounds like he's projecting," Grace said, returning her focus to the box. She reached down and found an old dish we both recognized, and she smiled. "I'm shocked this is still here."

I walked over, picked up the dish, and let my fingers run over the smooth delicateness of its surface. I had painted it in my first-grade art class and given it to our grandmother as a birthday gift. It was supposed to be an image of a heart but ended up looking more like a rear end, which both she and my sister found hilarious. It had remained on the wall until Grandma had painted them a few years back, and the painters had chuckled, packing it away.

Without her being here to share our laughter of the plate, it somehow felt colder in my hands.

"I miss her," I said and wiped the dust from it with the towels. I then set it up on the table in the corner, a proud badge of honor in this house. "I can't believe this place is mine now. It doesn't feel right without her."

My eyes took in the space I grew up in so many years ago, and I felt them well with tears. Our grandparents had raised the two of us here in Abilene before we went off to school, and Grandpa died not long after Mom and Dad. Grandma was all we had in the world for a long time, and when I was old enough, I had helped raise Grace with her. The memories of finding who we were with the support of the incredible woman who gave me this house came flooding through me, and I couldn't stop them from taking me over.

Hearing a sniffle approach, my sister stood to embrace me, squeezing me tight in her arms. "I know, Penny. I miss her too. But she loved you, and she'd want you to be happy with this house. I think moving out here is just what you need."

"What about Marcus?" I asked, rubbing my nose on the edge of my shirt sleeve.

"Honestly, I think you should have dropped him when you left." At the Devil's call, my phone rang, and Marcus's face lit up the screen. "Why are you still with that guy?" she asked. "Want a beer?"

I nodded and took a deep sigh as I typed out a message in response. I just wanted him to know that I missed him but was busy cleaning and couldn't talk. Grace passed one to me, and I opened it, taking a solid sip before setting it on the mantle and turning to the big bin full of cleaning supplies. I grabbed the paper towels and spray and said, "It's complicated."

"Sure, it is." I could feel her eyes rolling, so I reached out and smacked her with a roll. "What?" She laughed. "Sis, I'm sorry, it's just so plainly obvious how sucky this guy is. How long are you going to keep holding out a candle for him?"

"He's a good guy; he just ..."

"He sucks."

"Would you stop?" I asked, and then I cleaned a spot where grime had accumulated around the kitchen. It was relatively small, but it would work fine for living here alone. "We've been together for a long time; we just need to adjust to the long-distance thing." When Marcus and I were together, any issues we had disappeared, and he understood me on a level very few people did. My sister had never been able to understand it, but I knew she was just coming from a place of wanting me to be happy. But her way to happiness was different from mine.

"Okay," Grace said, wanting to dismiss the conversation, though I knew it would come up again soon. "Did you already install the internet and phone and everything?" Her subject change was less than subtle.

I took another sip of my beer and nodded. "Yeah, and there's a guy coming in to repair the AC on Friday, which is frustrating. A lot of money coming out before I find a job out here."

"It's January; you probably won't be using it much." Grace emptied the box of wrapping paper and excess dust and folded it down for the recycling pile. "How's the savings looking?"

"I've been smart with it, so I don't have to worry too hard for a little while, but I would rather get something going. I don't want to start skating on it now," I said, and part of me wished it had been under my breath.

My sister caught the comment. "I'm only taking a year off."

"Just make sure you know how to take care of the inheritance, okay? And that you can budget it. Mom and Dad gave you a lot, but it can disappear fast if you're not careful," I warned.

"Penny, I got my camera on sale, and I live with three roommates; please don't start big-sistering me now." I could tell she was getting irritated with me, and with how willing she'd been to come out and help me move, I didn't want to push her further.

"I'm not big-sistering you; I just don't want you to lose track, okay? But I trust you; do what you have to do."

"Oh my God, I didn't know she still had this," she said, disregarding the emotional sentiment I'd just made.

I turned to look at what she'd found and saw the first photo my sister had ever submitted to be published. It was the town newspaper's "Local Artists" section, and they'd included a photo my sister took of the horizon on the town square. It was a beautiful landscape, and it was no surprise Grandma had kept it.

"She was so proud of you, Grace. And so am I." I wrapped my arm around her shoulders and kissed the side of her head.

Doing this alone would have been impossible. But at least with my sister here, the memories could shine for a moment before they turned sad.

"What else is in that pile?" I asked, seeing the many photos filling a cardboard box, haphazardly shuffled around and in various states of fading. She loved keeping photos but could never find the energy to put them in albums. That would be an upcoming project of mine.

"Look," she said, and she pulled out a few Polaroids of Grandma sitting next to me as a young girl, placing my fingers on the keys of her old piano. The film was slightly yellowed, but it was still as clear in my head.

"She taught me how to play on that piano," I said, taking the photos from Grace and flipping through them.

"The first of many annoying years." Grace laughed. "You would be on that thing for hours."

I brought the photos with me and turned the corner into the dining room, where the dusty piano was stored. It had worn a cover for many years, so I did it the favor of pulling it free. The ivories breathed, and the wood slightly glistened, even in its old age. The stool had broken a long time ago, and with the small space at hand, Grandma hadn't bothered replacing it when her joint pain had kicked in, and there was no one around to play it. Instead, I pulled over the chair from the dining table, and though I sat slightly high for comfort, I laid my fingers on the keys.

When I pressed down on a C chord, the notes bent and ached out of years of being out of tune. My sister laughed from the other room.

"Sounds like it needs a tune-up. Did she ever clean that?" she shouted over to me.

"Probably not, knowing her," I replied. "Yeah, I will have to get someone out here to repair this, but it still works."

Running my hands over the piano keys, thoughts of days spent here with my grandmother at my side sank into my heart. It had been a hobby of mine I could practice while visiting from school since I didn't have a piano in my dorm room. It had been a few years since I'd played, but it was one of those things you don't forget, not with the way I'd thrown myself into music as a child. It had helped me survive the death of our parents when I was old enough to process it and had done the same after Grandpa died. Music was the constant, and my life had been lacking in it for a while.

"Do you think there're  a lot of kids around town nowadays?" I asked out to Grace, cogs turning in my head.

"Yeah, probably. There are more every year with the young couples that come through and want to start families out here. Why?"

"I was thinking of teaching music," I said, running my hands along the wood of the back bar of the instrument. "To kids, like for tutoring. Probably some adults too, but that way, I could keep teaching.

"I'd been working on a teaching credential back in New York, but I would have to go through the school district. But what if I teach out of here?" I stood, rounding the corner again to see Grace turning to meet me, still squatting on the floor unpacking. "I could fix the place up, make it like a home office for teaching piano."

Grace stood and put a hand on her hip. "You could, yeah. You'd probably make more as a teacher at a school, but if you can afford not to have to deal with all that nonsense, I'd say do it."

"I could afford it if I started soon and kept a few clients coming in regularly. I'm not paying rent, and I don't exactly live a life of luxury," I scoffed, looking around. "With what I have saved, it would be something just to keep adding to what I've got." It felt too good to be true when talking like this, but I also knew it would depend on who I could find that would want consistent lessons.

"It sounds like the plan is making itself, Pen," Grace said with a smile as she hugged me close. "I have faith in you. You can do this. Grandma knew you could; that's why she left you the house."

"I'm also the oldest of only two grandkids."

"Which means you better let me crash here whenever I want because that's what she would have wanted," she said with a grin, and her playful nature of finding the silver lining in the darkest night got me smiling with her.

"As long as you're back at school by next year. Got it?" I said, squeezing her hand.

"Got it," Grace agreed, and I knew even she recognized the privilege of having a free ride to college from Mom and Dad. She'd taken time off to pursue photography but had always planned on going back.

"Good, now let's move this couch because you'll need somewhere for all that crashing," I said and laughed.

# Chapter 4

OWEN

"Owen, how are you, you old son of a bitch?"

I shook David Adler's hand, firmly grasping it as I gave him an award-winning smile. "Mr. Adler, I'm doing all right; how are you? It's been a while since we've had you in the office, hasn't it?"

"That it has! You're just about the spitting image of your old man." That comment sat coldly within me, but I let it go. "And Lorenzo, isn't it?" He turned to my business partner, offering him a shake, as well.

Lorenzo slipped his phone back into his pocket to accept the handshake, and then he raised his hand in the air to summon the intern. "It's a pleasure, Mr. Adler. Can we get you anything, water, coffee?" The intern walked over, a young man with a pen shoved behind his ear and eyes hopeful for a raise that would never come.

"Offer me a Manhattan, but other than that, I'm fine with water. Thank you," he said with a chuckle.

The intern nodded and walked out, returning with a few glasses and a jug of water for the table. He exited without another word. A well-trained worker bee.

"Come on in, and we can chat, Mr. Adler." Lorenzo led Adler and me into the conference room, giving a word or two to the receptionist, Anne, at the front to hold calls until the end of the meeting. "I have to ask," Lorenzo continued, "are you the same Mr. Adler as Adler Tree Company?"

The question took me by surprise, but Mr. Adler laughed. "Yes, that was my older brother's company. He had me come in sometimes and handle estate business for him. Why do you ask?"

Lorenzo gave his charming smile, applying one of the first rules of establishing a good client relationship—find something to bond over outside of your work, and create a friendship. He was exceptional at making himself look appealing to those that paid for his time. "When I was younger, my family went to the tree farm to chop our Christmas trees each year. I take my nieces there now and help chop theirs. I recognized the name, and it brought back such good memories that I just had to ask."

A-plus, Mr. Jamison.

"I'll take that as a fabulous sign for our partnership, Lorenzo!" Mr. Adler said and then stepped toward the conference table and took a seat. "So, gentlemen, since last we spoke, the team over at Adler Real Estate has made plans for renovations in the downtown Abilene area to break down some of the smaller buildings and lots. We're trying to get a mall in there, and we think Tate Legal is the perfect firm to partner with and make it happen," he said, taking a sip from his water.

"I think that's an amazing idea, Mr. Adler," Lorenzo replied, already one to kiss the behind of anyone he could manage. "I think I speak for both of us when I say that we would be delighted to sign on with you. We have to clear any decisions like this by Mr. Tate, as you might remember."

"Of course." Mr. Adler nodded, remembering our owner. "How's he been doing?"

"Fine, last we spoke a few days back, he was relaxed as ever. I'm sure he'll be just as on board as we are to make this project happen," Lorenzo said, far too confident for my taste.

I jumped in, throwing a hand toward Lorenzo next to me. "Well, I think there are a few things we can discuss first, like logistics."

"Those always take some adjusting, but logistics are easy to handle," Lorenzo suggested, even though he knew I was the one that usually handled all the paperwork. It wasn't the first time he'd jumped in headfirst to a project.

"They usually are, but they're worth considering first." I reached out for a file from Mr. Adler. "Is this the proposal?"

"Indeed, go ahead and have a look. I wanted to present this in person, but feel free to take all the time you need to think it over." Mr. Adler leaned back in his chair, and while he looked comfortable, he seemed to understand my insinuation that another meeting would be needed.

Lorenzo barely looked over my shoulder as I turned through the documents in the file. I flipped across the existing grounds in the place they were looking to develop. It included two small stores that I knew from experience had been struggling and would most likely benefit from being bought out for their location. I would make sure the offer made to them was worth it; working directly with the rest of Abilene was important to me, and I did my best to keep a community built around us.

A few pages in had the details for two residential locations that would be uprooted by the building. "And what are the plans for these residential homes? Are you making offers to them, as well, to get a hold of the land?"

"Yes," Adler started. "We have investors very interested in seeing where this mall goes, so there's an ample budget for moving folks around." His confidence put an odd twist in my stomach, and I tried not to linger on it.

"I see." I continued to flip through the pages, looking at all the possible outcomes that might occur should anything from this deal go south.

"I think what my partner means to say," Lorenzo spoke up, "is that there're still details to hash out, but I think we can count on this deal being beneficial for both of our companies."

"Of course," Mr. Adler said. As he must have noticed my hesitation, he rose from his seat. "Why don't you two and Mr. Tate look those details over and get back to us in the next few days with a contract? We can go from there."

Lorenzo nodded and stood to match him, reaching out a hand. "Happily, Mr. Adler."

I tentatively rose from my seat as well, shaking Adler's hand in agreement. "We'll be in touch. We look forward to working with you, Mr. Adler."

"And I as well," he replied, taking one more sip of water and opening the conference room door. "Thank you for your time, gentlemen."

"And we'll make sure to get that Manhattan for you next time, sir!" Lorenzo called out to him as he walked out of the office.

Once he was gone and I was left alone with my partner, I chuckled and put my hands casually in my pockets. "You might as well have stripped and done a fan dance for him."

Lorenzo turned to me with a playful glare. "At least someone in this office is doing some schmoozing. You might keep the paperwork together, but I get us the clients. Besides," he said, shrugging, "he seems an easy sell. He's a familiar client; he worked with your dad back in the day."

"Well, the paperwork is what keeps the company going. Besides, Dad kept paperwork on napkins, and Joseph was never any better. I swear I'm the only one who has ever filed a thing," I said with a laugh.

"I'm serious, O. This is a good deal, and I think we need to take it. We can probably make any demand, and they'll give it to us on a platter. I can talk to Joseph tomorrow, and I promise he'll be behind us."

"That doesn't make it a good deal," I said, sighing and looking at the clock on my phone. "Listen, it's been a long day; let's sleep on it and talk more tomorrow."

"The kid's got you stressed, huh?" Lorenzo asked, taking a sip from his glass of water in the conference room. "Sometimes I worry about you, man. Don't go losing your focus on me."

I texted our neighbor that I would be heading home soon, and I didn't lift my head once as I spoke to Lorenzo. "I'm not stressed. And I'm not losing focus. We run this firm together; I just need to get some things sorted for Lilly."

He was silent for a moment, waiting for me to acknowledge him. When I didn't for longer than he deemed acceptable, his mouth formed a grimace. When I did look up, he was glaring. "Whatever, Owen, just make sure your head is still in the game. You're not the only one at stake here."

"I know, I know." I packed my things in my briefcase bag and slung it over my shoulder. "Rest, then we'll talk." I gave a wave to Anne at the front desk and the intern (whose name I could never remember) in the back, replacing coffee filters. "See you guys tomorrow," I said, striding out the door.

# Chapter 5

PENNY

I couldn't seem to find the meat.

Most of the aisles of this small supermarket on the edge of town were pretty low on stock, but I'd apparently missed the aisle for ground beef twice now. Tonight, I would be making my grandmother's spaghetti recipe while my sister was still around, as Grace needed to be back in Colorado for a shoot in a few days. It was something we could share with Grandma, being in that house again, and I didn't want her to leave before we had the chance to make it. But ground beef was the main ingredient, and I couldn't seem to spot it. Frustrated, I made my way back around and found the section sign just as I felt my phone ring in my back pocket. The section was remarkably bare, which was how I'd missed it, but I grabbed the beef as I answered the call.

I didn't look at who it was before answering, "Hello?"

"Is that how you greet your boyfriend?" I heard Marcus chuckle, but there was a touch of a serious offense to his tone.

"Marcus!" I shouted, nearly dropping my handbasket in the process. An old lady looked over at the exclamation, and I shooed her away with my hand. "I'm sorry, baby, I wasn't paying attention to ID; I'm at the store."

I didn't often like taking calls, especially in public, as it gave me the worst anxiety. But I'd worked through most of that, especially with having a long-distance boyfriend. It didn't make the nervousness for calls any easier.

"I shouldn't have called while you were busy," he said, and I immediately turned to placate him.

"No, it's okay!" I said, again, most likely too loud. I set the basket to balance on the edge of a section lip by the cheeses, and the rest of its weight leaned on my hip. "I can talk."

He didn't hesitate to jump in at that confirmation. "Good, because I had something I needed to talk to you about."

"Yeah?" I asked.

"You've only been gone a week, Penny, and I think we can both already see this isn't working."

I dropped the basket, and it fell to the ground with a crash. The contents, a can of tomatoes, some vegetables, and of course, the beef, all tumbled out and rolled under one of the shelves.

"What are you talking about?" My voice came from my own mouth, but it sounded garbled and far away.

"Penny, I'm not happy. I know you're not happy."

"I'm happy. Of course, I'm happy; what do you mean I'm not happy?" I said, but it came out more in a half-sob. "Where is this coming from?"

He was quiet for another moment, and all at once, I knew there was no saving this when his mind was made up. Three years were going down the drain with a single phone call.

"I don't think we've been happy for a while, Penny, and it took this move to say so."

I scoffed, clutching the phone firmly in one hand as I wiped tears with my sleeve and started reaching down to pick up my fallen groceries. The peppers almost slipped out of my hand, and one of them was bruised, but back in the basket, it went. The old woman spotted me again as she rounded the corner, and I ignored her judgmental glares. "We can't even talk about this? I could come back for a bit; we could talk this through, and—"

On the other line, I heard rustling in the background behind him and a woman's voice that sounded too real to be coming from the TV. I immediately changed my tune and flipped on him.

"Is there someone there?" I asked.

"No," he quickly said, but the rustling continued. "Penny, we're just—"

"Is there another girl there with you, Marcus?" I asked, and a lump formed in my throat as I realized the answer. I set the full basket of groceries on the ground and had to move over when a mother holding a baby on her hip needed to reach for the cottage cheese, and seeing my state, she gave me a pitied smile.

"Is that what this is about? You're cheating on me?" I asked, turning around so the mother wouldn't be totally present for my accusation. "You told me you weren't; you promised you weren't after what happened last year!"

Last winter, I'd found earrings in Marcus's room that didn't belong to me, and without any of his family nearby and with him giving me non-answers, I overstepped boundaries and snooped on his phone. I'd been right, finding text after text of random women he'd been talking to behind my back. Now it seemed one of them had potentially returned.

"I'm not cheating on you, and you're honestly being crazy, just accusing me of that!"

At the name-calling, I ran out of energy to give him at that moment, and I took a deep breath, stepping back from the call. It wasn't until I could breathe again that I put the phone to my ear and heard him yelling about me always using that "one time" time as an excuse to "police" him. I was over it.

"I think you're right, Marcus. I think we're done here. Send my shit, would you?" I said and hung up the phone.

I almost gasped, holding the phone in my hand like a murder weapon. I'd never done anything like that before, and the liberation it brought, mixed with the hurt building from his repeated betrayal, overtook me.

A hand rested on my back, and the woman with the baby approached me with a grin and a squeeze. "He's an asshole, and you did the right thing." She had no idea about the context of my situation, but there was something universal in what she'd overheard that she took the time to reach out. I was so thankful for that random act of kindness.

I sniffled, touching the baby on her shoulder lightly to brighten my heart. "Thank you." She handed me a napkin from her bag and sent me on my way to the checkout counter.

# Chapter 6

OWEN

From outside, I heard the soundtrack to Princess and the Frog being played at full blast. One of the characters had a saxophone; I couldn't quite remember which one and his tune echoed along the entryway when I opened the front door around nine-thirty.

"Hey, Lil!" I called out, dropping my bag by the front door and pulling off my coat. I dropped it on a hook and started tugging at the back of my shoes for a moment, then got frustrated and relegated to removing them while sitting.

She sounded absorbed in her movie, but at the sound of my voice, her little body rushed over to greet me. Her arms wrapped around my waist, and I recalled how tall she'd gotten lately.

"How you doing, Lilypad?" I asked, kissing the top of her head. "Have fun with Darlene?" I walked past her and sat on the couch to untie my shoes.

Darlene came over from the kitchen, an older woman with hair that had greyed years ago, despite having more energy than I'd mustered in a long while. "We finished all her homework, and I even got her to practice a song on the piano."

"Oh, you did?" I asked, surprised.

"But no luck on practicing technique." She chuckled under her breath at me. "But she did good on her homework and practicing her times tables, so I didn't push it."

I watched Lilly continue her dances to the giant alligator's song as the group in the movie made their way along the path of a bayou. She could choreograph a routine and have it memorized in a few minutes when she was in her playful zone.

Once my shoes were off, I followed Darlene into the kitchen, lowering my voice. "She had some trouble in her piano class; I don't know if she said anything to you."

"Barely," Darlene sighed, taking a sip of her drink. Lilly had most likely made her, as Darlene didn't drink liquor, and the cup was holding a swirly straw. "She's been a little off all day, though, and her answers were short when I asked how piano went."

I looked over the counter to make sure Lilly wasn't overhearing our conversation. "She was more or less kicked out of class for being disruptive. I need to find a new one for her or a tutor of some kind if she wants to keep playing." I sighed, getting a Coors from the fridge. I didn't drink often, but on nights like these, avoiding alcohol was my last concern. "I don't get why she's causing such a problem."

"She's a young girl," Darlene offered. "There's a lot going on in that little brain of hers. It's not just singing frogs," she said with a laugh.

"I know that. I just wish I knew how to help her more." I brought my hand up to my nose and pinched it after taking a sip of my beer. "Plus, we have a new contract coming up, so I'm going to be pretty busy with work. It's not what she needs right now."

"Hey, take it easy on yourself." A hand found my shoulders and patted lightly, and when I looked up, Darlene's kind and wise eyes found mine. "You're going through a hard time. But you're doing a good job. Everything will work itself out, and Lilly is a good kid. She gets distracted sometimes, and she struggles with the other kids, but she's smart, and she'll make it through."

41

I welcomed her support, as much as I didn't want to. "It's been hard without her mom here these past few years. I don't know how we would have made it without you."

Darlene's smile glistened, and she gave me a look that told me many memories were swirling around her mind. "I helped raise Fiona, so it's been great helping to raise her own daughter, too. It's been too long that my house has been without children's laughter." Her smile fell a little, and I remembered the way Darlene lit up when her own daughter had come to town. She'd gotten married a few years back and moved to Europe with her husband, so it couldn't have been easy for Darlene to be alone for so long. "A mother needs a child. And I've always been a mother at heart."

"That you have. Thank you for helping with her." I looked out to the living room. "She reminds me so much of Fi sometimes."

"I think we all miss her. But she would want us all to be happy. And that means working with Lilly to do what she needs best, even if we don't quite understand what that is just yet. It's a learning process." Darlene put her book and a few other things in her purse, zipping it up and pulling it up her shoulder. "So we ought to start teaching ourselves."

I took her words to heart, knowing that in the two years Fiona had gone, I'd seen Lilly grow into one of the most beautiful and brilliant young women I'd ever met. Even at nine, she was already mastering more than her school class could keep up with, and she understood concepts meant for high school and college. Now I just had to learn how to speak her language.

"Guess I got to get started then, hm?" I said with a smile, reaching into my wallet to pull out money for Darlene.

She smacked the bills away when I offered them to her. "You got me groceries yesterday, Owen; worry about that mess later," she said, wobbling to the door. I always slipped a few bills in her purse when she wasn't looking, especially with how much help she'd been offering for Lilly lately when I worked late at the office like this.

"Lil, come say goodbye to Darlene!" I shouted to the dancing bean in the living room.

She hurtled out, squeezing Darlene tight. "Goodnight, Darlene! Thank you for helping me practice today," she said, and her smile was glowing.

"It was my pleasure, sweetie. Have fun with your dad tonight, and I'm always next door if you need me!" She ruffled Lilly's head before slipping out, and I turned to Lilly in the quiet once she was gone. The movie had progressed to a softer moment, and I took the opportunity to step over and interrupt.

"Hey, Lilly, can we talk about some stuff?" I asked.

She nodded, sitting next to me when I took my place on the couch. Her little hands grabbed the remote and paused her movie, though she'd seen it a hundred times and surely wouldn't be missing anything. "What do you wanna talk about, Dad?" Even in starting the conversation, she sounded more mature than she should have at her age. With her mom gone, part of me worried she had grown up too fast.

"A few things. Music class."

"Oh." Her shoulders fell a solid half-inch, and her smile faded. "I'm sorry I was fooling around in class. I just didn't want the other kids to make fun of me, and they sometimes laugh when I do stuff that bugs the teacher."

I wrapped my arm around her and chuckled. "I bet they do; you're a funny kid. But Lil, you have to behave during classes, or your teacher's going to have a real problem."

"Then why doesn't she stop the other kids when they tell me I act weird or look stupid?" she asked, and I could tell it was coming from a place of deep pain and embarrassment.

"She should be. But sometimes, teachers don't always pick up on everything."

"She never said anything; that's why I threw stuff at Isaac and Thomas. They called me stupid."

My heart broke to see my little girl hurt, and I wished I could have done more to protect her. "You're not stupid, Lilly. Boys are, and usually, they don't have anything better to do, so they decide picking on people as their favorite hobby. But you can't be violent against them, and throwing stuff at them is not okay. I didn't raise you to do stuff like that."

"Mom told me I had to stand up for myself."

It was the first time she'd brought up Fiona in a few months, and it took me aback.

"You do, Lillypad. But not with violence. You stand up to people with words or let go of what they say. Because it doesn't matter."

"Yes, it does, Dad!" Tears welled in Lilly's eyes, and her fists balled up in her lap. "They just laugh at me when I try to use my words. Mom would have told me to do it."

"No, she wouldn't have," I said firmly, and I meant it. Fiona was a lot of things, but a perpetrator of violence for our young daughter was never one of them.

44

"If she were here, she would be able to tell me what to do because you never do!" At that, her little body slid off the couch and stomped off.

As sad as I was to see my daughter hurting so much, I lost myself in the emotion of her behavior. "Get back here, Lilly; we're not done talking!"

I stood to follow her down the hall, but she slipped into her bedroom and slammed the door before I could. I heard the lock engage from the other side, accompanied by a sniffle.

"Lilly!"

No response.

"Dammit," I muttered quietly to avoid her hearing my frustration. I walked back to the living room and put my face in my hands, catching one or two tears that made their way down. It was all I'd allow; I'd promised myself two years ago when I almost fell into a deep depression following Fiona's death that a few tears were all I would let break through.

After about an hour of wallowing and waiting to see if Lilly would make a guest appearance, I checked on her and found the door unlocked. I did my best to turn the knob with no alert to the girl inside, and when I peeked through the door, I saw her asleep in bed, curled up with her stuffed pig, Lucia. Fiona had given it to her for her birthday, and since Fiona's death, it never left her side at night.

I sighed, closed the door again, and went back to the kitchen.

Checking the time, I recalled there was a drink special going on at the bar down the street Wednesday nights to try and get people out more often. I'd gone out a few times after Lilly had gone to bed, especially after Fiona's death, but it wasn't something I'd ever made a habit. Before I ever even considered it, I'd installed security cameras around the house and the perimeter that all synced to my phone, so I often would just sit at the bar and watch the empty house.

Knowing I still had another few hours available, I pulled on a leather jacket I had stocked away in my closet and changed into my more casual shoes, an old pair of sneakers that still fit like a glove.

Before I walked out, I made sure to stop in Lilly's room and leave her a note in case she woke up and got frightened, as well as to kiss her on the forehead and silently apologize for everything I'd done and hadn't done, as her father.

After locking the door, I saw the light on at Darlene's and sent over a text, asking her to keep an ear out and that I would be back in an hour or so. She was familiar with the bar, and she texted back immediately, telling me to be careful and that she would look out for Lilly in case of an emergency.

I did everything right, taking care of my daughter and making sure she was safe and happy. So why did I still feel like such a failure as her parent?

# III. THE FOLLOWING DAYS

# Chapter 7

OWEN

The lights from the office conference room glared in my eyes, and I deeply reconsidered forgoing the sunglasses indoors today.

"God, Owen, you look a mess," Lorenzo said, slapping me on the back as he stepped in and set down his coffee.

"It was a long night," I said, ending it there.

"Get a night nanny for that kid, would you? Can't have you in the office looking like a soggy piece of stale bread," he said. He set his files down on the table and started going through his phone. "You going to be okay this morning?"

"Yeah, I'll be fine. Where's the kid with coffee?" I asked. Any other day, I would have remembered his name. But with the amount of alcohol that had been flooding through me last night and that had greeted my toilet this morning, I was lucky to remember where my work building was.

The night before had been a wonderful blur, though I was pretty sure I retained all my memories. I recalled having an incredibly taboo bathroom tryst with a hot stranger at Dave's, getting her and her sister a car home (I had walked over and was in no shape to drive), then stumbling across the street and flopping into bed. I'd checked on Lilly for a moment and found her in the same position I'd left her in a few hours prior.

When I woke up, I'd found myself hurling into the toilet, regretting drinking so much. I'd been able to put it away easier when I was younger, but it wrecked my stomach, something awful nowadays.

Randy (I recalled the intern's name when I saw his face again) stopped by with fresh hot coffee and some cream and sugar packets. I did my regular two sugars. Adding a cream was for days when my stomach was feeling more prepared for the time ahead, and this was not one of those days.

"Thank you, Randy," I said. He nodded with a hopeful smile, and I made a mental note to put a good word in with his agency.

Lorenzo sipped his own coffee once Randy had left, looking over the papers in his lap. "So, Adler wants an answer."

"What do you think?" I asked, swirling my red mini straw around the paper cup. "I'm behind it if you are. A mall is a pretty sure deal. They'll be bringing in more retail, and there are only a few locations to manage in agreement."

"Yeah, we've done more for much less." He chuckled. "I'm full speed ahead on it. I think it's a great idea. Plus, I'm sure your dad would have liked you working with Adler again, huh?" Lorenzo's shoulder nudged forward at me. "I think we'd be silly not to take it."

"Have you heard from Joseph?" I asked. Technically, the firm was owned by a man named Joseph Tate. He worked with my dad back when he was alive, and they owned the firm together, but he'd stepped back years ago. While he and Dad had originally started the firm together as partners, Joseph started running the show at some point down the line, and it became Tate Legal. Dad was a good enough friend and a smart enough businessman to go along with him. Joseph was living out his days at a golf course in Florida, but due to legal ownership and as part of the deal when Lorenzo and I took over, he still wanted us to clear any jobs this big with him.

Lorenzo nodded. "He's scheduled for a video call this afternoon. Didn't you clear your schedule with Anne?"

I gave him a vacant stare after a giant sip of coffee.

"Good point." He chuckled. "Anyway, Joseph said about the same thing. He's game if we are, and he knows and trusts Adler from prior deals."

I pulled up the budget for the demolition and relocation of homes on the planned lots and whistled. "Those residents will be getting a pretty penny."

"You're damn right. I wish *my* house was getting knocked down for a mall." He laughed.

I scanned further down the page. "So, do you know anything about the woman who owns this one, Ruthanne Desmond?"

"Ruthanne Desmond ..." Lorenzo put his hand on his chin to think it over, but he shook his head until realization hit him. "That's the place on Plumosa Avenue, right?" He reached for the file I was holding, looking at the outside. "Yeah, an old lady. I think she died or something. I'm pretty sure I egged it as a kid," he said with a laugh, clearly entertained by his immature past.

"She died recently?" I raised an eyebrow and took the file back, placing it in the manila folder in front of me. "That means ownership transfer, or we might be dealing with a repossession if the bank got a hold of it."

"Damn," Lorenzo sighed, shaking his head. "That would be pretty frustrating. What about the other one? It was two residential, right?" he asked, peering over.

I nodded. "Yes, the other one has actually been vacant for more than a year. I don't think we'll have a problem with it at all."

"So, the main focus should be this old lady, right?"

I nodded in agreement. "The house from the dead old lady, but yes."

At that moment, a roll of nausea ran through me, most likely agitated by the coffee I'd been consuming, and I stood for the bathroom. Lorenzo watched me for a moment, then understood as his eyes widened.

"Jesus, go!" he said, shooing me off and dismissing me from the conversation.

I took the olive branch and ran as fast as I could.

# Chapter 8

After recovering from my horrifying hangover that morning, Grace and I spent most of the day huddled around toilet seats and buckets in the living room. She recovered slightly faster than I did, and we'd both healed enough for a simple meal of light salad that night. I hadn't been able to go heavy on the spicy dressing I'd made, but it kept our stomachs where they belonged, particularly mine.

The next day, I helped her pack, making sure to get as many items of my clothes as I could find. We'd been swapping clothes since we were younger, so they somehow always found the same pile.

Returning after dropping Grace off at the bus station, the place felt a little emptier than I remembered. The dirt I still had to clean made it colder, as if the fire in its heart had been snuffed out as the dust had gathered. I set my purse on the couch and went into the kitchen for some water, noticing the sound of my own echo with each move.

I'd never actually been *on my own* before. After leaving here the first time, I'd lived in college dorms with a roommate. Then I'd lived with friends after school, and I'd been getting ready to move in together with Marcus. Now that plan was shot, and I was being uprooted to my hometown, to a place that no longer felt like home. Not without the family that once inhabited it.

Pulling out my phone, I scrolled through my texts and found the conversation from the guy I'd met at the bar the other night, Owen. I'd

52

given him my number, and then he'd surprised me with a text when I got home, just to make sure I was safe after the drive. That kind of behavior made me think there was a chance for a follow-up, but he'd been quiet since, so I didn't hold out a candle. Part of me wanted to cherish it for the delicious sin it was—an incredible one-night-stand with a total stranger.

He had itched something in me both physically and emotionally, and it made me crave the connection it'd allowed me to feel after losing Marcus. With Grace gone now, too, everywhere I went felt paralyzed with emptiness.

A moment of silence in the kitchen was all it took before I set about preparing the place for music again.

I dug through some old boxes in the closet, finding the printer I'd saved in my high school bedroom. Originally, most of its use went to scrapbooking, but today it would serve a professional purpose. Pulling open my computer, I went to a cheap design website I'd used when making business cards for myself. I whipped together a basic flyer— experienced music teacher seeking enthusiastic students for piano— and set it to print. I'd start with twenty and find a few solid places to hang it around town. Seeing the layout again might be nice, too, as it had been so long since I'd walked through Abilene.

Digging in my purse, I found my headphones and popped them in my ears, turning on my favorite dance playlist. I was determined to turn this into a way to force me out of my funk after what had happened with Marcus. And honestly, I was still processing what being here and taking care of my grandma's home meant to me. I needed the walk.

# Chapter 9

After excusing myself to empty the contents of my stomach, I was able to pull myself together to meet Joseph by video call. Thankfully, Lorenzo did most of the talking. I think my situation was clear from my blank expression for the majority of the meeting and the fact that I went through three glasses of water and two cups of coffee in an hour alone. Joseph Tate was old, but he was not inexperienced or stupid.

"It sounds like you boys have the plan ahead of you; just be ready for the work it'll take to get that house," Joseph said, coming too close to the camera for his reply and talking too loud into the microphone. His gray hair shone in the hot Florida sun that beat down on his back porch, where he was attending the meeting. "I remember Ruthanne; she was a sweet woman. She only passed a few months back, but they just got her estate settled, from what I heard."

"Do you know anything about who she had listed to inherit?" Lorenzo asked.

Joseph put his hand to his chin, scrolling through memories that were surely fading as the years went by. There was a reason Joseph's wife didn't let him drive anymore.

"Not too sure. You might have to look into that and see what you can dig up."

"We can do some digging," Lorenzo said.

"Adler's got a solid backing behind him, so buying whoever it is out probably won't be an issue," I suggested.

54

Lorenzo chuckled. "You say that now. Old homes like those can be a sore spot for people, especially if Ruthanne just passed. Be prepared for battle, then take the relief if it's only a debate. But go ahead and give Adler the okay."

"Of course, Joseph," Lorenzo said, giving him a dramatic thumbs-up. If I had a dollar for every ass my partner kicked, I would be richer than Joseph Tate.

"I'm trusting you both, and I know you're going to knock this one out of the park. Best of luck, boys!" Joseph said, waving as he started fumbling with his camera.

"Bye, Joseph!" both Lorenzo and I said as we watched him attempt to end the call. Lorenzo finally put him out of his misery and just ended the meeting entirely. Without a doubt, Joseph was still on the other end, trying to exit.

I took a deep breath when the call ended, loosening my tie a little. Joseph allowed us to take as much control as we wanted, and I'd been running the firm with Lorenzo for four years now, but I constantly felt like a kid trying on his dad's suit whenever we talked shop with our owner.

"Congratulations. I don't think he realized how hungover you were." Lorenzo laughed, putting away his things.

"I'm not much anymore, thank you very much. Work tends to sober me up faster than a cold shower."

"Been having a lot of those lately, hm?" Lorenzo mocked, but a memory from last night echoed in my mind.

Blair, the girl from the bar, with her legs wrapped tightly around my waist and me thrusting deeply into her as I pulled her ass closer to me, moaning into her ear.

I certainly would be needing a hot shower later.

"What time is it?" I asked, coming back to reality and remembering that Darlene needed me back today for a doctor's appointment. "Shit," I said, realizing how close to five o'clock it was.

"Crotch goblin calls?"

"God," I shook my head in disgust, shoving papers in my bag and slinging it over my shoulder. "Could you not call her that?"

"Sorry, man." He laughed. "Go home, go take care of your kid. I'll clean up the rest here."

"Thank you," I said, putting out my hand before running out the door. "Bye, guys!" I shouted to Lorenzo, Anne, and Randy, who I was pretty sure was still filing.

# Chapter 10

PENNY

On the walk into town, I dove into the music playing in my ears, shaking my hips at some beat drops. It entertained a few old people I passed while walking, and while I wasn't paying attention to what they did, it appeared one or two may have recognized me.

At the crosswalk for the street in front of the grocery store, I stopped and hung a sign with the tape I'd brought on my wrist. Just as I was patting it down firmly on the cold telephone pole on the corner, in view of most passersby, I felt a tap on my lower back.

I turned and saw a girl, probably younger than ten years old, wearing a pair of leggings under a fluffy pink skirt. The breeze that day was cold, so she had a sweater and a tiny scarf tucked around her neck.

She looked up at me with sweet, brown eyes and grinned wildly. "I really like your scarf."

That morning, I'd yanked on a scarf myself—one with piano keys all over it. I'd received it as a gift from a prior student a few summers back, and I thought it was hilarious. I wore it today just in case anyone commented on it and would be looking for a tutor.

It seemed luck was in my favor.

"Thank you!" I said. An older woman stood about a yard behind her, and I wondered who had asked who to go comment on the strange woman hanging up posters wearing a piano scarf.

"I play piano; that's why I like it," she said, and it seemed like the part the older woman might have pressed.

"You do?" I asked, performing enthusiastically for her. She had so much energy that it made me want to meet her at the same level. "You know, I play piano, and I teach it too. Do you practice often?"

She nodded quickly, too hard to feel completely honest. The older woman behind her tuned in.

"Not enough. She can struggle with focusing on practice instead of just clanking away," the woman said.

"That's a good thing!" I said, happy to hear she had a passion for exploring music on her own. "That means you want to play all kinds of things. You can do both, practice the serious stuff and get the chance to play anything you want!"

"Really?" she said, and her eyes went wide. It made my heart burst a little. "I wanna do that."

"She has been … looking for a tutor," the woman said.

I tried calming myself, so I wouldn't go into sales mode, but I couldn't help being thrilled to find a first potential client so soon. "That's wonderful; I'm happy to take on students for group or private classes. Can I give you my card?"

"Please, Darlene, please?" the little girl asked, throwing her hands together in a dramatic prayer motion.

We both laughed at her attempt to persuade. "Her father was looking, I mean. You have to talk to him first, honey," she said, turning to the girl. "No promises." She brought her attention back to me and nodded with a gentle smile. "But yes, we'd love a card."

Before I knew it, the girl's hands were firmly around my legs, hugging me tight in thanks. I gasped, looking down in surprise, but meeting her in a light embrace. "I'm Penny, by the way."

"Lilly!" Darlene called out to try and stop the girl before she landed, but I waved off her worry. "I'm sorry, she's very easily excitable."

"Again, that's great to hear," I said, rising from the hug with Lilly. "You're a passionate girl, and I hope we get to make some music together soon!"

"I can't wait to talk to Dad!" Lilly said in delight, returning to Darlene's side.

Darlene put my card in her purse and looked over at a tree just behind us. "Lilly, is it okay if I talk to Ms. Lewis really quickly? How about practicing your climbing skills, hm?"

I laughed, watching Lilly's excitement turn to the physical challenge of climbing a tree. It was amazing to see Darlene guide her so well while letting her explore on her own terms when it was safe.

"She's an adorable kid," I said, turning to Darlene.

"She is. She's a sweetheart, but she sometimes struggles in class. Gets picked on a lot, acts out, especially in new places, from what I understand," Darlene said with a sigh. "It breaks my heart." She brought her eyes up to me and looked me over once, then nodded. "She already adores you, so I'll definitely talk to her father, but do you come in for home visits?"

"I don't normally, but if you have an instrument there she's comfortable learning on, I'm happy to do so. Do you think that would help?" I asked.

"I do," Darlene replied. "And her father would be happy to pay, I'm sure. He just wants her happy, as we all do."

My lips pulled into a light smile, and I remembered why it was I loved teaching children. "I completely understand. And I'd love to do what I can to help," I said.

"Darlene, look!" we heard Lilly holler in the distance.

"Very good, sweetie!" Darlene yelled back, walking over to where she had climbed. "Thank you again, Ms. Lewis, and we'll be in touch!" she said over her shoulder at me, and we exchanged waves goodbye.

I watched the two interact for a moment in the tree, and I could tell how much spirit was in that little girl. And that one positive exchange and promise of a potential new client who would be positively affected by my tutoring gave me the boost I needed to continue my mission. I took the rest of the afternoon to hit the community boards at the grocery store, the local sandwich and coffee shops, and the park in the square next to the gazebo. I'd kept a lookout for any new places that had popped up in the last few years, but those were the locations I remembered being frequented the most growing up in Abilene. Surely, it would lead to a few bites.

By the time I started the walk back home, I was already a bit wiped out, so walking through the door felt like reaching the top step of heaven. I huffed and flopped onto the couch, watching a small cloud of dust form over me as I did. I didn't mind and closed my eyes to rest them, just as my phone buzzed in my back pocket.

# Chapter 11

OWEN

The drive home was quick, but I managed to catch every red light coming into town, and it only made me feel more agitated that I would be late. I despised tardiness, so I prided myself on getting places on time. I'd even set my car clock back a few minutes to ensure I was consistently early.

When I walked inside, Darlene was waiting by the door with her purse already zipped and her shoes on. Lilly was fastened and focused on the table, her shoulders hunched over a handout from school.

"I'm so sorry I'm late," I said, hanging my bag by the clothes rack.

"No apologies, five minutes isn't the end of the world." Darlene smiled mildly and then began to tell me about the encounter with the mysterious music teacher.

When Lilly also noticed me, however, it was over with the calm. She abruptly jumped up from her seat to greet me as if we hadn't seen each other in 37 years.

"Dad, she had a piano tie!" Lilly exclaimed, taking a breath from running around the room.

"I heard that bit already, Lillypad." I chuckled, untying my other shoe and pulling them both off. "Darlene says you two ran into her putting up posters?"

"Yeah!" Lilly started. "She was putting up posters all over town for music classes because she's looking for jobs, and she has a piano at home too, and she said that I have 'passion for music' a few times, and—"

Lilly was running on overdrive, the excitement taking her over as she nearly ran out of breath. With how distant we'd been from each other the last few days because of her prior music class, it was wonderful to see her so animated and excited to see me. Even if it was because she wanted to convince me to hire this young lady with a piano tie.

"You're going to hyperventilate!" Darlene said, catching Lilly by gently reaching for her back as she made her rounds. With a laugh at Lilly's antics, Darlene pulled a card from her purse. "Here's her business card."

Upon grabbing it, I had to laugh myself at their make and the extravagant colors covering the card; it was catered to children, I would guess. They were printed on cardstock, most likely on a home printer. But the design was nice, and it advertised in-home piano lessons by Ms. Lewis with a music note dotting the I. I was willing to look into it, but I wanted to ensure Lilly wouldn't act out again first. I didn't want to be blacklisted by every music teacher in the area, especially in a small town like Abilene. People already knew I was a widower and single dad, and I was judged and pitied by every old woman in town for having to do things on my own. Lilly's behavioral issues would only draw their attention stronger.

Darlene brought my own attention back to the card in my hands. "She said she's willing to come here and use Lilly's keyboard to teach her," Darlene mentioned. "I thought it might be nice for at least the first few times, maybe, to have her in her own environment? Somewhere safe that she trusts?"

"Thank you for getting her card, Darlene. I'll see if we can try to contact her," I said, not wanting to give Lilly too much to go on before I had the chance to sit her down.

"Really?" Lilly squealed, to my dismay. Her eyes went wide. "Can she be my teacher, Dad, please?"

I sighed, knowing I'd given keeping it off the table my best go. "We'll try," I said, and Darlene smiled as she made her way out. "We have to talk about some things first."

"You got this, girl," Darlene whispered to Lilly before stepping out the door, and I grinned. I was so glad to have a figure for Lilly to girl-out with sometimes.

We said goodnight, and I returned to the couch with Lilly at my side. She was waiting for me to say or do whatever it took to make this music teacher happen, and her perseverance to convince me also entertained me. Her hands sat properly folded in her lap, and her little toes twiddled against each other in her pink socks as she waited for my icebreaker. I playfully sighed, being a tad dramatic on the exhale, like I wasn't just stirring the anticipation for the little ball of energy sitting next to me.

"Dad!" she groaned when I sighed again. "What do we have to talk about for Ms. Lewis to be my teacher?"

I wrapped an arm around her. "Oh, that?" I feigned ignorance, which earned me a playful shove. We both laughed, and I nudged her next to me. "Well, Lilly, I think we both know you had some problems with your last music class. And the two before that. But, kid, I see how happy you get when you're playing. And you're good at practicing when you can focus on just the music, and you don't let other kids get to you. So this time, if you want this, we're going to set some ground rules."

At the serious turn of my tone, she sank slowly into her seat. She got quiet and didn't meet my eyes. I put a hand on her back to sit her back up.

"I love you, Lillypad. I want you to be happy, and I want you to play music and learn how to use it to get those feelings out. Because you've got a lot of 'em!" I said with a weak laugh, but it was true.

Since losing Fiona, I could see the emptiness that had grown and festered within our daughter, especially at her age, when support was needed most. She seemed to have so many things inside her that I just couldn't understand without the communication, and she often had no one to teach her the words. I struggled to connect with her at times, and it just came from a lack of experience—I'd never been without Fiona, either. We were both still learning how to stay afloat, lacking one member of our crew.

In the aftermath of Fiona's funeral and the adjustment to our new normal, my mom had helped me sign up Lilly for children's bereavement therapy after seeing what losing my dad had done to me as an adult. Lilly seemed to benefit from having a woman to speak to, but I remembered them hitting a wall and her getting too frustrated by talking to a stranger. I'd considered signing her up again, but I knew it would be a longer conversation and process to have, and this was something I could do now that might help. Now that my parents had relocated to a home in Florida, I was a bit more on my own.

Lilly remained quiet, and I rubbed her shoulder.

"Lil, I know you've been struggling a lot. You've been through a lot, more than most kids should." I sighed, wanting to take that weight off her but not knowing how. "But you've got to work with me here, okay? If you want to be in a music class, you have to be ready to listen to your teacher and not antagonize the other students. You're a big girl now, and you're talented. You can do this, but it takes passion, just like Ms. Lewis said. Right?"

She still wasn't looking up, but I watched a tear fall onto her pants where her head hung low. Her little head nodded, and I heard a sniffle.

"Right, it takes passion. And that means having discipline for yourself and for learning. Now, look at me." I lightly put my hand under her chin and turned it in my direction. I never held her face firmly, but she also never pulled away. "I love you, Lilly. You're an amazing kid, and you make me proud every day. You can do this."

Her lip, which had been quivering and dribbling away some tears, curled up. "I love you too, Daddy." She pushed her head into my shirt, most definitely leaving it covered in snot. But with my daughter, I wouldn't change it for the world. "I promise I'll practice super hard and focus and be a great pee-nist if Ms. Lewis can be my teacher, please?"

I was silent for a moment, taking in what she said before chortling loudly.

"What?"

Her blank stare told me what I needed to know, and she shied back before I hugged her tight again. "Honey, it's pi-an-ist, pianist."

"Oh, what did I say?" she asked, not even realizing what the other word sounded like.

"Never mind," I said, continuing, "but yes, we can contact Ms. Lewis about teaching you piano, okay?"

She yelped and wrapped her scrawny arms around my waist, squeezing me like a tube of toothpaste. "Thank you, Daddy, thank you, thank you!" The queen of dramatics, she ended by scrambling up to the top of the couch, splaying herself out, and pretending to pass out from excitement.

I let the kid watch way too many daytime shows.

"You're welcome, Lilly, and I meant what I said. I don't want to hear anything about you acting up with her, understand?" I gave her a firm eye, and she nodded. Even at nine, she had the maturity and sadness of a girl far past her age. I trusted her to be able to learn and improve in class with this new teacher. All her other classes had been for a group, so maybe one-on-one would prove the way to go.

"This is going to be awesome!" she said, rolling down the couch again. "Dad, I'm done with my homework tonight, so can I go make popcorn?" Lilly asked her attention already elsewhere.

"As long as you grab the garlic powder for my bowl, too," I said with a wink. "Want to watch a movie together?"

She brightened, nodding vigorously, and then she made her way into the kitchen toward the cabinet.

"Get the stove turned on for me, and I'll watch it, then come pick something out for us, okay?" I asked, grunting as I rose from the couch. I often felt older after serious conversations like this with Lilly, and my manner of getting up reminded me of that.

As I walked over and she scooted past me toward the remote, my phone rang. With it being after hours, I set it to Ignore for everyone but Darlene and Lorenzo.

Lorenzo's name popped up, and I sighed, calling out to Lilly. "I'm taking a quick phone call while I'm making popcorn, okay, honey?"

She yelped back a reply of an acknowledgment as I noted the handle of the pre-packaged stove-top popcorn wire was backward and would soon melt if left for another few minutes. "Lil—" I gasped, moving it with one hand as I tried to pick up the phone before it went to voicemail.

"Hey, Owen, I'm on a stakeout."

"Lorenzo?" I asked, turning my full attention to the call. "What did you just say?"

"You know that house on Plumosa that we need for the Adler deal?" he said in a whisper, forcing itself to be clear enough for a call. "I'm parked outside it. I wanted to scope it out, so we know what we're dealing with."

"Are you out of your mind?" I asked. "You're stalking them?"

Lorenzo sputtered lightly. "No, I'm not crazy. I'm just grabbing some food downtown, taking note of the neighborhood, you know?" I heard him munching on something.

"Just stop by, officially, during business hours. This is ridiculous!" I told him. It was also a huge liability, and it had more ways than any to go bad.

"I just stopped by for a second; all I could see was some young lady." He took a breath to swallow, and I almost urged him off the phone, but he cut me off before I could. "I just wanted to let you know I'll make a stop tomorrow with an offer for her, based on the budget from the proposal from Adler. Keep it all above-board. But yeah, she's kind of cute, so I'm making the stop," he said.

I scoffed. "And you called me for this, why?"

One of the kernels popped, and it started the process of the others going, smacking against the aluminum cover as it inflated.

"Sounds like you're busy at home with the squirt." Lorenzo laughed.

"Yes, *Lilly* and I are going to watch a movie and have some popcorn. Nice night in with just the two of us," I said, emphasizing her name.

"How picket-fence of you. Sounds boring as hell to me." He swallowed again and said, "I'll leave you to it then. See you tomorrow, partner."

"Good, go home, Lorenzo," I half-demanded, but I already heard the engine, so I wasn't worried. "Goodnight, see you tomorrow."

I hung up, stirring the popcorn lightly.

"Make sure it's not burned!" Lilly yelled.

Upon shaking the tin, I sniffed deeply and got the smell of tire rubber, which didn't bode well. My case wasn't helped when the fire alarm went off, beeping annoyingly and bringing Lilly over with her hands covering her ears.

Then she wordlessly reached into the cabinet, got the last one we had, and placed it on the fresh stove. "Thank goodness we weren't out."

"Oh, bye, Darlene," she said, hugging her on the side. When she saw me coming through, however, she jumped from her seat to come to greet me. "Hi, Dad!"

When I protested to stop her, knowing it might have come across as rude to Darlene, she stopped me. "I don't take it personally. She misses her father."

I nodded, hugging Lilly tight and scooting her back off to the table to finish her homework. "Thank you, Darlene," I said to the woman as I moved to let her out the door. "Really, and have a good appointment today."

"Just a checkup. Makes me remember I'm still alive," she said with a laugh. "Goodbye!" With that, the old woman took off walking down the street. She didn't drive anymore, and she insisted on walking to every location she needed to get to while remaining in Abilene. She proposed moving around on her own was the only reason she was still as nimble at her advanced age, and I couldn't help agreeing with her. I always offered a ride, but she put my gym-rat college days to shame with how much she walked.

"How you doing tonight, Lillypad?" I asked, taking a seat at the table next to her. I looked over her shoulder and watched her practice her simple multiplication tables. She was more advanced in mathematics than I had been, and it made me so proud.

"I'm okay," she said, but she was quieter than normal.

"Did you have a good day at school?" I asked.

"Yeah," she said. "A girl in my class got a piano for Christmas. She told everybody she knows how to play Beethoven."

I laughed, setting my hand on the back of her chair. "And she just got her first piano at Christmas? I would bet that she might be fibbing."

Lilly's eyebrows furrowed, and she gripped her pencil tighter, looking forcefully down at her math page. "Maybe, but she said her mom got her a private tutor."

"That still means she has to practice the piano and keep up with her lessons. A tutor doesn't just make you magically able to play the piano," I said.

"I know," she replied, sounding dejected.

My gears got turning, and whether it was from how much life I could see was missing in my daughter's eyes without music, or whether my defenses were down from a busy day at work after a night of drunken bliss, I said the next thing without thinking.

"Maybe that's something we can look into getting for you."

She turned to me with eyes wide. "Really? A tutor to help me play piano?"

"To help you *learn* piano," I said with a smirk. "And maybe. We can talk about it."

Just from that one inkling of hope, Lilly's attitude shifted completely. She smiled brightly as she flew through the page, completing equation after equation of two-number multiplication sets, dramatically signing off her name at the top of her sheet. She then shoved it in my face, her eyes gleaming.

"I finished my homework, Dad! And you can double-check them too!"

She was so overenthusiastic that I couldn't help laughing. "Okay, I get it; you're willing to impress to make this happen."

"No, I'm not; I'm just happy to do my homework!" Her smile could have been award-winning, and I knew at the end of the day I was a lost cause when it came to making her happy.

"You're not fooling anyone here, Lillypad, but okay, I'll think about it," I said, and I pulled her head in for a kiss. "Now go wash your hands and get ready for dinner; I'm cooking tonight."

Her brows scrunched together in apparent worry. "What are you cooking?"

"Don't look so terrified. Fine, I was going to make a pizza," I said, resigning to telling her my plan. I'd never been great in the kitchen, and it was honestly the hardest adjustment after Fiona's death—figuring out how to cook for and feed my daughter.

"Want me to help shred the cheese?" she asked, much too excited to turn down.

"Of course, I'm incapable of doing it myself, as you've implied." I laughed. "Now go get ready, or I'll start by myself and burn the house down."

# Chapter 12

PENNY

Tired, I rummaged for my cell phone.

To my shock, the text was from Mr. One-Night-Stand himself, Owen. I raised an eyebrow.

»Hey you«, it said.

Nothing too dramatic. It was a safe bet as far as flirty texts went. I hadn't expected him to follow up, but without anything better to do that would require me rising from my current flat position, I texted back not long after.

»Hi, right back at you«, I said. »What are you up to?« I was asking innocently but was comfortable going wherever he planned to roam with his answer.

»Sitting at home, slamming my head against a computer. Missing fun distractions and thought I'd say hi.«

»So I was just a fun distraction, huh?« I asked, pulling his chain.

»Not what I meant«, he texted back almost immediately, and I laughed at his paranoia of upsetting me. »I really enjoyed spending time with you and talking with you too.«

»I'm just kidding. It was a really fun night, and I needed the distraction too.«

»What are you up to right now?«

»Just got home from some errands«, I said, enjoying the sense of anonymity between us. I didn't exactly want my one-night stand involved in my professional life. »About ready to crawl into bed, honestly«, I added.

»If only I could join you«, he said. »Cuddling with you sounds lovely.«

I smirked, refreshed by how willing he was to flirt over text. It scared some guys off, but it used to be part of my M.O.

»And what would that benefit be?« I teased him. »Are you specifically good at cuddling? Maybe good at getting people to fall asleep?«

He matched my energy, texting me; »I would say I'm skilled at knocking people out, with enough time in front of me to wear them out properly.«

*I raised an eyebrow as my smile grew. I do like some exercise before bed. Especially with a partner.*

»I think working up a sweat should be required. It makes you more likely to bask in the melting pleasure of ... sleep.«

His addendum made me laugh. *Definitely, the s word you were going for there.* »Absolutely«, I wrote.

He was quiet for a second, and then the text came through louder than the others. »I'd love to give you a lot more pleasure, Blair. «

After lingering on the fact that he still called me by my middle name—which was not fake, just not the name I told people I knew better than one night—I almost sank into a puddle right there on my grandmother's living room couch. I squirmed, remembering the feeling of his hands all over me on that bathroom sink. My legs squeezed together instinctively, and I picked up my phone again to reply.

»Maybe we can make that happen. I think getting on top would be a lot of fun.« I grinned. »On top of my sleep habits, I mean.«

By the time he texted back, I was already slipping into my bedroom to have some fun at the memory of him taking me the other night when my inhibitions had been low, and my heartbreak had me wanting affection. I'd told Grace that Blair had become a kind of alter-ego, and she was the one fueling my rebound sex-capades.

At least *Penny* was reaping the benefits of Blair's bravery.

»Hardy har har«, he replied, but I was already off in my own world.

# Chapter 13

PENNY

*Does taking water bottles to her home seem like I'm trying too hard?*

I took one out and set it on the table next to the notebook I'd purchased for my new students at the only stationery store in town. Next to that sat a newly sharpened pencil and a music stand, ready for use. I was waiting to see where each student stood with their skills before purchasing the music guide books I would be using for them, especially with individual lessons.

In many ways, this first solo class with Lilly was a trial run of what my potential future could look like in Abilene. Her dad had apparently approved and was paying for the classes, but he was so busy with work that I hadn't had the chance to meet him yet; most of my interaction had been with Darlene. I tried not to let my mind wander, but it was a lot of pressure to put on meeting a young girl. All she would want is someone to connect with to teach her piano. And that was something I knew I could provide.

At one-fifty, I straightened my colorful mid-length skirt, tucking in the pink blouse I'd paired with it, and went out the door. When we'd met before, Lilly had seemed to enjoy my default attire of outlandish youth, so I dove headfirst into it.

When I made it to their house across town, I saw Darlene with her again. She must look after Lilly often, and I hoped I'd meet her dad one day. Lilly smiled and jumped off the porch to greet me when she saw me walking up. I wanted to bottle that excited energy, worried it would fade.

"Hi, Lilly, Darlene. This is such a beautiful house!" I said, stepping up the porch with my tote.

"Thanks, it's my dad's," Lilly said, opening the door to lead me inside.

"Mr. Michaels is a lawyer and has a hard time leaving the office," Darlene said quietly as she ushered me through. "A wonderful man and father, just busy."

"I completely understand," I said, and upon entering the living room, I saw the classroom-esque setup they had put together. Lilly's piano was set up facing the back window with lots of natural light; her bench looked like it probably sat at the right height for her, and her music stand was clipped to the back of the keyboard, making it easy to move around if need be. Next to that setup was another keyboard, older and a little more in disarray. The bench on that one was mismatched, but the keys looked loved, which was the most important part of a piano. A table sat off to the right of the older piano. It held two water bottles, freshly sealed.

"You're all decked out to learn some music in here, aren't you?" I said with a smile, shoving the two I'd foolishly brought with me deeper into my bag. "Most people don't have two pianos to work with; I was expecting just teaching her on one."

"It's my mom's piano!" Lilly said, and I knew she had decided to use it.

"Without Fiona here, it was just sitting around," Darlene said, and with her tone, I immediately understood she was no longer in the picture. "The one Lilly plays was through her private school; they all had to have the same one."

"That's silly; every piano can play the same music. They just have their own personality," I affirmed with a nod.

Lilly seemed to like that, and without another word, she flopped onto her seat.

Darlene watched her and nodded in a laugh. "Well, she's all ready, so I guess that's that." She looked at her watch and sat on a chair in the kitchen, clearly wanting to give us space while still being aware of how the first day was going.

"You're welcome to stay," I said, "but I'm also comfortable watching her if you need to go anywhere."

Darlene looked surprised, turning to Lilly to ensure it was something she'd be comfortable with. The girl's eyes were wide with excitement for our class, so Darlene nodded. "I may run some errands while you're here ... I'll only be just a few buildings down at the bank."

"Of course," I said, sitting at the second piano next to Lilly. "We'll be great here."

"Okay," Darlene said, sliding on her jacket. "My number is on the fridge, as is her father's anything happens. And Lilly, follow your directions and have fun, sweetheart."

Lilly's little head nodded hard, making her hair sway. "Thank you, Darlene; see you later!"

Darlene waved one last time before heading out, and I could tell she had wanted the time to herself.

"Okay," I asked, bringing my attention to Lilly. "Let's see what you've been working with so far, and we can start there or adjust to something else that will help you."

Lilly dug her hands through the music bag at her side. Individual pages of short songs and warm-ups crumpled into one another in the pink satchel, but she pulled out a bound instructional book.

"This is the one my last teacher gave us, but I hated it," she huffed, but she set it on the stand in front of us.

"Why did you hate it?" I asked, taking a look at the book. It was a typical instructional, starting with individual notes, then scales and chords.

"The songs were all so boring. We never played anything fun."

"Hm," I said, squinting as I went through the song listings. She was right on one thing—their reference material for songs all came before 1960. Most of them were classically based, and the first three pages were ones by composers Lilly probably wouldn't even have been able to pronounce yet. "I can see what you're talking about. But I've got a compromise for you."

"A compromise?" she repeated, and I could tell she might not have been fully familiar with the concept, especially as an only child who appeared to have gone to private school.

"Exactly. See, learning the basics is kind of crucial for piano. You need to learn those few first steps of walking to learn how to run or play the kind of music you want. But it can be frustrating when the music you're practicing with isn't as fun to play."

I laid my fingers on the older piano's keys, and I noticed some dust sitting between some of the keys. This piano had once been very loved, though it seemed to have gone forgotten for a while. I was proud to be the person to help bring light and song to it again.

Looking around, I saw a poster for Star Wars on the wall beside the mantle, signed by some famous names. I raised an eyebrow and pointed it out.

"Do you like watching *Star Wars* with your dad?" I asked.

"Sometimes. I like the loud music they play when Darth Vader comes in."

"Perfect!" I said, turning back to the piano. "Watch." Starting with the A and E keys, I played the simple two-chord melody of the "Imperial March" from *Star Wars*. "This was one of the first songs I learned because I recognized it, and it was fun when I could hear it myself and make the song I knew."

"Whoa, that was just like it!" Lilly exclaimed.

"And it's very easy to learn," I said, showing her the keys directly on her own piano. Just these two here, and you keep the beat here."

I gave her the example with my own playing, and she then put her hand on mine to do it with me. She seemed to learn well by applying it physically herself, so I made a mental note to give that avenue of learning to her as often as possible.

"But to play this, you need to know and understand these individual notes and how they work together. Then you can use them to build songs that you recognize, not just the dusty ones in these old books."

I showed her a melody I'd based on the same march I'd adapted from simple creative exploration over the years. It was one of my favorite things to show off to new students to emphasise other ways of learning and teaching yourself in a way that engaged your own interests. Once you had a structured passion for the music, it's easier to go back and relearn things you missed by looking at your skill weaknesses and building them up.

Seeing the recognition of possibility on Lilly's face drove me to continue the lesson with as much positive energy as I could muster. Knowing she was taking in what I was teaching her motivated me and kept me excited that I didn't even notice when Darlene opened the door and walked back in an hour and a half later.

We'd spent the time chatting and learning about each other through the lens of music. Lilly had told me her mother often played music, and though she didn't say more about it, I could see it as being a connecting piece between the two of them.

"With her focus fully engaged in the lessons I was giving her, Lilly's behavior was wonderful," I mentioned to Darlene when we chatted after finishing our lesson. "I can understand why she might struggle in group settings—she needs that attention to succeed in something she's still building confidence in, like the piano. Lots of reassurance. But she's a great little girl, and I'm so glad she seemed to like the class too."

"Like it?" Darlene asked as she poured herself a soda in a glass, waiting for the fizz to fall. "She loved it so much she forgot to use the bathroom for an hour and a half." She laughed.

"I'm so sorry about that," I offered, but she waved me down.

"No, it's fine! She used to use it as an excuse to leave class, so this is a big difference!" Darlene smiled, sipping her drink. "It's so nice to see her smiling again. I won't bore you with everything today; I know it was your first class."

"We can keep talking more later if you want," I suggested. "I hope we can work together again. She's so much fun to be around."

"She really is," Darlene said with a smile. "Want a soda for the road?" she asked.

I nodded. "I'd love one." I grabbed the cola from her hand and swung out toward the hallway, just in time to hear Lilly come out of the bathroom, hands still drying. "I'm heading out, Lilly, but thank you for a really cool class! I hope I can keep teaching you; you've done a great job today!"

"Thank you, Ms. Lewis!" she said with a smile.

It lit up my heart and fueled me for the ride home. "See you guys later!" I said and slipped out.

I stopped to get a burger and fries on the way back, treating myself to a milkshake to go with it. Celebrating my first class felt like a poor excuse, but being on my own for the first time, there was no one to tell me that fact.

As I pulled into my grandma's driveway, I noticed a green car parked across the street with its lights on inside. It wasn't one I recognized, but until it caused a problem, there was no worrying over anything. When I was inside and in the process of locking the door behind me, I watched the car pull out and exit the cul-de-sac, but I tried not to dwell on the feeling of paranoia in my stomach.

I took some time inside to relax and put on *Gilmore Girls* as a comfort show, enjoying the meal and quiet. I didn't often enjoy being alone, but nights like these made them seem a bit more tantalizing.

Around six o'clock, there was a knock on the door, drawing my attention from Rory's fight with Dean again. Despite the fact I'd seen the entire series at least three times, I still loved watching the drama unfold. At the same time, I felt my phone buzz, and I saw a text from Owen pop up. I groaned, wanting to focus on that instead, but I paused Netflix to answer the door and was surprised to see a man I didn't recognize in a business suit.

"Hi there, is this the home of the late Ruthanne Desmond?" he asked, looking down at something on his phone in reference.

"Yes," I answered, my eyes wary. "She passed away earlier this year. Is there something I can help you with?"

"Oh, I work with a law firm in the area, and we're just checking in with people we've noticed are new around town." He was being much too vague, and part of me worried this was some kind of scam or scope-out for a robbery. "It's a small town; we like to welcome people in, make them feel like they're home.

"That's a weird thing for lawyers to do. And I'm not really new in town; I grew up here," I said, my eyes scanning around the inside of the house for emphasis. "I'm Ruthanne's granddaughter, Penny."

"I see, well, Penny, I'm so sorry for the loss of your grandmother. I personally knew her a little, so I offer my deepest condolences," he said, and it felt very canned. "Are you caring for her estate here after her passing?"

"Yes," I said, "she owned it, and I needed to come back for some paperwork, so I'll most likely be staying for a while."

"What do you do?" he asked, and I wondered when the small talk would end.

I squinted, not wanting to tell him anything more than absolutely necessary. "I'm a teacher. Listen, is there anything else I can help you with? I was kind of busy." Standing straight, I tried to imply I was doing something important. And hey, relaxation and texting a hot guy were important to me.

"Of course," he said, nodding and stepping back. "Well, welcome to the neighborhood, and please let me know if there's anything I can do to help you adjust or if you have any need for a lawyer. I'd be happy to help." He flicked out a card from his suit pocket, holding it between his index and middle finger.

I took it, if only just to get him to leave. "Thank you. Have a good night," I said, closing my door and turning the deadlock as loud as possible.

Examining the card, I didn't take note of anything and simply tossed it in my junk drawer. The situation was weird, but I guess small towns like Abilene had a way of making the most normal of interactions feel odd.

Once I was comfortably back on the couch and curled up in my blanket, I opened the text from Owen.

»Have you ever seen Teeth?«

I laughed. »That movie with the carnivorous vagina?«

»That's the one. It came across my feed, and I needed to know if that's the standard for horror nowadays or if it was just a nightmare all guys have.«

»I think that might just be you.« I chuckled. I was thankful he was turning to things like ridiculous movies to have an excuse to text me.

»Ain't that the truth, shiver.«

»Just wait until you have a guy bite your labia and ask if it was sexy.«

I hoped that made him laugh, however true it was. I'd hooked up with a guy in college who'd insisted that was the way he'd always made girls orgasm.

»God, that sounds like a nightmare. I'll have to get in there myself and show you a real good time. We can have a movie night together. and it could be fun.«

While I was surprised he wanted to see me again, my stomach twirled, and butterflies inside it found wings at the thought of Owen's mouth between my legs. Marcus had done it less than five times throughout our relationship, and I'd basically had to beg him to do it for my sake.

»You've gotten good reviews then?« I asked, egging him on.

»It's hard to tell over the gasps and moans, but yes. And I enjoy it more than most others. Getting to taste my partner and feel them writhe on my lips.«

»I bet that's a line«, I teased. But as much as I wanted to deny it, I felt the arousal drip within my panties, even so, gushing in delight at what this man could do to me, could *make* me do, just at the thought of another night with him.

»Guess you'll have to find out soon.«

# Chapter 14

OWEN

I'd been up texting with Blair all night, and it left me worked up until the morning. I didn't have time to handle it myself before getting Lilly, so I was left tortured during a long and arduous work day. Thankfully, Blair had been providing me with plenty of material to keep me distracted.

»And what would you be wearing?« I asked, continuing our conversation, curious to see how filthy she could get at one o'clock in the afternoon.

»What I normally wear, probably a blouse and skirt. But it'd be drafty without panties on«, Blair replied.

I smirked, happily fantasizing about the visual of her in a skirt, blowing up just enough to spot that she was bare underneath. The thought of it nearly had me reeling, but I was pulled back to reality by Lorenzo.

"Are you logging into the call?" he asked, grabbing our coffees from the intern. "Adler's expecting us at three, and according to the file, he can be a stickler on time."

I looked up from my phone and shook off my craving for afternoon delight, returning my focus to the meeting with our new contract partners at Adler Real Estate. I had to admit that I would much rather be curled up next to Blair, a light layer of sweat covering us after a quick toss in bed.

"Hey, Owen? You going to tell your brain you're at work now, or what?" Lorenzo asked, shoving a coffee in my face. "Drink; you don't want to be sitting out for any of this."

"I'm not; I'm fine," I said, but I took three strong gulps even so. "Sorry, I'm on."

"Good, so are we," he said, and then he flicked on the camera and opened the call. "Hello, Mr. Adler!"

"Afternoon, boys, how you been?" he asked. If he were here, I knew his entrance would come with another grand handshake.

"We're not too bad, Mr. Adler, and yourself?" I asked.

"Just fine, just fine." Adler nodded with a smile. "So, I hope you boys have good news for me!"

Lorenzo started, "We think you'll be happy to hear, Mr. Adler, we spoke with our owner, Joseph—"

"And how is old Tate?" Adler interrupted, and the pleasantries began running.

"He's just fine and says hello to you," I said with a customer service smile.

"Anyway, Mr. Adler," Lorenzo continued, "we spoke with Joseph, and he agreed to sign a deal."

Lorenzo's hand went out toward the screen, and Mr. Adler didn't seem to register he was offering a "handshake" digitally. A silly concept, but it would surely win Adler over.

"That's wonderful news; I'm glad we're making it happen, but are you alright there, son?" Adler asked, leaning forward into his camera. He got close enough for us to see directly into his eyeballs, much too close for comfort.

"He meant to pretend to offer you a handshake, sir," I clarified, taking the wheel for a moment. Lorenzo, however, frustrated with his own fumbling, seemed placated. "Anyway, we're having our receptionist, Anne, send over our forms and a copy of the contract and agreements for you to sign, laying everything out. There're a few retail locations here that you'll be clearing out, but we've found those are often pretty easy to manage, especially with the budget you're presenting."

"Our backers are very excited about this venture," he said.

"But we've started doing some research," I said, building steam, "and it looks like one of the homes you're interested in moving is owned by a woman who recently passed away." I went through the file folder of the Plumosa residence, pulling out the information for Ruthanne Desmond.

"Yes, I remember seeing something about that house. The other is vacant, right?" Adler asked, rubbing his chin.

"Yes, it is, so it'll be an easy swoop in," Lorenzo said.

"It will be," I reassured, but brought the focus back to the file I had in hand, "but it looks like this one was passed down to the granddaughter, Penny. We're still ... investigating, but we'll be doing an offer pass in the next few days to present her with the relocation opportunity. We just have to hope she'll be willing to take the offer instead of attorney-ing up and making our job harder."

"I'm sure you boys can be persuasive!" Adler offered, winking too dramatically.

"That we can be, sir; we'll be sure to secure that location for you," Lorenzo said, but I stopped him.

"Of course, there's only so much we can do, and if the owner isn't willing to sell, the best we'll be able to do is offer services on another comparable location or guide you on how to move forward without her land. Obviously, the contract will go into all those policies and disclaimers," I said.

"But enough of the little details; they always come together," Lorenzo said, referring to my presentation. It irked me to no end how willing he was to try and one-up me during meetings, and he often didn't leave me a choice but go along with it.

"That they do, and once we have this mall up and running, boys, you'll be first on the list for the opening weekend! We already have seven stores signed on, and we're looking to get at least five more; that first sale period will be quite the deal!" Again, he got much too close to the camera and nudged toward us.

Lorenzo and I looked at each other for a moment and nonverbally acknowledged we had to schmooze, and then he continued, "We'd be happy to, Mr. Adler."

"So can we get some of the paperwork from you on your budgets to present to the home owner and businesses? We'll start putting together a file to present to Penny Desmond at the residence with those details as soon as next week," I mentioned, though I knew the work to start this would be occurring immediately and would not let up until the project was through.

The problem with big contracts like this is the priority it has to take because of how crucial it is to get through. That would mean late nights, weekend work, and less time to focus on my daughter, who had already struggled with the amount of work I had brought home. As thankful as I was for my job and the safety and security it brought us, there were times when I wished I could step back and focus on the things that mattered to me, like time with Lilly, instead.

But that day had yet to come. Today, I belonged to Tate Legal.

"Definitely will get our man on sending over the files. I never much know how to deal with the digital part of all this," Mr. Adler laughed. "If I had it my way, I'd mail everything over to look at by hand, but my wife says all the tree-killing isn't worth it. What can you do?" He shrugged, then smiled. "All this sounds great, boys."

"We feel the same here, Mr. Adler," Lorenzo said with a grin. "We're looking forward to continuing work on this project!"

The three of us finished our pleasantries, which consisted of Mr. Adler taking a few tries to press the End Call button. Once we were off the meeting, I slurped the remaining coffee in my cup and stood to ask Randy for another. "That went well, I think," I said to Lorenzo. "I want him to get his head out of the clouds if we can't get that last residential unit, though."

"Come on, when's the last time we haven't been able to secure?" Lorenzo asked.

"Two summers ago. That house on Lexington. We offered her a mil on a three-bedroom house, and she still turned it down," I said.

"That contract sucked ass, and I didn't even do much research on it to start. I think with a better first impression, we can make sure to get it off the first few contacts before they have much time to think it over." Lorenzo smoothed back some of his hair. "When I stopped by, she seemed kind of into me. I think I could make the offer, and she'd take whatever it was."

"Jesus, just don't get us in a sexual harassment lawsuit while you're out there, okay?" I said, but I wasn't worried. As much talk as he could be, Lorenzo was harmless. Being a predator required more of a spine, which Lorenzo lacked.

"I'm not, don't worry, but let's get that file put together ASAP. My sister's wedding is coming up in a few weeks, and I could use a date if this works out; that Penny girl is cute."

"Keep it professional," I said, shoving the file into his chest. "And get to work reading through whatever he sends over by this evening; I'll make sure to have Anne call again in the morning if he hasn't," I said, calling the last bit out. Anne gave me a thumbs-up from her desk. "Thank you, Anne!" I yelled over to her. "Now I'm out of here."

I pulled my coat on by the door, shoving my notebook into my bag and throwing the strap over my shoulder. Randy dashed over with a fresh coffee, which I'd requested despite being about to leave the office. I knew I was running low at home, and I wouldn't be stopping by the market for the next day or so with all the work ahead of me.

"Thank you, Randy," I said with a nod. "Bye, you all, get some sleep. Going to be a long few weeks."

We said our farewells, and I headed out the door back home to Lilly and Darlene. The drive home was plagued by some icy roads and drivers losing control, so I had to take my time. It was late in winter, but it had rained the other night, and a cold front had blown through and frozen it all at once.

When I pulled in, I saw Darlene and Lilly walking in their bundled-up coats, and Lilly's hands were flapping around in her mittens. I was at least glad she wore them, as it had been a point of contention until I had the chance to get her fingered ones.

"I've got good timing," I said, smiling as I opened my arms to Lilly. She ran to me, hugging me tight with a grin so wide it nearly disappeared under her scarf. "Someone's had a good day. How was your first piano class?"

"It was amazing, Dad!" she said, hugging me close as I stood, making my neck crane down. "She showed me how to play music using Darth Vader, from *Star Wars*, and she asked about my piano recitals, and she said she liked my outfit, and—"

Sounding like she'd been rehearsing this all day, Lilly nearly ran out of breath. Darlene patted her back, just coming up from trailing behind her on their walk. "I don't know about you, but I could use some cocoa. Let's get our frozen behinds inside." She laughed and huffed out steam.

"Of course, sorry, Darlene." I chuckled and grabbed one of her bags, then took an arm to help her in. "Did you guys go into town?"

"Yes, I needed to pick up something from the store," she said, then reached into one of the bags on her shoulder. "And your coffee, I got more."

I smiled, nodding in thanks. "That was very sweet of you, Darlene."

"Oh, it's nothing," she said as we made it to the door, and Lilly dinged the bell, just like she does every day. "Not twice!" Darlene said when Lilly tried to.

Lilly dove into the house, laughing and sitting on the floor by the couch to take off her mitts and shoes. She was tapping her feet the entire time to an invisible beat, and seeing her with so much joy made me light up.

"She loved it, Owen," Darlene said quietly, behind the cabinet in the kitchen where Lilly couldn't hear us. "I haven't seen her smiling like that in years."

"I'm glad," I said. So the teacher was okay? I'm assuming they weren't some murderous fiend, or you would have called."

"Oh, she's great," she said. "She's sweet and patient, understanding. I left for a bit to get my medication, not far. I came back, and it was like listening to two old friends. I think it's really good for Lilly. This teacher is good at teaching kids who struggle with focusing, and I think that's something we've been learning about Lilly over the years."

I sighed. "Yeah, I struggled with that too. Looks like she inherited more than just my good looks." My sardonic laugh was welcomed by Darlene, who patted me gently on the back.

"She inherited more than just you. Seeing her on the piano ..." Darlene said, shaking her head in what looked like disbelief. "It was like looking at a picture of Fiona, but it came to life and was making music again."

I was quiet, still tender in talking about Fiona. Being one of the biggest helps over the last few years in caring for Lilly, Darlene had seen me at my worst and hadn't judged me for a moment. She'd lost her husband a long time ago, and she'd regaled me with stories of the pain that wound caused that she said could last a lifetime. Sometimes I feared that would be me, longing for my wife to be at my side again for the rest of my existence. But Darlene helped me feel like there was a light at the end of the tunnel. Plus, she made great chicken soup, and she loved taking my daughter to the movies.

"Fiona would be proud of how far you've come," Darlene said quietly before going to meet Lilly. I caught her glance for a moment but let it go and turned my attention to dinner.

Lilly came over to us and interrupted the heavy conversation with her dramatic sighs.

"Dad, are you cooking tonight? I'm so hungry I could eat a horse," she said, drooping over on the counter.

"You really ought to get her in acting lessons, too," Darlene said with a laugh, kissing Lilly's head. "I'll see you tomorrow, honey."

"Bye, Darlene!"

"And practice your scales like Ms. Lewis said!" she hollered, making her way out.

Lilly yelped, "I will!" and waved out the window. She came darting into the kitchen, running into my leg and holding it tight. "So what's for dinner?

# Chapter 15

PENNY

"Bye, Seamus!" I called out the window to the young boy and his mother. I'd taken on another client in addition to Lilly, a kid around twelve who already knew a lot and was more in need of someone to help discipline him to keep practicing regularly.

It was so promising to get a second client, and with the income, two regular classes would bring, along with the savings I had, I didn't have want for much more. Grandma's house was totally paid off, so without rent or a mortgage to pay, my frugal lifestyle had finally seemed to pay off.

After saying goodbye to Seamus and Mrs. Morgenstern, I went inside and started cleaning up what little had been put out for his lesson—a glass of water and some extra grapes. I liked having snacks out for the kids, but I often opted for grapes because of how little they spilled on the piano if the kid didn't wash their hands and how having the nutritional option always pleased the parents.

I poured the water from Seamus's cup and started nibbling on the last few green grapes in the bowl. My phone rang as I was setting the empty dish in the sink, and I picked it up and shoved it in the crevice of my shoulder so I could wash the dishes.

"Hey, Gracie," I said, turning on the water and getting to it. "Sorry about the noise; I'm cleaning up from a lesson."

"No worries, and a lesson? Did you get another client, or is this that little girl from before?" she asked.

"It's another one! A boy, twelve, and he's skilled already, so it's just helping him on upkeep. His mom wanted a private tutor, and I guess those aren't in big supply here." I placed the few dishes I was drying on the rack, turned off the water, and wiped my hands on the towel finishing the job on my jeans.

"That's incredible! So you're actually doing it; how's it feel?"

"Really good, as strange as some things are. Just being in this house and calling it my own is weird. Like wearing Grandma's clothes."

"That's a weird way to put it," Grace replied, "but I see what you mean. But how is that Owen guy; are you still talking to him?"

I tried to hide the slight blush and nodded as I spoke, though I knew she couldn't see me. "Yeah, we're texting a bit. *Texting*-texting, you know?" I tried to insinuate what I was talking about with my voice, but she didn't pick up on it. "We've been sexy texting."

"You're sexting?" Grace laughed. "Damn, sis, I didn't think you had it in you. I'm proud of you."

"Thanks, I was hoping you would be," I said, grinning. "We've also texted other stuff, like how we're doing or about our days."

"Have you swapped pics yet?" she asked.

"Like ... like nudes?" I chuckled. "No, we haven't. But I was thinking of trying it, or at least seeing how he'd react. He seems like he's still into me."

"He looked older, you looked hot, and you screwed him in a bathroom. He'd be an idiot not to still be interested."

"There was one thing ..." I said, nervous to tell her my secret. "He calls me Blair."

94

"Your middle name? Is that what you told him that night?" Grace seemed entertained but surprised, nonetheless.

"Yeah," I said with a sigh. "And now I can't take it back, or he'll think I'm crazy for giving him a fake name and lying to him."

"It's your middle name, so it's not entirely fake. And you're a girl meeting a strange guy in a bar; that's totally normal. If anything, though, I would clear the air sooner rather than later if you want to keep talking to him."

"I do," I said. "He just makes me feel … God, I can't even really explain it. Like my stomach is going to burst into flames, but all the flames are nervous butterflies." I shook my head, flopping down on the couch with a huff. "Marcus hasn't made me feel this way since we started dating."

"Then that's a sign, sis; you gotta go for this Owen guy. Go after what makes you feel good."

"I am, I think." I smiled wistfully at the ceiling, remembering the feeling of Owen's hands on my thighs.

"In other news," I said, changing the subject before I got too distracted, "I've been doing research on stuff Grandma was working on here in Abilene before she died, and it looks like she was in the middle of establishing a benefit foundation. For kids in low-income homes to learn music."

Grace was quiet for a minute, but I swore I heard her smile. "That sounds like Grandma."

"She has all this paperwork started, but she never got to finish. And I think I want to do it, Grace, in her honor," I said, sitting up with the passion rousing in me. "I'm making enough to live off of with just two clients. So why not volunteer my time to teach kids for free when they're struggling to afford it?"

"That sounds amazing, Penny; just make sure you're not running yourself too thin. Besides, don't most foundations come with some kind of financial backing?" she asked. "You're not going to be able to fund a foundation all by yourself.

"That's where I got to thinking," I said, "what if I put together a benefit concert, then use that as an opportunity to take donations and sign-up sponsors for the foundation?"

Grace scoffed. "You've been doing a lot of planning, huh?"

"I've been a little bored, I think," I said. "I'm so used to the New York lifestyle of having seven projects on my hands and needing to make the subway before rush hour. Everything here is a bit slower, so I'm making the projects on my own. And Gracie, it feels amazing. Like I have all this freedom I've never known before. And it's all thanks to Grandma."

"She did it because she believed in you, Penny."

"She believed in both of us."

"True, which is why I have her to thank for my tuition from the inheritance. I wouldn't still be at school without her."

I smiled, wishing I could hug my baby sister and reminisce over our lost grandmother together. But for now, she lived a few hours away, so digital hugs would need to suffice.

"This whole thing really has been a mixed blessing, in a lot of ways," I said with a grin. "I miss her, but she's helping us even after she's gone."

"That's what family does," Grace assured, and I laughed with her.

Suddenly, the doorbell rang.

"Hey, someone's at the door; can I call you back?" I asked.

"Sure, love you, sis!" Grace said, cutting off the call after I said the same.

Getting up from the couch, I strode over to the door and looked through the peephole. I saw that lawyer guy from the other day, and with it being still bright out this time, I wasn't afraid of the interaction. Unlocking the door, I opened it to him, smiling in a way that made my skin crawl.

"Good afternoon, Penny; how are you today?" he asked. Today, in contrast to the last time, he had a suitcase at his side.

"I'm fine; what can I help you with?" I asked.

"My name is Lorenzo, and I'm with Tate Legal. I apologize for not introducing myself properly the last time I was here. Can I come in to chat with you for a moment? I have some questions to ask about your late grandmother's estate." He handed out his card to show proof that he was who he claimed, and along with his matter-of-fact tone and the fact that he didn't press to enter without permission, I'd allow it.

"The estate?" I asked. "I mean, sure, if you like. Come on in."

I stepped away from the door to let him inside and moved us over to the kitchen. "Can I get you anything to drink?"

"A glass of water would be fine, thank you." He opened the two buttons on his coat, taking it off to hang on one of the dining chairs. "Warmer out than I thought today."

"Yes, especially for winter," I replied, handing him a glass. "So, what did you want to talk about? Was my grandma in some kind of trouble?" I asked, hoping it wasn't true.

"No, nothing of that sort. I'm actually stopping by to give you some good fortune." He placed his briefcase on the counter, and it landed with a *thunk*. He opened it, handing me a paperwork file in a manila folder. "We're working with a real estate development company interested in taking this home off your hands. We're willing to offer you a large sum, which, in this area, would most likely allow you to have your pick of the land. It would also give you funds to relocate or do whatever you'd like."

"You want to buy the house?" I asked with a laugh, finally understanding what all this fake charisma was for. "Look, I'm sure you're willing to offer whatever, but I'm not selling."

"Of course," he said as if he were prepared for me to turn him down. "I understand that, especially after losing your grandparent, selling her house is the last thing on your mind. However, I think it could be a very helpful opportunity for you. I'm happy just leaving you some of these offer details to look over, and we can check in with you soon, maybe a few days."

He closed the briefcase, leaving me with the paperwork, which I hadn't done so much as open.

I shook my head. "I'm happy to hold onto this, but I can tell you right now, I won't be selling. My grandmother's house means a lot to me, and I'm making a life for myself in it. So I'm sure it'll disappoint your clients at the development team, but just let them know I respectfully decline their offers."

"You haven't even seen the offer yet," he said, getting pushier. "At the base, Adler Real Estate is willing to offer you upwards of $400,000 for this location, which is a steal for a three-bed, two-bath."

I took the number in stride, knowing I'd never pictured that kind of money in my life but not even knowing if it was comparable to the market. Even so, it wasn't something I'd be considering.

"Thank you for stopping by," I said, moving back out toward the hall. "I don't think I'll be needing your services. You can tell them I decline." I stood by the door, waiting for him to follow suit.

He got the message, standing and meeting me at the entryway. "I understand it's a lot to process. You have the paperwork, and my card is in there, so let me know if you change your mind. We'll be in touch."

"I don't think I will," I added, shuffling him out the door. "Thank you so much, Lorenzo."

"We'll call you next week!" he said on his way out, but I slammed the door in his face too fast for him to fully get it out.

Once the house was quiet again, I huffed and pulled out my phone, redialing my sister.

When she picked up, I didn't hesitate before starting.

"You'll never guess what just happened."

# Chapter 16

OWEN

A week later, my workload started to infringe on my home life more than I'd like it to.

"Dad, can you come help me reach the cereal?" Lilly asked from the kitchen.

I signed my name on one of the contract pages, then flipped to the next to start when I returned. "Yeah, honey, one second!" I got up with what I thought was enough time, but just as I slipped into the kitchen, I watched a shower of cheerios fall onto my daughter's head.

"Lil!" I yelled, running in to try and catch it, but failing miserably. A few pieces landed on the lip of my pajama pants, making me sigh. Lilly was standing with her hands at her sides, the image of youthful innocence and eyes widely staring at me. "I'm sorry for yelling; I just wanted to stop the avalanche." I chuckled, showing her I wasn't mad.

She sheepishly waddled to the cabinet to get the broom and dustpan. "Sorry, Dad, I thought I could reach it."

"You're getting taller, but I don't think your spurt has hit quite yet. But your mom was taller, so you've got time." I gave her a grin as I took the broom for her. "You hold, I'll sweep?" We took these positions often, as making a mess was relatively common around here.

"Yeah, I'll get it," she said, kneeling to ready the dustpan. I swept the excess around us, including some pieces that had slid under the open dishwasher door. "They got everywhere."

"I can see that."

When we'd put the pan and broom away, she turned back to her bowl and the now emptier box. "Do you want any? I think there's enough for two," she said, peering inside. "Did you already take out the toy?

"You did when we opened the box; that's why it was all mashed in and spilled," I replied without turning my back as I grabbed a small bottle of orange juice smoothie in the fridge. "But no thanks, kid, I'm okay."

I heard her filling her bowl with milk, and I often worried she would overflow it. But it was a success, and she took her cereal to the coffee table to sit on the floor by the couch. "Want to watch Looney Toons with me?"

The show had been a favorite of ours to watch on Saturday mornings like this, and I had been glad to introduce my daughter to a cartoon that had shaped me growing up. It was quality time I held dear, but my morning workload needed my full attention.

"Not today, Lil, I have to go through some work stuff, but I promise I'll make you a delicious lunch later, okay?" I drank my smoothie and brought it back to the table with me. My phone buzzed, and I saw a text from Blair, accompanied by some heart emojis.

»What sounds better, breakfast in bed after sex or breakfast in bed after sex?«

I grinned, typing back quickly, »I think both options are great; can we do one right after the other?«

»You tell me«, she replied, and a photo was delivered with the text.

Making me quiver, she had taken a photo of herself wearing only her panties, though they weren't covering much, honestly. She was draped over a counter, looking over her shoulder and holding her breasts in her hands, with her light brown hair cascading over her shoulder.

In a word, *divine.*

I barely had the chance to reply in thanks and salivation before Lilly hopped over to kiss my cheek and skip off again. My phone was shoved into my pocket to avoid her wandering eyes seeing something they shouldn't. After that distraction was gone, I sipped my coffee, diving back into the engaging world of real estate law.

I found it fascinating in many ways, and I enjoyed helping people like Adler build their dream location while still having the security and structure of an office job. But as it was a position my dad helped put me in, I often found the work more grueling than I'd like it to be. My origins of interest with my law degree were in environmental law, which was how I'd met Fiona.

Being away from Lilly, however, was a drawback of the job.

With my cup of coffee still steaming by some miracle, I sipped away and continued reading, going line by line down each page to search for any loopholes we should be aware of. Adler was trustworthy, but this was typical of any contract we did. And this contract was big.

Another twenty minutes or so went by, and Lilly came swinging back in, wanting to get started for the day. There was still a while for lunch, but she was bored with it being a weekend. She was a kid, and I couldn't blame her, but it was tough to focus.

"Lilly, can I get another half hour in?" I asked.

She complied with only a small frown, heading to her room to play with some of her dolls and their outfits. Lilly had grown up as an only child, so she was used to needing to entertain herself. It made me feel guilty at times, leaving her unengaged, but I was only human. I was only one parent, and I did what I could. She came rushing out a few minutes later, hollering something about her music class, and then I heard the notes of the piano. It was a lovely ambiance to work in, honestly, and it made for a fast pace of reading.

Ten pages later and nearly at the bottom of the coffee cup, I looked up to Lilly's hopeful face grinning at me. "Can I help you cook lunch?"

"Sure, you can; I just need to finish this up," I said.

"*Dad*," she whined, "you said 'half an hour' an hour ago. It's almost one o'clock."

"It is?" I lifted my phone and checked the clock, shocking myself. The phone then rang, and Lorenzo's name flashed. "I just have to take this, honey; I'm sorry, then we can make lunch."

This time, her huff was audible, and she went back to the living room, pulling up a show to watch while waiting.

I picked up with a sigh. "What's up?"

"Sorry to call you on a weekend, man, but I stopped by the Plumosa house last week with the paperwork and wanted to update you."

I scoffed. "Last week? Why did you wait so long? Have you at least been making progress on the other resident's home?"

"Well, I was hoping she would have called me, but seeing as it's been a silent phone line since I gave her my card ..." He trailed off but came back to promise, "And yeah, I filed all that, the house is already in transfer. But we're still shit outta luck for Plumosa."

"Why?" I asked.

Lorenzo sighed. "She rejected, didn't do so much as open the file to see the offer, even when I mentioned how much it was for."

"She didn't even open it?" I groaned, rubbing the bridge of my nose. "So this is going to be a fighter case. Great."

"Hey, Joseph said it; we're going to knock this one out of the park," Lorenzo said, reassuring me.

"Dad," Lilly interrupted, "can I practice for you for the concert?"

"Not right now, Lilly," I said, waving her off. I would need to take another few minutes at least on this call, and I needed to focus. "Lorenzo, have you reached out to her again yet?"

"No, I was going to leave that up to you after the week mark. And here we are."

"Okay, go ahead and give her a call Monday morning, and next time, please tell me after you make a proposal out in the field," I told him. "I need to be kept up to date."

"I wouldn't call Plumosa downtown 'the field,' but sure thing."

"Dad, Ms. Lewis said we each get to have a solo if we want it, so I wanted to practice the one from Princess and the Frog, but just the beginning before it gets fast, and—" Lilly's voice rattled next to me, turning into an increasingly loud buzz. She came up to the table and tried to curl up into my lap, but I was still holding the file in one hand.

"Also, Owen, how high did Adler clear us for the offer hikes?" Lorenzo asked, adding another layer to my focus and bringing me back to the call.

"I think starting on an extra five-hundred increments and clear it with them before surpassing six hundred."

"Dad, did you see the flyer I left on the table?" Lilly pestered.

"Lil, hold on!" I yelled louder than I wanted to. My fist slammed on the table, rattling it a little.

I hadn't meant to yell, but between my focus on the documents, the call with Lorenzo, and her asking about the piano, I had let the frustration spew out in anger. Lilly grew quiet and her eyes widened again, but they filled with tears this time.

"I don't want lunch anymore. And I'm not doing a song for the concert," she said, the last few words dripping with sobs as she got up and ran into her bedroom.

"Damn, dad of the year," Lorenzo said quietly after a few moments, infuriating me further.

"Shut the hell up. And yes, just make the offer again; I gotta go," I said, wanting to be off the call immediately.

"You got it, chief. Talk to you later; go after the drama queen."

I seethed as he hung up. While it was one thing to acknowledge Lilly had a hard time with emotions, I didn't appreciate his tone when teasing me about her, and I wouldn't tolerate any of it *about* her. I made a mental note to approach him about it later, but for now, I had a bigger task at hand.

"Lilly?" I asked, going down the hallway. Her door was shut, and I heard the faint whispers of a hiccup on the other side every few moments. "Lilly, can I come in?"

"No, you're gonna yell at me again," she said, her little voice cracking. She sounded like her face was stuffed in a pillow.

"I'm not going to yell at you, honey. I want to say that I am sorry; can I please come in?" I made my voice soft and gentle, one that she would find comforting rather than startling, as she had only minutes ago. I loved my daughter more than anything in the world, and I hated myself for making her feel so upset with a reaction she did not deserve.

Lilly was quiet for a second; then I heard her mumble, "Yeah," into her pillow.

With relief, I turned the door handle and went in, finding her face down on the bed with a water stain already forming on her pillowcase

105

under her face. I sat next to her on the free space on the mattress and then lifted her feet onto my lap.

"Lillypad, I'm sorry for yelling at you. I was just focused on work and stressed out, and I needed some space. But you didn't deserve being yelled at," I told her, caressing the back of her head. "I love you, honey."

She remained silent, not giving me any kind of response outside of the occasional hiccup and sniffle until I was done speaking. Seemingly taking in the apology, she made me sit as she slowly turned around, her head coming around last to draw out the last second of suspense.

My daughter, the drama queen.

"If you promise not to yell at me again," she said, considering it, "I forgive you. Under one condition!" Lilly turned her head up to meet my eyes and gave me the most serious and stern look I had ever seen on her.

"Yes?" I asked.

With my affirmation, she reached over to the bedside and grabbed her backpack, giving me a piece of paper with the label "Charity Music Concert: Admit One," and the front was designed to look like a ticket.

"So you're going to have a solo?" I asked, looking at Lilly as I took the ticket. "The Princess and the Frog one? It's pretty fast," I said, knowing what she'd reply.

"That's why I'm doing the beginning!"

I laughed, bringing her head forward to kiss it. "I can't wait to see it, kid."

"You're coming?" she asked, her brows scrunched together in hope.

"Of course, I am," I said with a smile. "I have to meet your favorite new teacher, right?"

# Chapter 17

### PENNY

"Are you sure you don't mind coming down a few days early?" I asked, putting the phone in the nook of my shoulder and shoving my things in my purse to prepare to leave. I always forgot something, but each time I got closer to a full bag.

"No, really, I could use the time off," my sister replied. "I've been in a literal ghost town for almost a week. I need to see someone not wrapped in a feather boa or covered in cobwebs."

"That sounds wild. I can't wait to hear all about it."

"On the three-hour drive, you'll have the chance to. I'm in Dodge City."

The news came out so quickly, I scoffed. "Dodge City? Jesus, I'm glad I called now. But you have to help me set up chairs in the yard when you get here, okay?"

"Yeah, of course," Grace said. "Got to get it ready for the big concert this weekend!" She let out a small squeal at the end, making me laugh.

"It's a charity concert, but I'm nervous about it. I've only ever worked with the kids one-on-one. Having everyone together for the rehearsal will be a little terrifying," I admitted.

"That's why I'll be there." I heard some rustling, and then Grace said, "I've got to let you go; we have one more thing to shoot, but I'll be done when you get here. I'll text you the address."

"Got it. See you soon, have fun!" I said.

Dodge City was a hike from here, but it was worth it to get someone else on my side to deal with all those kids—but more importantly, their parents. I was never one for being a good parent diplomat, but my sister was charismatic and kind after working in customer service and retail on the side during high school. Most moms might even remember her from the ice cream shop downtown.

Knowing the drive would be long, I grabbed my comfortable cardigan and scarf, then hiked my bag onto my shoulder and went out the door. Then I came back in, grabbed my coffee, and went out again, locking the door behind me. The drive over was smooth at nine in the morning, and I'd driven it back in high school with some friends one time, so the road wasn't completely unfamiliar.

I blew through some true crime podcasts on the way there, pulling up in a rickety old town that did look like ghosts were the main residents. The antique buildings had shutters falling off, and you could almost imagine a shootout happening in the square between the general store and the saloon. There were residential homes leading into the town center along Wyatt Earp Blvd., the address Grace had sent to me, but the entire city was stationed around being a historical sideshow. That said, an Applebee's sat adjacent to the historical museum, so it was clear who the community catered to, often with happy hour margaritas.

My car rumbled along the pavement and pulled up against the Brewing Company Grace had sent me to. The shooting team had clearly called it a day before noon, enjoying the late winter morning breeze, just late enough for the sun to warm you from the chill. They were circled around one of the tables in the back, and three of them were wearing old-style saloon dresses and corsets, hair done up with tendrils and feathers everywhere. It looked like they'd had a fun morning, but my sister looked wiped.

"Hey, you!" she said, rising from her chair to meet me. "Want some food before we head out?"

"No," I said, "I had a big breakfast this morning to tide me over, and I thought we could grab some road snacks on the way."

"Sounds like a great plan," she said with a smile, and then she turned to the group at the table. One of the men asked if it was that time already, and she replied, "Yeah, I have to go help my sister with some stuff. But thank you guys for an incredible shoot. I'll be around the area; let the agency know if you're looking for another photographer again!"

She passed around hugs and smiles, ever the people-person, impressing everyone she met. When she felt she was through, she took one last swig of what was once a very hefty mimosa goblet and then followed me out the door.

"So, tell me about this old west shoot, huh?" I asked when we got in the car and started the trek. As I pulled out of Dodge, literally, I took the chance to continue admiring the scenery. "This place is so cool."

"It is, especially when you're taking photos of sexy boudoir girls," Grace said, and she accompanied it with a dramatic sigh and slinked down into her seat.

"Wait, really?" I asked, shocked as I turned onto the main road. "You're doing sexy shoots now? That's incredible; I'm honestly shocked you have it in you!"

"Why?" she asked with a laugh. "I get to drool at hot girls all day while being a respectful photographer, and it got me a number the other day. Her name is Simone."

Another longing sigh and stare out the window.

110

My sister was such a hopeless romantic, especially regarding her relationships with women. She'd only dated one guy since high school, from what I knew, so she was constantly being wrapped around the finger of whatever cute lesbian found her that week.

"Of course, her name is Simone," I said with a chuckle. "Are they paying well, at least?"

Grace nodded, turning her attention back to me. "Oh, yeah, they're rolling in the dough. That's why they were able to afford me for the whole week. I've seen a lot of feathers in places feathers should never be," she said, laughing. "But really, it's a fun gig. I'm having the time of my life. But enough about me," she said, smacking my arm. "How about you; send any risqué pictures yourself lately?"

I couldn't stop my cheeks from reddening a little. "Maybe. They've gotten good reviews so far," I said candidly. "Look, I just want to focus on this concert and making sure everything goes perfectly. I need to ensure I have a place in the community secured if something happens with those real estate jerks."

"Yeah, what's been up with that?" Grace asked.

As she dug through the map and we found a place to stop that had milkshakes (a road trip requirement for the Lewis girls), I spun her the tale of the first drop-by with Lorenzo, followed by his car stalking me for a day or so, then his visit with the offer to buy the house.

"I just don't know how far he's willing to go, you know?" I said, handing the cashier at the window my card and taking one of the bags and a Neapolitan shake for Grace. "Since I'm not paying rent, I have some money set aside, and I have the money coming in from my students so far, but I want to make this foundation for Grandma work. And that's going to take putting in some unpaid labor."

Grace took a fry from the bag and shoved it in her mouth, despite not mentioning being hungry. "Just make sure you're not overdoing it, okay?"

"What are you talking about? I never overdo it."

***

"Grace, I think I overdid this."

I took a deep breath, placing my hands on my head to calm my pulsing heart through my temples. "The chairs are sinking in the grass. I know at least one kid has a fidgeting problem, so he's going to get mud everywhere."

"Okay, hold on," she said, taking off some of the chairs from the grass. The stale winter rain from the last few weeks had made the grass eternally damp, making it easier for the chair's plastic legs to be gobbled up into the dirt. "Here, grab that tarp."

I turned to see the tarp she was referring to, currently covering a layer of the roof on the old shed. "We can get another one later or move this back, but if we lay out the tarp, it'll stop the chairs from sinking in a little."

"Will it be enough?" I asked.

"It's going to have to be; it's almost four," she noted, looking at her phone. "Come on, help me spread this out on the grass."

I followed her instructions, slightly annoyed yet entertained at how strictly she fit the lesbian stereotype of handiwork and resourcefulness. Once we had the grass covered by the blue plastic tarp, we carefully set the chairs along it, trying to avoid any holes we'd made previously. Twelve chairs I'd borrowed from the old church (after schmoozing the ethnic foods women and talking about Grandma) were set up to accommodate the six students I had signed on and their parents. I'd set out a few more on the actual show day, but this would work fine for the rehearsal. Each spot had enough space to hold a keyboard in front of their chairs, and I'd already confirmed with five students that they'd be supplying their own. One of them only had a full piano in their family's home, so I would be letting them use my keyboard for the duration of today and the show.

At three fifty-nine, the first knock on the door alerted me, and I happily answered it, greeting the adorable little boy with glasses I'd only just signed on this week. His mom was excited about the chance of free music lessons. The next kid, the twelve-year-old I'd been teaching for a few weeks, came by. His mom left within a few minutes, with my allowance, to run some errands while he had a sitter. I could tell he was often left to his own devices, which I understood. The next two girls to show up were new, and I had been talking with their parents by email this past week. I helped all the kids with their keyboards, and the one boy I was loaning my own to was shuffled and taken care of out of sight of the other kids. Lilly arrived around five minutes past, with Darlene shuffling her through the door, carrying her keyboard.

"Can I help you with that?" I said to the older woman, taking hold of one edge of the keyboard while she grabbed the slipping stand.

"Thank you!" she said, huffing. "These things are portable, but not portable enough!"

"I know, right?" I laughed. "Thank you for bringing it with her."

Lilly had already slipped into the crowd of children gathering outside, where Grace was guiding them into their seats and setting up their keyboards with the extension cords we'd installed. She was a natural social butterfly, but I could see how her lack of attention, mixed with a need to chat, could get her in trouble.

Once it was four-twenty, I called rehearsal beginning, casting the last as a no-show. I would be contacting Caroline's parents by email that night just to make sure everything was okay, but we had to get started.

"Okay, everybody, I'm so happy to have you all here! Thank you so much for joining me to participate in the music show I'm setting up to raise funds for kids just like you, who want to learn music." I turned my attention to the parents, mostly sitting in the row behind their kids. Darlene was helping Lilly get adjusted in her seat, adapting to the lumpy foundation. "Thank you so much for your patience as we put all this together," I said with a smile.

"I know I've spoken with most of you before, but just to reintroduce, I'm Penny Lewis. My grandmother was Ruthanne Desmond." I saw one or two sad, sweet smiles on the parents in front of me, remembering. "She taught kids out of her home, just like I am today, because she cared about the children and knew how important bringing music into their lives was. So thank you for doing what you can to help continue her incredible legacy by joining me in raising funds for the Ruthanne Desmond Foundation. It's already benefitting the community, and it's only the beginning." I didn't directly reference Winston, the boy with glasses who would be continuing free classes and be the first beneficiary of the scholarship, but I watched his mother hug him into her shoulder at that point.

"Without further ado ... let's make some music!"

The rehearsal, to my disbelief, went much smoother than expected. By the end of the night, I was so thankful to have Grace there at my side. As I was teaching the kids the piano lines they'd be learning one by one, then how to play them together to create a choral sound (while still engaging their individual skill levels), Grace was keeping the ones getting distracted at bay by helping them go over finger positions and chord letters when it wasn't their turn to play. The parents were also pretty calm and understanding, and I was proud to get to show them the positive influence music could have on their kids. The twelve-year-old, Seamus, got into a bit of a tiff with his mother, but she had been micromanaging, so Grace noticed and commissioned her to help with refreshments in the kitchen.

After about two hours, every kid was bouncing off the yard gate walls with lack of focus, so we decided to call it a night.

"Thank you so much, Ms. Lewis!" Lilly said when I called the rehearsal to an end. "I can't wait to go home and practice for the show. My dad is coming too!" We walked outside together as I waved to some of the other students and Grace, who was helping people get to their cars safely.

"My dad got us a car today, isn't that cool?" Lilly said. "There!" She waved down a black Hyundai whose driver pulled up along the street and popped open the trunk. He offered to get out and help load the keyboard in, but I waved him away, showing I would do it.

"That's wonderful; it'll be great to have him here, and what a cool car, you're right!" Darlene chuckled behind me with the piano stand at my energy with Lilly. "Have you been working on the beginning of 'Down in New Orleans?'" I asked her, loading the instrument into the back.

"She definitely has," Darlene said, putting in the stand after me. "While I'm with her, she goes over it a few times each day."

"I'm just happy I get to play a song I know, none of that Back stuff," she said, giving me a *yuck* face while shaking her hands.

"Are you talking about Bach? There's a time and place for him, trust me. But you can learn that when you're older." I looked over at Grace with a smile. She was doing the same for Seamus' mother and not missing a beat in offering physical labor. "For now, just have fun with the music. Explore the sounds you can make and fall in love with it. That's what music is for."

Lilly was delighted by my answer, wrapping her arms firmly around my waist in a hug. "You're the best, Ms. Lewis."

Darlene gave her that moment, realizing how thankful she was for this class and, by extension, me as a teacher. It touched my heart that I was such a positive influence on this young girl who was still building up an image of who she was and how she saw the world. Amid all that prepubescent confusion and development, she looked to me for guidance and support. It made me want to do better, be better, for kids like her.

They were our future, after all.

I took a second to pull my thoughts together by rebinding my heartstrings with this little girl's smile and opened the back passenger door. "Hop on in because the sooner you head out, the sooner the concert will be!"

"Whoo!" she hollered, jumping into the car and buckling up as Darlene did the same.

"See you next week, Ms. Lewis!" Darlene yelled from her seat as the driver pulled off with them in tow.

One week. I had one week to pull the rest of this together.

Phew.

# Chapter 18

OWEN

"Owen, don't forget to sign this last page!" Anne called out to me, making me swerve back into the office. "It's the last one, I promise!"

I huffed and pulled the pen from my shirt pocket, clicking it to sign the sheet. I was already running late to beat the traffic, and I felt my phone buzz again. I was terrified that it was another nude from Blair, which I had certainly appreciated, but I didn't want anyone else in the office to see. We'd been texting pretty consistently but keeping things more or less casual—we both knew so little about each other— kept it exciting.

Once I had signed the sheet, I pulled my phone out to see another text from Darlene, checking in to see what time I would arrive at the house to pick up her and Lilly, as they had the keyboard again and could use the lift.

"Okay, nothing else?" I asked, clearing with Lorenzo, Anne, and Randy.

Each shook their heads, and Lorenzo added, "Just make sure to read through the next formal offers I drafted to give Plumosa Ave, and we're good. Go have fun, enjoy Lilly's concert, and tell her we said good luck."

I smiled, nodding. I'd been talking about it all afternoon and stressing how quickly I needed to leave the office. And now, I was burning that candle a little too close. "Good, then I'm out of here."

"Oh," Lorenzo mentioned, "I was going to try and stop by the Plumosa house again this afternoon, maybe catch her home from work in a good mood for a proposal."

"Okay, thanks for staying on top of it, Lorenzo," I said, but my mind was already out in the parking lot, where I needed to be. "See you guys next week; get some rest!" I yelled, going out the door.

Once in my car, I sped home, nearly blowing two stop signs in the process. Lilly and Darlene were already waiting outside for me, and Lilly was wearing her shiny dress she'd picked out that morning with all the sequins that change color when you rub it a certain way. I'd told her that when she got bored between solo songs to play with her dress, which she loved, and I was sure Ms. Lewis would appreciate the tactic.

After four weeks of lessons, I was excited to finally be meeting the teacher that got my daughter so excited to learn piano, something I'd been trying to get her to connect to for two years now. She definitely had an affinity for it when she focused, and she used to bond with Fiona over it, so I know she loved it too. But finding the right way for her little brain to learn while getting so easily distracted and lost in her own world made keeping a consistent teaching schedule hard.

Ms. Lewis must have been one hell of a woman.

I pulled up, opened the trunk, and grabbed the keyboard out of Darlene's hands from where she had it leaning against the wall. Lilly followed me with the music stand, swishing in her fluffy dress all the while.

"You excited?" I asked with a laugh. "Everyone at the office knows and wishes you good luck!" I dropped the keyboard in the trunk, did the same with her stand, and then pulled her in tight for a hug. "I can't wait to see you play up there."

"It's not a real stage," she said, grumbling when I dad-handled her, making me laugh more. "Ms. Lewis made her backyard into one, and the chairs kind of sunk in the grass."

"I'm sure it'll be an amazing show," I promised her. "Now get in and buckle up. Darlene, do you have her address?" I asked.

"Sure," she said, pulling out her purse for the exact house number, I guessed. "It's on Plumosa Avenue."

My brow lifted, not remembering there being too many people on that block

outside of the one we were addressing for work. That was why that location was such a win—it and the other house that wasn't currently occupied were the only ones on the general land Adler wanted.

"Plumosa, you're sure?"

Darlene nodded, finding the invitation to the concert. "Here it is, 2402 Plumosa Avenue."

Hearing the house number, I had to force my jaw to stay up when it wanted to drop to the floor. "You're joking." Darlene seemed confused, and I looked back to make sure Lilly was engrossed in her music through her kitty headphones, how she often decompressed before big events. I whispered to Darlene, "That's the residence we've been working on at the firm. We're trying to get her to sell the house."

Darlene's eyes widened, and she shook her head. "And you had no idea?"

"No," I said, sighing and turning the corner onto Plumosa. "I've been so busy with work, and you've been taking her to the lessons. There's no way you could have known unless you gave me the address directly."

"It was on the invitation playbill flyer Lilly gave you the other day," she said.

I blanched. "It's on my desk; I just haven't had the time to read through it."

Darlene frowned a little, glancing back at Lilly before turning to me as we pulled up along the winding road leading to the Lewis house. "Just make sure this is a day for Lilly. She worked hard, try to leave work behind for a little."

"I know, I will," I said, sighing. "It just always seems to find me first."

Our little caravan made it to 2402 Plumosa Avenue, and once we were parked and all out of the car, I took the lead with the piano as Lilly followed with the stand. Penny Lewis had placed lights all along the entrance. It was still bright out, but it would make for a beautiful ambiance when we left at the end of the night.

Lilly went ahead of me, looking around at the lights and the poster Penny had set for the event. *Charity Concert to benefit the Ruthanne Desmond Foundation.* In the bottom corner of the banner, there was a small photo of Penny. She was young, pretty, with light brown hair cascading softly over one of her shoulders.

But one thing stopped me in my tracks.

It was a photo of Blair, the girl from the bar with whom I had been having ridiculously sexual text conversations. She was my daughter's piano teacher and the owner of the house we were trying to claim.

"That's Ms. Lewis?" I asked; my tone of shock made it clear something was amiss.

"Yes, I'm Ms. Lewis, Penny, nice to—" I heard from the front door, but when I brought my face up to meet her with wide eyes, she matched them. "Owen?" she asked.

I shut her down fast, not wanting to raise suspicion in front of my daughter. "Yes, I'm Lilly's father; I don't think we've met yet ... Penny." I said, squinting my eyes a little at her name.

In front of both Darlene and Lilly, her cheeks turned the color of roses, and I hated how cute it looked on her. I'd fantasized about bending her over my cabinet to compare to the gorgeous photo of her ass she'd sent me, but now we had a bit of conflicting interest.

Darlene took the lead, breaking the silence. "I'm going to get Lilly inside; why don't you two chat!" She led a hyper-focused Lilly into the backyard, and I could hear her exclaiming about the decorations and how hard Ms. Lewis had worked on dressing up the place.

Blair—*Penny*—and I stood eye-locked.

She was the first to speak once we were alone, and she checked to make sure no other families were approaching yet. "I have to keep taking care of the kids, but can we talk afterward? I promise, I can explain things, and we can ..." she drifted off, and I nodded in reply.

"Of course, today is about Lilly; that's why I'm here." I cleared my throat. "You have a lovely home, Penny." I practiced saying her real name out loud as a way to make the situation *feel* more real in my head.

I heard Penny acknowledging other families at the door, and I didn't want her to get overwhelmed on a big day like this, so I continued to the backyard to meet Lilly and Darlene. The yard was decorated with small flameless candles that would surely become more present as the sky darkened slowly this evening. Penny had also put up a big sign hanging from a tree next to the house. It was the same

122

as the one out front, but this one had a big arrow drawn on it in black ink.

Lilly was setting up her piano on the small stage Penny had established with the woman Penny had introduced as her little sister that night at the bar. I tried to slink to my seat next to Darlene, giving me the most curious stink-eye I'd ever encountered. I waved a hand toward her down low, showing I didn't want to talk about it, and she didn't continue to press. She'd said it first; today was about Lilly.

Slowly but surely, the families filed in, and kids between what looked like six and thirteen filled up the spots on the small stage. It seemed pretty cramped, but Lilly mentioned they were doing one group number and would then clear off. Lilly was swirling on her stool behind her keyboard, stretching her hands. It was wonderful to see her so focused and excited; she was always one to enjoy the spotlight of a stage.

Penny's sister caught sight of me while helping one of the boys up on stage, and her eyes bugged out. All I could do was slink slightly lower in my seat, but I realized that if I did that too much, the chair would sink into the dirt, even over the tarp Penny had laid out.

After around twenty minutes of people loading in and seats filling with children and loved ones coming to see them perform, Penny came on stage, using a small microphone they'd hooked into a sound system that looked like it came out of a highschooler's parent's garage. Knowing what I did about this house, it more likely came from their grandmother, but I couldn't see the woman they'd described hosting rock band rehearsals.

"Thank you, everyone, for coming by today. We're so excited to show off all the hard work we've been doing!" She looked around at the students and seeing how enthusiastic she got when teaching, as well as knowing how charismatic she could be from my own experiences, and I could easily tell how Lilly had fallen in love with her. She seemed to make it very easy to do.

"My grandmother, Ruthanne Desmond, taught piano out of her home for years, just like I'm doing today. She gave back to the community, so I'm doing the same. Some of these students have been working with me for a few weeks, but most of these amazing kids have been receiving free rehearsal lessons to prepare for this event. Today, we're raising funds to allow students whose families are struggling financially to receive assistance and scholarships for free music lessons and opportunities. It's something my grandmother wanted to do all her life, and I'm so proud to be able to continue that dream in her honor. Thank you for all of your support, and we hope you can enjoy the work we've done." She clapped her hands together, being the perfect presenter and spokesperson for this foundation. "Now, without waiting another second longer because I know my kids are excited to play for you ..."

She turned her head to look at the children on stage, and they responded enthusiastically, "Let's make some music!"

It was adorable, and I'd never seen Lilly so happy to participate in class.

The students, together, performed an iteration of "Don't Stop Believin'" by Journey, allowing some of the more advanced pianists to take the lead and play more complicated chords and sections. Lilly's head bopped up and down as she very carefully played one hand of chords for the chorus, a slower beat that she could handle. Every once in a while, she could toss in a second hand for a section, but she mostly focused on her right.

By the end of the song, the parents and family in the audience were so thrilled that they shouted and roared for their students. Darlene and I were two of them, standing for my daughter. Lilly seemed to find it a little embarrassing, but I glanced over at Penny, and seeing how much pride she had in the children, I could tell how much it meant to them both.

After the applause, the stage cleared, and each of the students had their moment for solos. Darlene got very into each performer, reaching out to the parents cheering the loudest, and telling them how talented their children were. Once the time came for Lilly's solo, it became clear it was more of a duet. She was doing some opening lines of the Finale version of "Down in New Orleans" from *The Princess and the Frog*. It tickled my heart to see her so delighted in the simple keys she recited, and I could tell how hard she'd been working to focus on the melody she was playing.

Darlene and I stood once again for her "solo" with the young girl with straight black hair at the piano next to her. Penny and her sister joined in the applause, as they had for the other students, but Penny's smile was brighter. Darlene's eyes had tears in them when I watched her turn back.

"It's been a long time since I've had a child to tear up over while watching them perform," she said, and she squeezed my hand. I squeezed back.

Toward the end of the concert, Penny took the stage with the last student, who stood following their last notes of "Don't You Forget About Me" to do a fist in the air, a la Bender in *Breakfast Club*. His dad, a grumpy-looking man with white tufts spewing from under a shaggy mop of hair, returned the fist.

Penny laughed as the young man made his exit, and I admired her for letting these kids get creative with the music choices they performed.

"We're so happy that you've chosen to spend your evening with us. I'm so proud of each of these students, and I hope to work with them all again in the future. I know I'll see some of them next week at their respective lessons!" She smiled and looked back at Lilly and one of the other children, a cute little guy with glasses. "Other than that, our donation bins remain at the entrance to the house, and we're so grateful for every dollar in there. It means kids like these can learn to play without stressing their families in times of need. Thank you so much, everybody!"

Penny Lewis received a standing ovation from every member of the audience and all of her students. She was glowing.

And as much as I hated to admit it, I missed seeing that glow.

# Chapter 19

"Everybody ready?" Darlene asked, looking around at the rest of the parents and kids gathered by the house entrance. After taking in pianos that were staying here and loading the others into their respective cars, everyone gathered inside to discuss going out together to celebrate. She and some other parents coordinated to hit Mama's, the diner downtown. It was within walking distance from the house—I could see why the real estate company was interested in the land, at least—and it further solidified the community I was trying to create.

"Let me get our coats," Seamus's mother said as she pulled them from the pile on the couch.

"I can get mine, Mom," he said, taking the coat from her hands and tugging it on. He was constantly looking for ways to find independence from her, and I hoped she'd notice soon.

The kids all squabbled, excited from the rush of the performance. Lilly took the lead in socializing with some of the other kids her age, including Seamus and Caroline, who had overcome a lot to perform today. Yesterday, it seemed, she was having piano troubles, but she was also prone to stage fright. I was delighted to receive her call that morning, out of wanting to help her overcome that fear.

I grabbed my own coat, making sure everybody made it out the door so I could lock it. "Grace, did you lock the back?"

"Yeah, we're good," she said at my side, shoving her hands in her pockets.

"You're coming too, right?" I asked Owen, who had been straggling upon following Lilly. I could tell he wanted to talk to me but didn't quite know how to take the initiative. He'd said he was a lawyer, so I was surprised at how nervous he seemed to be. I made a mental note to ask his legal advice on the people trying to buy the house, but that would be at least after a milkshake or two.

Owen looked at Lilly, then at Darlene, who was having a wonderful time socializing with the parents ahead. Most of them knew her anyway, as a neighborly woman in a small town who could often be seen walking to all her errands and appointments.

"Yes," he said, "I think I can squeeze it in. I cut out of the office early for the show."

"Perfect," Grace said, shoving him forward and into me a little so it would seem obvious if we didn't walk next to each other as the procession of parents and children proceeded down the sidewalk toward Mama's. Owen and I took caboose, ensuring we didn't lose anyone along the way. Really, it was an excuse to stay and talk to him.

"Man, that office must keep you busy if getting in a stop at the diner is cutting deeply into your schedule," I said, placing my hands in my pockets to keep them warm in the chilly air. It was just about getting dark—we'd timed the concert perfectly; it would have been too dark and cold to do after the sun went down.

Owen nodded with a chuckle. "Yeah, they keep me busy. Work is ... it's actually something I wanted to talk to you about, but first ... who is Blair?" he asked.

I huffed, having hoped we could wait until later for this talk, preferably accompanied by something to ease my nerves. "It's my middle name. I just introduce myself like that when I go out sometimes; it's a girl thing, I..." I sighed. "I'd just gotten out of a big relationship, and I was so nervous that night. By the time we ... you know," I kicked at the ground with the back of my heel, the bashfulness seeping through, "You already knew me as Blair, and it felt silly to tell you my first name is Penny."

He nodded, and I kept trying to meet his glance to find a response. But all he said was, "I understand."

"I didn't mean to lie to you, Owen," I said, and I meant it. "I've really ..." I lingered, my voice getting soft. "I've enjoyed talking to you these last few weeks, and I didn't want you to cut me off because of that."

"No!" he said too loudly. The crowd ahead of us noticed and turned back to check, making him grumble and wave them off. "No, it's not a big deal. You know, we're still getting to know each other."

He was surprisingly responsive, enough that it felt suspicious. As we strode along the sidewalk, I watched his body language, a firm gait, and hands clenched in his pockets.

"There's a lot we still don't know about each other, and I think that is part of the fun," he said quietly, nudging me along my side. "That's why I was hoping to talk to you, so we could do that. Because I have some things I need to tell you, too."

We came up to the downtown's excuse for a strip mall, which meant the diner, a few shops, a grocery store, and a handful of smaller eateries. There wasn't much to do around here, but if there were, it was in this central area.

I nodded. "We can." I hopped up to Grace and Darlene, leading their respective packs. "Why don't you guys head in? I might be a little behind; I'm going to talk to Owen for a little bit."

Darlene was already the life of the party, taking the hollering kids inside to play at the two coin machines next to the checkout counter. Grace stopped me for a second, but then she nodded. "Be in soon, okay? Everybody's here for you," she said, hugging my side as I held the door.

"We will, but they're here for all of us." I smiled brightly. "Get me a strawberry milkshake?"

"Of course, and fries for the table."

"I was counting on it," I said to her, laughing. I let go of the door and met Owen back outside. "We can chat for a little bit. As long as we don't get frozen out," I said with a grin.

"Of course. I just ... so you've been the one teaching my daughter the whole time?" he asked, and it came with a hand over his face. "And the texts too." Thankfully, his distress ended in a laugh. "I'm surprised I didn't find out somehow anyway."

"I know, and I'm sorry for keeping my real name from you. I guess that could have easily solved the problem, hm?" I said. "But Lilly is ... she's a wonderful student. Seeing her grow and being the one to help guide her hands as she learns is one of the most rewarding experiences I've ever had." I brought my eyes to his and was happy to see that he had met them. "May I ask something that might be candid?"

"Yes," he said, but the crinkle in his eyes and along his forehead told me he was concerned, so I treaded lightly.

"Lilly's mother ... does she play music? Lilly has mentioned her before, particularly about her favorite songs to play or things they used to do together to practice, and I just didn't know how present she is in Lilly's life." I did have my own ulterior motives for knowing about Lilly's parental history, but I didn't make any of that known to him.

Owen turned from me to lean against the wall, looking out at the street ahead of us. It had just been covered in a light sprinkle of snow this morning, so it shone in the bright sun. "Lilly's mom ... Fiona, died about two years ago in a car accident." He didn't seem to have the strength to say extraneous words about the event. I didn't blame him.

"Lilly loved playing piano with her. It made her feel close, and she's been struggling with her mom being gone still. We both are." He got quiet for a second, his eyes lingering on the ground before coming back up again. "But that's why I'm so glad she's putting it into her piano. She's been happier than ever while still being focused and attentive, working with you," he said. "You've been such a positive influence on her life. On our lives."

Our eyes met, and we held contact for a moment. He turned away first, and I wished he hadn't.

He turned his gaze to the ground again, shuffling his feet in boyish nervousness. "I don't want our relationship to affect the one you have with Lilly. And you just came out of a relationship, as you said—"

I cut him off. "I'm making my life over here, I only just broke up with Marcus the day you and I met, but I'd been distanced from him for a while." I sighed. "I came out here to take care of my grandma's home, and I started building a life for myself. I don't really have anything else," I admitted sheepishly. "I've got Grace, but she travels and goes to school. I can't ask her to stay in a little town like this." I took a deep breath and looked at Owen next to me, who I'd noticed had turned his whole body to face me. "And that night with you, even for what it was ..." I reached out to touch his arm. "I haven't felt that alive in a while, either."

Owen reached out and put his hand on mine, and he held it there, rubbing his fingers against my own. "Me too," he said. It was fewer words than I wanted, but I knew he meant them with the seriousness of his tone.

We stood there against the wall for a moment, still and silent. Our hands remained entwined on his coat, and it wasn't until he started feeling my fingers shiver from the cold on top of his that he covered them with his other hand.

"Let's get you inside."

I nodded, feeling the cold hit my core. He let me walk in first, holding the door behind me and, shocking me, placing a hand on my lower back on the way. It felt so comforting and intimate, even while being in such a public place.

The families were sat at a table-booth combo toward the back, and the waiters were just bringing out the drinks, so we hadn't missed much. Darlene and one of the other parents noticed us coming back in together, and Darlene gave me a knowing smile. I blushed unwillingly as Owen pulled out my seat next to Grace and let me slide in. Of course, the minute she realized, Grace turned to me with wide eyes and a smirk. She approved.

"And Darlene ordered you a milkshake? You haven't had dinner yet!" Owen said, looking at the ginormous shake, along with a glob of whipped cream and a cherry, in front of Lilly.

She grinned and nodded, shoving a spoon in and mostly getting whipped cream. "She said to celebrate my performance!"

Darlene gave Owen a sheepish smile, and he chuckled. It was great to see him so concerned and supportive of Lilly, even with needing the help of Darlene. I couldn't imagine how hard it must have been to lose Lilly's mom so suddenly like that, and from what I'd seen of Darlene interacting with Lilly, it was a mutually beneficial relationship as Darlene doted on her like a grandchild. Until I noticed Lilly kept using Darlene's first name, I'd thought she *was* Lilly's grandmother.

"Ms. Lewis, can we raise a toast to you?" Caroline's mother suggested. "It's silly, but I'm so proud of getting to see my little girl on stage, finally."

Caroline huffed, the dramatic pre-teen in her ignited with embarrassment. "Mom."

"I mean it," her mother said. "To Ms. Lewis," she continued, raising her glass toward the center of the large table, and all the other parents and kids circling it joined in.

"Only if I can include Grace in my toast. And Grandma," I said the last part quietly. I wasn't great at receiving praise and compliments, so it made me nervous about getting everybody's eyes on me at once for anything positive. But in each of their shining faces, I saw Grandma's eyes shining back at me.

Grace laughed and nudged my side. "This is all you, sis."

Everybody cheered, raising their glasses to me, and I smiled gratefully. "Thank you, everybody. It's been such an honor working with your kids. I only just arrived back in Abilene a few weeks ago, and I had no idea what I was doing then. But now, building this community with you all around music gives me a purpose. And now, I don't think I could be anywhere else," I said, offering a small smile to Owen by the end of the speech.

# Chapter 20

OWEN

Throughout dinner, I was racking my brain about how to get Penny out of that house without ruining the tentative relationship both Lilly and I had with her. I ordered a coffee, and then with the incessant buzzing of my phone, I huffed. Darlene looked at me from her seat, noticing I'd mentioned being off from work for the evening. My shoulders raised in an innocent shrug as she knew how invasive work could be for me.

I checked my texts, and Lorenzo had asked if I still wanted him to stop by this evening. Remembering all the balloons and posters up outside of the house and that he knew Lilly had a music concert today, I panicked.

»No, not tonight. Stop by on Monday; I have some things to file first. Thanks for holding off, I appreciate it«, I texted back, driving my point home. I didn't want him to see all the decorations and make the connection that Lilly was taking classes from the woman we were trying to get out of her house.

Not to mention the fact that I'd been exchanging lewd texts with her for weeks after a hookup at the local dive bar.

The hole I'd dug for myself was beginning to give way.

My attention turned to the kids who had made themselves comfortable in the diner's small "arcade," which was much too generous a word for the few machines it contained, including a pinball machine, Big Buck Shooter, and a few coin crank machines next to the ATM.

"It's my turn, Seamus," Lilly whined, crowding up along Seamus and some other kids at the pinball machine. "Darlene gave me quarters for it."

"Go play the shooter game," he said, shrugging toward the old machine in the back with accompanying guns.

Obviously distraught, Lilly fumed, walking over to spend her money on the coin crank machine next to the ATM and the bathrooms. Caroline soon found her and offered to show her how to play Big Buck Shooter, which she now apparently found cool because another girl wanted to play it.

I loved watching her interact with Caroline, just to see her happy and playing with other kids without the worry of being mistreated. By sharing this small event they all put on together, Penny had given my daughter new friends she had something in common with, minus the snotty attitude that often came with students in paid music classes. Lilly seemed so happy.

Not wanting to alert anyone, including judging parents, that anything was wrong, I turned toward Darlene. "I'm so sorry, girls, but I'm going to have to run home. Darlene, would you be willing to stay with Lilly for a while longer?"

"Of course," Darlene said. "She seems like she's having fun. I haven't seen her play much with other kids like this."

"Caroline has always been very friendly with other kids," her mother said, and I could tell she worshipped the girl.

"You have to go?" Penny asked, and the look in her eyes told me she'd wanted more time together after dinner.

Unfortunately, with how soon all things could unravel, I had to cut the time short. "Yeah, I have a big project at work, and my partner just let me know about some issues that I need to handle." It wasn't entirely a lie, but it wasn't nearly enough of the truth for my taste.

"Just let me know when you're ready to leave with her, and I'll order the car," I told Darlene, buttoning up my coat as I prepared to leave.

I walked over to Lilly, and she had the Buck Shooter gun pulled up to her chest, ready to aim. "How's it going here, ranger?" I asked, ruffling her hair a little.

"Dad, I have to focus, you're not supposed to hit the deer, just the bucks!" she said, taking another shot. The gun didn't physically react when she did, but the sound made her jump back a bit.

"Good shot!" Caroline said at her side, nudging her a little.

Seamus looked over at them from pinball and rolled his eyes as Caroline stuck her tongue out at him.

"I have to slip out, Lilly. I'm going to get a car for you and Darlene when you're ready to come home, and I'll meet you there," I said.

To my shock, Lilly didn't drop a beat, not even turning away from the screen to talk to me. "Okay, Dad, I love you, see you there!" she said.

After all my years of having Lilly pretending to weep in my arms, flailing out in a faux death at mentioning I had to leave a function for work, seeing her barely respond at all was a double-edged sword. I was so proud to see her becoming independent and unshakable when I was not there with her, but part of me wished my little girl would beg me to stay and play with her again.

But Lilly was making her own friends and finding happiness without me, and that meant I'd been doing my job as her dad right.

"See you at home, Lillypad," I said quietly so as not to embarrass her in front of Caroline. I kissed her on the head and slipped out the door of the diner toward my car.

I hopped in quick, wanting to rid myself of the cold winter air freezing me to my core. After the new year, the fun holiday spirit always wore down in me, and the slush left afterward for weeks felt like the mess left in Times Square after the ball drop. Just a sad reminder of days already past you.

I sped home, doing my best not to catch any ice and go skidding, but I was on a mission.

From the moment I got inside, I was on the hunt for my files on the Plumosa residence, and the deal we had cut out with Adler. Maybe there was a loophole that would allow us to transplant things, so she could keep the house. It had been done in real estate before, but the costs would be astronomical, and I doubted Adler would find it worth it. He could, however, catch on to my conflict of interest and get the entire firm removed from the case.

That was my bigger fear.

As I was nose-deep in some of the case files by my desk, my phone buzzed again, this time showing a call.

I picked up. "Hi, Lorenzo."

"Hey, so how come you don't want me to stop by? We were all set with that next offer. If we can get her signed before the weekend, we might be able to start working on demolition," he said.

I swallowed hard, imagining that beautiful home Blair's grandmother had made for herself, where my daughter had discovered her love of music again, beat into the ground with a wrecking ball. Less than a day ago, that house meant nothing more than a paycheck to me. But now …

"I just want to hold off. Intuition," I said, my brain scrambling to come up with an excuse. As I spoke, I got the text from Darlene saying the two of them were ready to be picked up. I huffed silently, trying to focus on putting the order in for the car while talking to Lorenzo.

"You've never been one to go with your gut, what's going on?" Lorenzo asked, intrigued.

I held the phone off my ear and put it on speaker to finish the order, sighing when it was complete. "I … I have this bad feeling that we're going to have issues with the foundation or with deconstruction," I said, hoping I wasn't coming off too flighty as I tried to think of an idea. "Plus, we've been looking into it; right, this old woman who just died, she was a neighborhood favorite. Are we sure we won't have protestors, things like that?"

Lorenzo laughed. "I mean, sure, it's possible, but it's nothing we haven't taken care of before. Why, are you hearing anything around?"

"No, not yet," I said. "I don't think anyone knows we're developing, so they probably just haven't rounded up yet."

"Are you okay, O?" Lorenzo asked. "You sound a bit off, was Lilly's thing okay?"

"Her recital?" I asked, then nodded despite not being seen. "Oh, it went great. She did great," I said with a smile. "I'm so proud of her."

Lorenzo was quiet for a moment, most likely taking stock of my tone and thinking about how to proceed, so I cleared my throat to jump in first before he asked too many questions.

"Listen, can we just hold off until next week? I can talk to Adler if he starts pressing, but I would just appreciate it," I said.

He seemed to take a moment to consider the request, then he said, "Okay, I'm trusting you here. But you're acting weird. Go have a drink or something, get laid."

"Not really the problem here," I said, but my sex life was, in fact, a *big* part of the problem. Granted, Penny would still be Lilly's teacher, but I wouldn't have been half as emotionally invested if I hadn't met Penny at the bar.

"I'm just saying, it might help," Lorenzo said, then chuckled. "Talk to you later; get some rest."

"Bye, Enzo," I said, then I hung up the phone.

With a huff, I stared down at all the pages in front of me. Details describing the bones of the house, the structure of the land it sat on. Then the plans for the mall to be placed on top of it—it seemed the Lewis residence would soon be the base of a department and shoe store. In any other case, I wouldn't even look at the profile of the current resident we were relocating, aside from information I thought might be useful to inspire them to take our deals. To manipulate them into accepting.

I'd faced many ethical dilemmas in my life as a lawyer, most of which still held a twinge of guilt for me. I went into my work wanting to help people, it was why I'd originally gone to law school. But somewhere along the way, between raising and needing to support Lilly and furthering my career, I lost sight of that. And I hadn't realized just how distant that dream felt until looking at the picture of Penny on her profile. Her smile gleamed, and I could tell it wasn't the most recent photo, maybe from a year ago. Her eyes, brown with lighter flecks of what could be pure gold, stared back at me, naïve to my motives to literally rip her home, all she had, from under her. Right when she'd started to feel at home.

I wouldn't be the one to take that home away from her. But until I could figure out a way around it, there was no way I could tell her the truth. Not without her turning away from me entirely.

139

And to be perfectly selfish, I couldn't lose that feeling in my chest that she'd awoken for the first time in two years. The first time I'd truly felt alive since losing Fiona, a caveat I hadn't mentioned to her earlier.

I heard thundering steps outside, signaling Darlene and Lilly's arrival. Darlene opened the door, and I waved over from my desk, still breathing off the realizations from the end of the call. "Hey, girls," I said, walking over to greet them.

Lilly looked more exhausted than the time I'd taken her to Disneyland for three days. I laughed when I saw her, and Darlene set her bag down with a huff.

"I found *someone* with the older girl, Caroline, doing what they called 'sugar shots' by the video games. There were six empty packets on the chair next to them," Darlene said with one brow raised. Lilly didn't look up. Instead, my daughter flopped on the couch and closed her eyes to rest. "She was bouncing off the walls for about fifteen minutes, but she started nodding off on the car ride over."

"It was just so much fun; I got so tired!" Lilly said, her eyes still closed. "Ugh, and now my stomach hurts," she groaned.

I grinned as I approached her and placed a hand on her cheek. "You are pretty sugar sensitive, Lillypad, but I'm glad you have fun. Just try to remember this cruddy, tired feeling. It'll help you in college," I said, making Darlene laugh at my side. Lilly didn't understand the joke, but she was also barely paying attention as she began falling asleep.

"So, it was lovely to see you talking with Ms. Lewis. I'm glad you two can finally meet," Darlene said with a knowing smile.

At that, Lilly's eyes burst open as if someone had passed her another sugar shot. "Dad, are you and Ms. Lewis friends? You looked like you'd met before." She rolled over onto her side, then pulled herself up.

"No," I said quickly, too quickly for Darlene not to notice. But then again, she had seen me grab Penny's hand on accident once at the diner, so she must have known something was up. "No, we first met today. I just thought I knew her from the address, but nope." I popped the sound on the P.

With a raised brow, Darlene eyed me, but she knew better than to keep pressing.

Lilly, on the other hand, piped up, "Are you going to ask her out on a date?"

Darlene chortled in response, but I waved my hand over my daughter's face. "No, she's your teacher, why would you ask that?"

"She doesn't wear any rings, so she's single," Lilly said, matter-of-factly.

I chuckled. "That just means she's not married, but anyway," I said, nudging Lilly softly, "I think it's about time you brush your teeth and get ready for bed, huh?"

"Your dad's right," Darlene said, taking my lead. She walked over and hugged Lilly's head into her side, and Lilly wrapped her arms around Darlene's waist. "You did incredible today. I'm so proud of you."

"Thanks, Darlene," Lilly said earnestly, hugging her tight. "I'm so happy you were there."

"Wouldn't miss it for the world," she said, then turned toward the door as Lilly got up to start the bedtime process. "Goodnight, Owen." Darlene came over and hugged me, taking me by surprise.

I squeezed the older woman tight, thankful she was in my and Lilly's lives. Without her, I don't think I would have survived getting on with Lilly after losing Fiona. Knowing she had most likely taken care of Lilly's leg of the bill at the restaurant, I dug in my pocket once we pulled

141

away. "This is yours for today," I said, giving her some money to help cover her and Lilly's cost, as well as a little extra. I hadn't helped cover her groceries this week.

"You know I don't like taking this all the time," she said.

"I know," I replied, "but you've still got bills, and you spend a lot of time taking care of my daughter. So let me help."

"All right," she begrudgingly said, then she pulled me aside for a moment. "You said Ms. Lewis' is the house you're demolishing?"

I swallowed hard, realizing she was in on at least part of my lies to Penny. "Yes. But I'm going to do something. I just don't know yet."

"I'm trusting you, Owen." Darlene was stern, as quiet as she was, to avoid Lilly noticing her from down the hall.

At that moment, my phone buzzed. I pulled it out to check, ready to curse at Lorenzo, and I saw Penny had sent me a message.

»It was so nice to meet you today, the real you. Lilly has an amazing father.«

Darlene continued as if she knew I'd heard from Penny. "Ms. Lewis is a good woman, and so was her grandmother. Help protect that home."

"I know. I'm going to try."

# Chapter 21

When Lilly walked up my driveway for her next class, Darlene wasn't with her. Instead, Owen stood at her side, holding her piano. His boyish smile, despite being older than me by a few years, made my heart melt.

"I thought it was about time I came by for a session," he said, bringing the piano in and setting it down on a stand in the corner.

"Hi, Ms. Lewis!" Lilly said, coming up to give me a big hug. "My dad was super excited to see you again!" she exclaimed.

His eyes widened, and he turned to her. "I just said I wanted to bring you to class." He looked sheepishly at me. "She thinks some crazy stuff after seeing us talk at the concert."

"Crazy stuff?" I asked, letting Lilly go get her piano set up. I gave him a little smile as I turned the corner to get my notes from my bedroom desk. "I might have to hear about it later." Winking, I turned around to go check on Lilly. "Got it all plugged in and secured?"

"Yeah, just like you showed me!" Lilly said with delight.

"Awesome!" I said, pulling my own stool out to sit next to her at my keyboard. "Well, Owen, if you'd like to stay, I ask parents to hang out over on the couch there, just to give us some space in the lesson. But you're free to watch all you like!" I said, too enthusiastic for my taste. I was using too much of the "client voice" I utilized so often as a

143

music teacher. It sounded embarrassing and like it was coming from someone else when I heard it out loud.

"You bet," he said, pulling out his phone and moving over to the couch. "I have a few work emails to get to, but I would love to stay." His smile was soft and genuine, making me glad he was willing to watch the learning process between us.

Worrying Lilly would be nervous about having class in front of her father, I went over to Lilly to start warm-ups with her, keeping my voice lower than I normally would. She seemed to love having Owen watching, using it as a performance opportunity, which made me laugh to myself. It was clear who she admired and wanted to acknowledge her.

I looked over at Owen a few times throughout the lesson with Lilly to find him gazing at the two of us, enjoying the small and barely comprehendible notes that came together to form a semblance of a melody by the end of the hour-long session. Lilly often struggled sticking with one piece for long periods of time, so I'd found giving her space to explore the notes for a few moments during transitions led to more productive learning. As I taught her one line, I would give her the chance to repeat it back to me once, then again with however many "silly" notes around it that she wanted. But then she had to play it again as written, followed by another round of unique and improvised notes around the melody. Often, they were discordant and didn't make sense, but when they were harmonizing, or she found a note combination that was pleasing to her ear, her eyes lit up, and she remembered the note. During the next round, she would keep that note and move on to some other exploration.

Watching her learn and comprehend the notes and how they worked together when given the chance to play was incredible. Owen must have seen it too, because he hadn't taken his eyes off us for the last fifteen minutes.

After we completed a line and Lilly went wild with the extra notes on the playful round, I banged on the keys (lightly, so as not to damage the piano), making loud and aggressive notes toward the bottom of the register. Lilly was giggling, which almost made me want to ignore the clock coming up on the end of the day's lesson.

"You did wonderful today, Lilly. You've improved so much since we started playing together!" I said as we finished up and started cleaning the instructional papers that had strewn about.

Owen came over to the piano to meet us, his hands casually shoved in his pockets, though it seemed he might be hiding nerves. It only made me want to meet his eyes that much more, and when I did, I knew I had helped cause those nerves. Something in that brought me satisfaction.

"You two sound great," he said, patting Lilly on the back as she packed her bag. "You're a lovely teacher, Ms. Lewis." He winked at me when Lilly wasn't looking, and I blushed.

"Thank you," I said, standing and clearing off my station so I could help Lilly with hers. "That's why I love doing solo lessons. So you can teach students the way they need to be taught, not how a class is run."

"Your class is so much more fun than the other dumb classes I took. And my dad likes you!" Lilly blurted out. Girls her age were infamously tactless, but just in the little amount of time I'd known her, Lilly often made that fact sink home, especially with her impeccable timing.

"I'm glad. Your dad is pretty cool himself, you know," I said, smiling at her. "And he raised a cool kid!"

We high-fived, and Lilly's grin was nearly wider than her cheeks. That was the expression I loved seeing on my students' faces as we left the classroom.

Lilly unplugged her piano and handed Owen the cord adapter, so he took both that and the piano himself. I offered a hand, pulling the adapter off him as he wobbled out the door. Soon, I would manage to see if I could get a second piano here, so students who rehearsed at home wouldn't need to lug their instruments back and forth. *Maybe that could come with another fundraiser*, I thought, making a mental note of the idea. Right now, I was just excited about how successful the fundraiser last week had been. Winston would be receiving free classes for the next six months, and there was even a little left over the targeted budget that I was using to get plywood and start building a platformed stage and audience in the back for future recitals that could be broken down after a show. I was tired of being at the mercy of all the grass and mud in the backyard.

"I'm going to put this in, then I'll be back," Owen said, hobbling out to the car. I had half a mind to follow him to help, but Lilly distracted me by talking about some songs she wanted to do at the next recital, which I hadn't even started planning yet. Her excitement ended when I brought up that the ice cream shop across the way had premiered a new flavor I was interested in trying, white chocolate raspberry pie.

"We should go get ice cream!" Lilly suggested when Owen walked back in.

Owen pushed his hair back from where it had fallen out of place, then put a hand on my lower back. "I think we'd be able to manage some ice cream," he said. "Not all that often I get to have the afternoon with her."

"Right, aren't you normally busy in the office during the week?" I asked.

"I took some time for a developing project," he said, and he rubbed through his hair again. "Do you have another student or plans after this?" he asked, changing the focus back to me and the ice cream, which I couldn't refuse.

Surprised at his inquiry, I shook my head. "No, I was just going to do some chores around the house and maybe go grocery shopping tonight. I wouldn't be overstepping?"

"Not at all," Owen said. "In fact, as you've heard, I think Lilly would enjoy you coming. We both would." He smiled.

I grinned, nodding. "Then I would love to come."

After packing the rest of our things and grabbing our coats, we were out the door.

On the walk over, Lilly strode between us, holding our hands in each of hers and swinging between them. With the three of us together, something about it felt so normal, so easy. Owen seemed to notice it, too, because I caught him smiling at me once or twice when Lilly swung around us.

At the ice cream shop, Owen opened the door for us and placed his order. "I'll take a scoop of vanilla in a waffle cone, please," he said.

I chuckled at him. "Could you get any plainer with your ice cream?" I asked, and then I turned to the counter. "One scoop of the white chocolate raspberry pie, waffle cone! Thank you so much," I said as the server constructed my cone. "Thank you!"

Lilly pondered the available options, taking stock of everything before making her decision. "I'm going to get two scoops of mint chocolate chip in a sugar cone!"

"One scoop," Owen corrected for the worker, and Lilly groaned as she took the single scoop cone. "Hey, at least you're getting ice cream, missy."

"I would keep that deal if I were you; it comes with ice cream," I whispered to her, but loud enough for Owen to hear. He found the comment entertaining, smirking into his cone as he paid for our treats. "Can I help?" I asked, knowing we hadn't talked about him buying my ice cream too.

"Nope," he said, shoving me aside as he completed the transaction. "Think of it as a tip for class."

"Dang, I wish my other students would tip me in ice cream. Usually, all I get are cranky emails," I said, and I laughed as I took my first bite. "This is incredible. You have to try." I grabbed one of the sample spoons off the counter and dug it into my cone.

"I wanna try!" Lilly said, and I handed her the spoon. She shoved it in her mouth, and her eyes rolled back in what looked like utter contentment. "That's so yummy. I want to get that next time, Dad!"

With a grin, I turned to Owen. "Want some?"

I didn't say it in a way that sounded sexual, but he made me giggle when he wiggled his eyebrows lightly. "I don't know; that's a wild flavor."

"Sometimes, you need to change it up with a little wild," I said.

We didn't break eye contact as he took the spoon from Lilly's sample, took a small flavor scoop of my cone, and then sucked on the plastic. Both Lilly and I watched in anticipation as he took a moment to judge the flavor, then nodded in approval. "It's delicious."

"Told you!" Lilly taunted, already getting chocolate chunks on her cheeks by how hard she was diving into her cone.

We hung around the ice cream parlor for a short while, making a table in the back our own as we chatted about the concert and my plans for my music classes.

"I want to keep the one-on-one structure, but after I fix up the back for the concerts so we can get more people in the audience, I want to create an area inside that is solely for lessons, rather than the makeshift space I use next to the kitchen," I admitted. "I have a lot of plans; I just don't know how I'm going to do them."

"It sounds like you've got some great goals for the house," Owen said, looking down at his hands before taking a sip of his drink. "It's beautiful land, and it's so close to the downtown area."

"I know," I sighed, scooping the last of the ice cream left in the base of my cone before eating it. I almost didn't continue, but something in the trust I'd built with Owen with this new realization about who we were made me want to be more honest. "God, and now I'm dealing with some real estate developer who wants to offer me money to let them demolish the house. It's awful."

"What, really?" he asked, and he seemed genuinely interested in letting me vent, so I continued.

"Yeah. I haven't even opened the file they gave me with the offer," I said, "but apparently, it's a lot. And I don't *need* the money, but they've been hounding me like crazy. One of their agents keeps showing up at my house, but I keep pretending I'm not home." I laughed darkly, remembering the one time I'd hidden behind the curtain when I'd recognized that lawyer pull up across the street. "I'm sorry, I don't need to be spilling all this to you."

Owen nodded lightly, looking down and then back up at me as he took in the seriousness of the situation. "No, I'm glad you did. I, uh ..."

he stuttered, something I didn't see him often do. "I hope that situation can calm down for you soon."

"Me too," I said with another sigh, this one deeper. "For now, all I can focus on is you little nuggets." I rubbed Lilly's head next to me, messing with her hair.

Lilly fussed at me, pressing the brown strands back down on her scalp like glued pieces. "I'm not a nugget. I'm a Dino nugget!" she demanded, standing and nearly knocking over her chair in the process.

"Lil!" Owen said, doing the same to make sure she didn't spill anything.

"Might be a good time to go; I still want to get some of that grocery shopping done," I said, standing with them both. I didn't want the evening to end, much the opposite, but I also didn't want to keep them longer than I was welcome to.

"Oh, of course," Owen said, turning to me once he saw Lilly was settled. Her focus turned to the birthday cake design catalog beside the register. "But can I ask, are you busy tomorrow night?"

I was even more taken aback than the ice cream offer, knowing a night engagement would probably mean without Lilly. Alone time with Owen sounded phenomenal, but I couldn't promise it wouldn't end similarly to last time.

"After a lesson at the same time as today, I'm all clear," I said.

"I'd very much like to take you to dinner," Owen said, a kind smile meeting me in the process. "Maybe on a real date."

In her ritual-perfect timing, Lilly took the chance to come back over. "Are you asking out Ms. Lewis?" She seemed thrilled at the concept and turned to me to see my answer. "Well?" she asked impatiently when I took more than two seconds to respond.

"I would love to, Owen," I said with a smile to match his own.

"Yes!" Lilly cheered, darting out from between us toward the door. "Best! Ice cream! Day! Ever!" Each word ended with a punch or kick to the open space around her until Owen swung his arms around her.

"All right, that's good, Lillypad," he said, bringing her swinging arms down so she wouldn't take out one of the presentation stands. "You're not allowed to be more excited; it's *my* date," he said with a laugh.

"I'm happy she likes it," I said with a nod. "Makes me feel better about saying yes."

Owen grinned at me, then turned to Lilly again as we all strode out of the ice cream parlor. "Don't worry; I'm excited too," he said to her, and I couldn't help agreeing.

# Chapter 22

OWEN

When we got home, Lilly was nearly bouncing off the walls, and I'd guessed only half was from the sugar in the ice cream we'd eaten with Penny.

"So where are you going to take Ms. Lewis?" Lilly asked, sitting on the couch to yank off her shoes and relax.

I grinned. "Not sure yet, but I'm thinking about doing Angelo's in Salina." It was the next town over, and as Abilene was somewhat lacking in fancy places to take a date, it was an old faithful I'd kept in my back pocket since taking Fiona there a few times. The itch of betraying her by bringing another woman there stuck in my side, but the excited look on Lilly's face kept the discomfort from lingering.

"Angelo's?" she exclaimed. "That place is super fancy! Mom always used to wear a dress when you went there, with her fancy jewelry!" Lilly squinted her eyes at me, raising one brow. "Are you gonna wear your shiny suit?"

I set down our things and joined her on the couch, scooping her up in my arms to sit on my lap, where she curled against me in a cuddle. "My shiny suit ... you mean the one I wore to the wedding last year?" A close family friend of mine had gotten married, and I'd brought Lilly as my date. It'd been her first foray into "adult" environments, and she had dressed to the nines right along with me.

"Yeah, you look great in that!" Lilly said.

"I don't know, Lillypad; it might be a little *too* fancy." To be honest, I was afraid of scaring Penny off, for whatever reason.

"No way, she'll love it! Then she can wear a super fancy dress, and you can have your fancy date at Angelo's! That's what I would wear; she probably would too."

I chuckled. "Lilly, the last time I took you there, you got pasta sauce all over your dress."

"So tell her to wear red!"

Her solution to the problem made me laugh, and I squeezed her tight in my arms, making her squeal.

"You're squishing me; I'll suffocate!" she yelled, trying her best to wriggle out.

I laughed as she squirmed. "That's a pretty big word."

"It was a bonus spelling word last week!"

"Okay, so spell it, and I'll let you go," I said, holding her in a firm bear hug.

Lilly groaned, admitting defeat but for a moment. "S-u-f-f-o-c-a-t!"

I laughed, giving her one last squeeze before letting go. "You forgot the E, honey."

She huffed once she was out and flopped on the couch next to me, panting dramatically.

"Oh, you're fine," I said. "Bet you'll remember the E next time, though."

Turning her head to me as she huffed, Lilly stuck her tongue out and rolled to sit up next to me. "No squishing in spelling; it's against the rules."

"Okay, okay," I said, plopping a kiss on her head before sitting back. "So you'd be okay with me taking your teacher on a date?" I asked. Even with her being nine, I respected her wishes as my daughter and didn't want to make her feel uncomfortable by pushing the boundaries with a teacher figure for her.

Lilly's nod was forceful, and she wiggled her head into my side, despite how hard she'd worked to get out of it only moments ago. "Yeah, of course! You and Ms. Lewis would make such a cute couple, and then she could always be around, and we could all go hang out or go get ice cream together, and—"

I knew if I let her go on, she would list all the activities she dreamed of us doing together. It delighted me that she was so pleased with the idea, but I also wanted my relationship with Penny to grow at its own rate, without worry that my daughter would insist on me getting her a ring in the first week of knowing her. That was just something I was not prepared for.

Since losing Fiona, my heart had known an emptiness that I never thought would be filled again. I was prepared to live with that hole for the rest of my life when she died, but Penny made me laugh and smile in ways I hadn't thought I was still capable of. I found myself wanting to please her, wanting her to be proud of what I was doing.

So how could I continue to court her while lying to her about my company's motives with her house?

I pushed those thoughts out of my mind, focusing on cuddling with my daughter. These were the moments I craved that I'd felt I'd been able to relish in more since meeting Penny. Seeing Lilly perform and grow in her music, seeing how Penny encouraged her and lifted her in times of struggle ... made me want to become closer to her even more.

"I just want you to know, if you were ever not happy about someone I was ... interested in ..." My hesitation in putting a label on

154

anything made Lilly giggle. "I want you to tell me. I want you to be honest with me about how you're feeling, okay?"

Lilly looked up at me with those beautiful big brown eyes that reminded me of her mother. Her gaze only broke when she wrapped her arms around my waist, squeezing me tight. I met her hug and did the same, holding her in my arms and being thankful for my relationship with her.

"I'm happy for you, Dad. I want you to be happy too! And Ms. Lewis makes me happy, and she has made you happy. So that's good, and you should keep doing it." Her face was bright with hope, which softened my heart even more.

"You make me happy too, Lillypad," I said, and I kissed her cheek softly, then left a big slobbery wet spot on it, making us both laugh.

"Dad, ew!" she said, rubbing the saliva off with her shirt sleeve. "Gross!"

I rubbed her head, playing with her hair a little. "Well, now you're all messy. Why don't you go get washed up and ready for tonight, okay? We can have a late dinner and some popcorn while watching a movie together. Sound good?"

Lilly smiled brightly, pushing herself off the couch. "Are you picking this time or me?"

I sighed dramatically. "No, I won't make you watch *Mission Impossible* again with me. Jeez, I put it on for you once, and I never live it down," I chuckled. "How about Pirates of the Caribbean?"

We were both huge fans of the series, and it was one of those movies that we could watch together and equally find fun in. The first time she saw it, Lilly had watched the series twice a week.

"Only if you do the Jack Sparrow voice!" Lilly said with a smile.

I nodded and said, "Of course." It was the only way to watch it with my daughter.

After she ran off to wash her face and get changed into her comfortable pajamas, a favorite of movie dinner nights, I moved into the kitchen to prepare a snack for us both. We'd eaten before her lesson, and with the ice cream, I thought some meat and cheese baguette sandwiches plus some popcorn would be enough to tide us over for the evening. Once everything was sliced and prepped, I plated them all onto a wooden board—Fiona and I used to love entertaining with charcuterie boards—and brought them out to the couch, along with a bag of popcorn that was indeed *not* burned.

When I returned, Lilly had already pulled up the movie, making for a quick beginning. Her favorite part of the charcuterie boards was always the salami, and I'd learned to cut her a few extra pieces, or I would be lacking by the end.

We cuddled throughout the movie, and she delighted in my Jack Sparrow impressions, which I always accompanied with the hand motions of a drunken sailor. She was old enough to know why he often slurred, so she found my fake drunk accent entertaining. I hadn't slurred like that since college, so the caricature was the only thing she knew of me this inebriated.

Around nine o'clock, Lilly's mouth started drooping into a yawn, as much as she tried to hide it. She loved staying up as late as possible and often waited up for me when I came home from work. But the sag of her head, even while a clashing swordfight happened in front of her, told me it was time to take her to bed. I paused the movie when I saw her eyes close for more than ten seconds.

Gently, I kissed her head in my lap, then pushed some hair behind her ear. "Honey, I think it's time for bed."

She grumbled against my waist, squinting up at the light above her. When she found the TV stopped and turned to the Netflix home screen, she turned back to me. "Is it over?"

"Yes," I lied, less out of malice and more out of ease. "You fell asleep. We can go back and watch it again after I get out of work Thursday, or you can watch it tomorrow with Caroline while I'm with Ms. Lewis," I said and smiled, thinking of my date the next day.

I scooped Lilly up in my arms, her little legs swinging over the crook of my elbow. She leaned her head back and yawned, giving into the exhaustion.

"Come on, Lillypad. We still have to brush your teeth after snacks."

"Aww," she moaned, but with how easily I knew bad habits could form, I'd always been firm on avoiding one or two "lazy" nights that could turn into cavities and root canals.

"I'll do it with you, come on." I kept her in my arms as I took my toothbrush to her bathroom and set her down on the lidded toilet. I squirted toothpaste on both of our brushes, then got them wet and handed Lilly hers. "Cheers," I said, holding out my toothbrush to her.

Even in her weakened state of needing rest, she smiled lightly, meeting my toothbrush in a toast. "Cheers, Dad."

We brushed our teeth in silence, sometimes making faces at each other to try and get the other to laugh. At one point, Lilly spat a little down her chin and onto the sink, making me laugh as I sputtered and rinsed.

I hadn't had a night with my daughter, laughing and smiling and being there for one another, for a long time, and I missed them dearly. Working at Tate Legal took a toll on me, and years of Lilly's life I would never be getting back, and after seeing the joy she had to share, how could I not make that my priority from this point forward?

After cleaning up, I scooped her up again—despite her wiggly protests—and dumped her into her bed like I had when she was a little girl. She'd gotten too big to really throw her and make her bounce on the mattress, but it still made her giggle.

"Night night, Lillypad," I said, sliding her between the sheets and making a form around her body with her comforter.

She wriggled a little, looking like a bug. "Goodnight, Dad," she said with another yawn, turning over in the comforter to remain tucked in while on her side. "I love you!" she added, and I felt she meant it wholeheartedly.

I smiled at her as I turned around to close her door. "I love you too, sweetheart."

When she was safely in bed and unconscious—I heard snoring within minutes—I went to the cabinet to pour myself a drink and do some reading before bed. My dad used to have nightcaps, and it was a habit I'd slowly found myself picking up while destressing. Of course, I enjoyed the taste of the whiskey I mixed, as well as the garnishes I decorated them with.

I mixed a light Old Fashioned, stirring in my ice, thinking of how thankful I was for the positive difference Penny had made in my life, in Lilly's life. Without her and the music class, Lilly was thriving in. I might still be struggling to connect to her. But after sitting in on their rehearsal today and seeing the light it brought to Lilly's eyes, I knew I owed part of that to Penny.

Before I could reconsider, I pulled out my phone to send a text. It wasn't too late, but it was late enough that there was a chance she wouldn't answer.

»Thank you for today. I'm so glad we found you.«

I set down the phone to take a sip of my drink and was surprised to find it buzzing almost immediately.

»It's a good match for all of us, I think. I'm just thankful to have such a wonderful student with a supportive family.«

I smiled, thinking, too, of Darlene and how much we considered her a member of our family. Especially in the last two years of losing Fiona, Darlene had become a constant in all of our events and planning, at first for ease but then out of love.

»That she does«, I replied. »I hope you're having a good night.« I knew it had only been a few hours since seeing each other, and I didn't want to jump the gun and push her away. But more and more, I found her smile lingering on my mind for longer than I thought possible.

»I am; I'm tucking into bed early tonight to do some reading.«

»Oh?« I asked. »I was just about to do the same. What are you reading now?«

The dots blinked for a moment as she typed, and then I read, »Don't make fun of me, but Dracula. Old favorite. What about you?«

With a chuckle, I replied, »No judgment whatsoever. Comfort reads are important, and Stoker is delightful. Very sensual«, I added, but I regretted it the minute it was delivered. I then sent, »I'm reading through some work documents, to be fair, but Dracula sounds more fun.« Hoping the distraction was enough from my sensual comment, I remained afraid of coming on too strong. But her reply sent me reeling.

»Sensual is something Dracula does well; you're right. That's why I like it so much.«

I grinned, taking that as a sign she was comfortable talking about things of a more sensual nature.

»Maybe you ought to take a break from work for a bit and relax.«

Upon reading that, I knew I was past the checkpoint.

Grabbing my water and a document or two, though I was hoping I wouldn't be reading them, I went off to my bedroom and closed the door. I'd stopped leaving it open for Lilly about a year ago, trusting her to knock if she needed anything. Once I was reclining, I replied to Penny.

»I could do with some relaxing, I agree. Did you have anything in mind?«

It was quiet on her end for a minute, and I was terrified I'd pushed too far. But a photo arrived, giving me the promise of what caused her delay.

In the picture, the lights were low, and Penny was lit up only by what looked like a candle at her bedside and moonlight through the window. But even in the shadow and cut off from below the neck, I could see she wasn't wearing a single thing. The silhouette of her body was somewhat difficult to make out in the darkness around her, but it wasn't impossible.

And God, it made me miss her, and that night in the bar.

I texted back, »You look like you're having a great night. Now I just wish I were there with you to make it even better.«

From under the covers, just in case Lilly burst in, I started stroking myself through my flannel pajama pants, and it didn't take me long to harden at the thought of her lying next to me in nothing but the moonlight.

»That would be perfect. Keep me nice and warm with all that body heat. And my bed's a lot comfier than the sink at Dave's.«

»You might be helping me feel warm right now, even,« I texted, wanting her to know what I was doing at that moment.

»Me too«, she said and groaned mentally at that image in my head.

As I texted her, »Thinking about you dripping on me again«, I moved my hand up and down my length, now tenting in my bottoms. I thought about her ass and how incredible it felt to grip in my hands when I was inside her at the bar. I teased my head, sliding the small bits of precum over me to give the stroking some lubrication, and I found myself thrusting into it more and more.

My free hand scrolled to read through the text she sent over as I moaned.

»I'm wet just thinking about it. I want you to bend me over again, but when you lifted me and fucked me against you, that's the part I think about most often.«

I was so sensitive at that point that I could have finished, most likely without another thought. But I eased off to bring myself closer to completion without hitting it yet, just in time for her to send a photo of her fingers, covered in her juices as she licked it up.

»Like it?« she asked.

»You look delicious. I'm so close.«

The little dots flickered again to show typing, but a voice message appeared this time. I wasn't too familiar with them, so I turned it down as I kept stroking and pressed play.

Her voice was gravely and breathy, and I could tell she was amid her own playing. "I'm so close to coming for you, too, Owen. I can't wait for you to taste it."

Any hope I had to avoid orgasming then and there went out the window, and I made a mess along my sheets at the thought of her touching herself the same way. I came fast and hard, rocking into the

161

orgasm as I spurted and imagined doing the same into Penny, feeling her squeeze tight around me, stroking into her.

I was left out of breath; head flopped on the pillow with a few beads of sweat dripping down my forehead. I'd masturbated regularly, but I hadn't orgasmed like that in a long while. It wrecked me even more, knowing Penny was at the forefront of it.

»Was that as incredible for you as it was for me?« I asked by text.

Her reply came a few minutes later, just after she did, by my guess.

»Amazing, she replied. »I'm glad you liked it too. I haven't done something like that in a long time.«

»Me neither. But it was amazing like you said.« As I typed I found my eyelids getting heavier, and I could tell I was somewhat emptied in more ways than one. I'd make a mental note to do the sheets in a day or so when I was planning on doing laundry anyway.

»But I am getting sleepy …« she texted, and I chuckled at how cute she must look, all cum drunk. »Good night, Owen. Thank you for such a nice evening ;)«

I replied, »Night, Penny. Sleep tight, and talk to you later.«

# Chapter 23

PENNY

"Okay, now remember to finish up with some hand exercises, if you can. You want to keep those muscles flexible and pain-free so you can keep playing." I pressed my fingers onto the keys and rang out a quick C chord, showing the end of my lesson with Caroline Singh. She'd been keeping up her skills, but she often rushed, and getting her to slow down and listen to her body would be the focus of our next lesson.

"Do you have the piece of paper with all the stretches on it?" she asked, looking up at me as she twisted her hands too roughly. "I was gonna do stretches with Lilly tonight. She's coming over to my house tonight!"

"Oh?" I asked as I tended to her hands. The tendons along the muscles and joints can be very temperamental if they get inflamed, so I pressed my hands on hers. "Gently. Yeah, I'll be right back." I rose to head to the back of the kitchen and find the printouts I'd made for students, all neatly sorted in a file along the back wall. When I hung things properly and kept them out of the way, they had much less opportunity to turn into a messy pile the first chance they got.

I dug through the papers, sorting through charts and notes when I heard a groan from the pianos. "Did you push them too hard?" I called out, finally snatching the right file. "Hold on."

As I stepped back toward the kitchen, I saw a green car I was pretty sure I recognized outside through the window. It was parked along the front of the house, though not blocking me or the spot where Caroline's mother had pulled in a few minutes ago to pick her up. I gritted my teeth and tried to put on a good face for Caroline as I pressed a hand to her back to help relax her shoulders.

"Here," I said, "practice these at home, and make sure to go easy." I brought my attention to the clock sitting on the mantle, reading that our time for today had ended.

Caroline sat up from where she had been hunched over, curling her bent fist into her elbow to try and stretch it out. She would break her wrist at that rate, so I made sure to show her mother the paper when I sent her out.

"Just make sure she's doing it gently before and after practicing. She mentioned the wrist pain again this week. I think it'll help so she won't have problems playing. That and practicing her form to keep her hands supported," I said as I closed their trunk, now filled with the long keyboard case that stretched up to their back seat, which was currently flat.

Mrs. Singh nodded with a sigh, opened her door, and slid into the driver's seat. "And you said the wrist braces would help?"

"Yes," I said, "but try these first to see how it goes. It might just be better to build up the strength in those muscles instead of relying on the supports first. That way, she can keep playing while getting stronger, and if she needs more, you know what to do."

"Thank you," she said, and Caroline flipped on the music in her mom's car. Currently, some Adele song from a few years ago was playing. "I see how hard you're working on getting her to practice and take it seriously."

"Only because I saw how happy she was to perform," I admitted. It was true, Caroline shone that day in the backyard, and it only served

164

as a proving point that she, like some of the other kids I'd been working with, just needed the connecting drive. "She's doing great," I said, louder than need be, and Caroline laughed a little in the seat next to her mom.

"Thank you, Ms. Lewis," Caroline said. "I'll do the exercises."

"Awesome, pal. Can't wait to hear about it!" I said, grinning and giving her a thumbs-up. "And have fun with Lilly tonight!" I added.

Mrs. Singh rolled up the windows and pulled out from the house's driveway. I waved back, turning my head and still seeing that one familiar car. Someone was in the front seat, maybe on the phone or reading, and I couldn't tell if it was indeed that lawyer from the other day. I had yet to ask Owen about advice on dealing with him if he kept coming by, but I made a mental note to bring it up again tonight on our date.

Trying to put it out of my head, I walked back inside and put a pot of hot water on. I stood in the kitchen for a few minutes on my phone as I considered a teabag, just enough to hear the pot hiss at me. Once I'd decided on raspberry mango (the fruity sweetness was always refreshing after a lesson), there was a knock on the door. It wasn't very hard, and I only assumed it was because they knew I was home.

I set the hot water to medium and grabbed the bag to prep, then went to the door with a sigh. I saw the same slimy guy from last time through the peephole, with that same stupid briefcase probably filled with the same icky offer to buy the house. Gran would turn over in her grave if she found out I sold this place to become the foundation of a mall. As tempting as the money was in moments of stress, it would never be enough to get me to sell.

"Penny?" I heard on the other side, then another knock. "It's Lorenzo from Tate Legal."

165

"Right!" I said, looking through the hole. "I'm so sorry; I can't talk today."

"I'll just be a minute!" he hollered, offering me another glowing smile.

My stomach lurched, and I swiftly came up with a new plan. I spotted my purse and tossed my makeup and hair product inside, then grabbed my travel mug from the shelf. "I'm heading out the door in just a minute!" I yelled through to him.

"Really, I think we can—" he tried to say, but I cut him off.

"Yeah, I'm super busy this afternoon, then I won't be home all night!" I said, but when I said it out loud, I realized it sounded like an open invitation for a robbery. "But I have security cameras!" I added, however much of a fib it was. As I yelled out to Lorenzo, I plopped the teabag in the travel mug and gently poured water over it, making a little steaming pot of salvation. I had extra sugar in my car, and I didn't want to give this guy another minute of opportunity.

I yanked open the door, surprising Lorenzo, who stumbled into me as he'd been leaning on the frame.

"Oh, you're heading out?" he asked, looking like a disappointed door-to-door salesman.

I slung my bag over my shoulder, bringing my coffee to my nose to smell the raspberries. The familiar flavor calmed me, and I nodded. "Yes, sorry about that."

"Did you have a chance to look over that proposal I left you?" he asked, not wasting a moment before jumping.

Without giving him another second, I pushed on toward my car, clicking the lock and opening the driver's door. "Not really. Listen, I'm not interested in selling."

Lorenzo followed me down the path. "I think at least considering it could be up to three times what the house is worth—"

"Thank you for the offers," I said, "but you really have to let it go." I jumped into my front seat, embracing the wall I'd put up between us and hoping he would step off once the car started.

"You run a music program, right?" Lorenzo threw out, just loud enough that I could still hear him with the window rolled up. "Is your home classroom up to code? Have you updated and paid permit fees to teach out of your home?"

That claim made me turn my head and scowl. I started the car, then rolled down the window halfway, just enough to talk over. "I'm still working on getting all my permits and applications in. I'm not good with paperwork," I said.

Lorenzo gave me a curt nod, and a smile behind his teeth told me he knew he'd found my sore spot. And the muscle did, in fact, ache.

Politely, he said, "I just want to make sure your students are getting their highest quality education." He tapped a pencil from his jacket pocket against his temple, winking at me. "You have our card if you want to chat. We'll check in with you again soon, Ms. Desmond."

"It's Ms. Lewis," I said, and I glared at him as he stepped away from the side of my car, allowing me to pull out safely. Once I was out in the street, I watched him in the mirror as I drove slowly down the straight block, making sure he was heading toward his own car to leave. I'd circle back in about half an hour to make sure he'd run back to the rat alley he'd come from. That Tate Legal team must have been a piece of work to send him out on trips.

Either way, he made my skin crawl as I drove to the square and parked in a quiet park area to put on my makeup and get ready for my date with Owen. I normally followed a routine before a big night like that, but tonight, we'd work with what we could manage.

I didn't have high expectations for the evening, so I went light with my makeup and hair, leaving it simply enhancing my natural features. I did add some lip stain to add color to my face, though I knew Owen had a habit of making the rest of the color find my cheeks. Once I was presentable and could see myself actually being someone who put effort into her appearance, I realized I had completely forgotten I'd worn a T-shirt and jeans for Caroline's lesson. It wasn't my preferred date getup, by any measure.

I checked my clock with a hefty sigh and waited another ten minutes before swinging back home to change. When I pulled up, I noted that the spot Lorenzo had been in was empty, and I realized how unsettling and nerve-wracking it was to have him waiting for me to come back home. I was glad I was seeing Owen tonight, and I considered my stance on asking him over, if only just for an added layer of security.

Concerning that, I had no idea how this evening would go, based on the fact that we already knew each other on that level, and it would be like taking a step back in getting to know each other again. But doing so around Lilly had been wonderful, so I knew that the evening would be a good one no matter what.

My confidence stirred within me as I left the car and walked up to the door, but it sank again when I saw an envelope taped there, the name *Tate Legal* typed out on the addressee. That battle still needed to be seen through.

# Chapter 24

OWEN

As the clock ticked further and further past five o'clock, the lump in my throat grew bigger and bigger.

I'd come home a little early to make sure Lilly was all set for a sleepover with Caroline. It had been a while since she'd had someone ask for her to stay over, as she'd struggled to connect with the other kids her age. Even at school, it often took a teacher matching for other students to engage with her, or so I was told by the various educators she'd gone through. Lilly herself often pretended she was more popular, though I could see in her eyes where the hopeful fantasy collided with the harsher reality of her lack of friends. It broke my heart to see my daughter so lonely, and when Caroline's mother called, I almost asked if she had the right parent. There were at least three years between the girls, and I had heard from Fiona's childhood just how cruel young girls could be.

Lo and behold, Caroline was expecting Lilly tonight for an innocent evening of movies and pizza snacks, and Lilly appeared to have gotten stuck in her suitcase.

"You're going for one night, sweetheart; you don't need to overpack," I told her, walking into her sitting on the luggage to make it close.

She frowned up at me as she hopped on the lump, yanking on the zipper along the side. "But Caroline said we can play dress up, and I won't have my favorite clothes there!"

"Don't you think you can borrow some of hers, even if they're a little big on you?" I asked.

"No, I want her to think I'm cool and fun and have awesome outfits, Dad," Lilly said with a sigh, offering one last hop before admitting defeat and sliding off. "I can take out a few things."

"Okay," I said with a chuckle, kissing her head. "We're leaving in a few minutes, so make it speedy. I have to make it back downtown by six." I wandered back out to the living room, adjusting my collar one more time in the mirror.

I often focused on my appearance, but it was even more so tonight. My shirt was firmly pressed, though it ended up looking *too* pressed, so I yanked the bottom and the collar a bit to break up some of the edges. My hair was more voluminous than usual after I'd tried using a special conditioner for men's curly hair. It ended up looking frizzy, so I'd tamed what I could and left the rest up to Penny. Just like Lilly, I couldn't get my mind off how I would look to my companion for the evening.

My daughter skipped out to the front door a moment later, wearing three different jackets at once and dragging her suitcase behind her. It seemed she'd discovered the secret many flyers learned in the security line at the airport.

"I'm ready!" she said, yanking her suitcase so hard that the wheels jammed. "Can you help with my bag?"

I grinned, taking it from her and lifting it, only to discover just how much she'd been able to pack, even with wearing half of its original contents. "Of course, my regal queen," I said, performing a

170

deep bow, making her laugh. If I could do nothing else, at least I could make my daughter laugh.

"Thank you, my lord!" she said with a giggle, then followed me out into the driveway.

Once Lilly and her things were secured in the car—she had to yank a layer of one of her jackets to keep it from catching in the door—we were off to Caroline's. She and her mother didn't live far, but it was more out of the way than I wanted to be at this time to get to Penny's to pick her up for dinner out of town. The drive to Angelo's wasn't far, but with the timing, I was worried about hitting traffic.

At Caroline's house, her mother attempted to get me in and socialize, but I tried to press I was on a tight deadline and needed to get back on the road.

"Are you sure you can't stay for some cookies; we just made fresh ones!" Mrs. Singh said.

"Cookies?" Lilly yelped, and with that, she followed Caroline in, and the two girls were off in their own world. I tried not to think about how much sugar she'd be consuming tonight, but tomorrow was a day off, so recovery wouldn't be too bad.

"I'm sorry, Mrs. Singh. I really do have to—" I started.

"Have fun with Ms. Lewis!" she said with a wink, and I wondered how she knew that's where I was headed. Apparently, more than just Darlene and Lilly had seen me flirting with Penny that night after her show.

Back in the car, I checked the clock, panicked, then hustled out of the driveway, nearly hitting an ice cream truck on the way out. I was met with an aggressive honk, but I didn't have time to stop. I had a date to catch.

By the time I made it to Penny's place, that old house that constantly reminded me of the secrets I'd been keeping from her, she was sitting on her front porch, wearing an adorable polka-dot dress and red pumps. Her hair was tied down in a half-up braid on top, and then it cascaded freely down her shoulders to lay against the cleavage her dress allowed. I felt like the luckiest man alive to be taking her out tonight. I couldn't wait to get her on my arm.

She walked up to the car, smiling, as I pulled up and rolled down my window. "Cutting it a little close? Is there a reservation?"

"Yes, but I know the owner, so we shouldn't have any problem wrangling our spot," I said, going into park so I could get out and help her into the passenger seat. I wanted tonight to be filled with all the romantic gestures she deserved and the ones I had missed getting to perform since Fiona died.

My mind almost melted into the memories of Fiona—I often took her to Angelo's, and I prided myself on all the charming acts I would perform when we went out, like pulling out her chair, providing a supportive and loving embrace on her lower back as we walked. It was in my nature, and rather than linger on the heartbreaking memories of a life I once had, I welcomed the chance to do them with Penny, to create new memories with her.

Once she was inside, we drove off, speeding along the highway toward Salina. Penny laughed at the playlist I had on—Happy Jams, one that Lilly often enjoyed. But once Love Shack by the B-52s came on, she couldn't mock me any longer.

"I don't often like bringing up the age difference, but I wouldn't have considered you to be an 80s music fan," I said. It was true, there were most likely about ten years between us, but it wasn't anything that hindered me from wanting to see her.

"The B-52's aren't just an 80s band, Owen; they're a lifestyle." She laughed. "It was one of my mom's favorite bands, and they're just so much fun to dance to; how could you not be a fan?"

I chuckled, making a left turn. "You're right on that," I said with a smile, and the drive continued.

We chatted and discussed music tastes, our favorite movies and books, and everything under the sun we could squeeze into the ride. Thankfully, she didn't bring up work, but we did get into talking about our favorite cuisines. I was delighted to find that Italian food was at the top of her list.

"You're going to love tonight's meal, then. Angelo's has the best pasta on this side of the Atlantic ocean."

Penny sputtered out a laugh. "That's certainly an opinion."

"The right one. You'll see."

And see, she did. We got to Angelo's just in time to make the reservation without much stress, and when we arrived, the owner clapped me on the back, giving me the small-talk of how long it had been since he'd seen me. When Penny slipped to the bathroom, I quietly whispered about Fiona to Angelo, just so he would be aware of the situation and not bring up the change in partner. He'd spent many years seeing me with Fiona at my side, and the last thing I wanted was to make Penny uncomfortable on the first real, nice date I'd had the chance to take her on.

However, all anxiety about things going wrong went out the window when she returned. I ordered us a fine Cabernet and some bread, and the conversation pacing from the car picked up where it left off.

"How have you never seen Rocky?" Penny asked in utter disbelief.

"It's true," I said. "I was just never much of a macho guy, so I didn't really have an interest in it. Then it became so much of a classic, with all the sequels and spinoffs, that I just never got around to it. I've seen the workout montage scene, though, so I'm pretty sure I can wrap my head around the rest."

"You most certainly cannot!" She laughed, dipping her white bread into a vat of oil and vinegar pooled on a plate before us. "It's more than just a movie about a guy becoming a boxer. It's about transformation, self-discovery, and his beautiful dog, Butkis."

I chuckled, following her with my own piece of bread. "Stallone is quite the performer; I'll say that. "Eye of the Tiger" has been on my workout playlist for years." I took a bite of the bread, and a little of the oil dribbled down my chin.

Just as I was about to take a napkin to it, Penny instead reached across the table and placed her bread along my chin, scraping up the excess oil and vinegar. I sat still, almost in shock at the action, but we both laughed when she took a bite.

"What? The flavor tastes better coming directly from the source." She giggled, and I couldn't help smiling even wider.

We each ordered our own meals—I had to avoid the instinct just to order two plates of the carbonara bolognese, the plates Fiona and I once got—and once they arrived, I watched as Penny's mouth began to water at the sight of her pasta. I'd gotten myself the bolognese, but she'd opted for the cheese ravioli with a side of meatballs. An interesting choice, but I was thankful for the opportunity to steal some from her as I offered her my own.

"Jesus Christ," she said, digging into her pasta. "You will never hear me say this again, Owen Michaels, but you may have been right. This is absolutely delicious." She took her fork down the center of a ravioli and cut it in half, offering me some on her fork. "You have to try this. Then try it with the meatballs."

"Can't say no to that," I said, biting it off her fork and then using my own to chip off a small chunk of meat from the ball she'd already dug into. Once I tasted both of them together, I knew she was right. The flavors went so well with each other, and the spices of the meat cut through the rich cheese of the ravioli perfectly. I'd had just the cheese ravioli once when I'd brought Lilly here—it was her favorite dish, and she always insisted I have some so she could eat some of my pasta too—but trying it with the meatballs changed the game.

We enjoyed our meal with more chit-chat, and because we were so stuffed from the pasta, I asked for some zeppole to go. The dusted, donut-like dessert was always a favorite of mine, but taking it home meant we could allow the food to digest more, as well as provide for some comforting atmosphere if the night decided to continue. And I hoped it did.

"Thank you for this incredible dinner, Owen," Penny said as we left the restaurant. "This place is so good, and I can't wait to try those zeppole!"

"Who said you're getting any?" I laughed, placing my hand on her back as we walked out to the car. I rubbed little circles along her skin outside her dress as I unlocked the door and let her in.

"How about you come back to my place, and we can share them?" she said.

Perfection.

On the drive home, I casually placed a hand on her thigh, not in a way that was overly groping, but one yearning for more touch. She met it by taking my hand in hers, setting it back down in her lap as she ran her fingers over my skin, sending bolts of electricity through me.

Back at Plumosa Avenue, we strode into her home, a bag of Italian pastries and chocolate dipping sauce in tow. I tried not to get ahead of myself, but it was difficult not to look forward to where it might end up with how the evening was going.

Once we were inside, Penny turned to me as she walked into the kitchen. "Care for a drink?" she asked.

"I would love one. Surprise me," I said. There weren't many drinks I wouldn't partake in, so it wasn't too much of a gamble. I took the time to make myself comfortable on her couch, popping open the takeaway box to try a zeppole. It had been so long since my last indulgence I simply couldn't stop myself from taking the leap. At the first bite, all regrets left my mind. "Oh, Penny, you've got to try some."

"Well, don't eat it all then!" she said, coming over to join me with two drinks in hand. "I made you an Old Fashioned. I hope that's okay."

I grinned, taking the drink from her. "It's perfect. One of my favorites, thank you." I took my first sip and enjoyed it, relishing in the whiskey she'd chosen, one of the darker ones, but flavorful, nonetheless. "I didn't take you for a whiskey girl."

She chuckled, leaning back and taking a sip of her own drink before setting it on the table next to the zeppole container. "I'm not, really. I keep it around for my sister. I prefer rum, so I made myself a rum and coke."

"Well, your sister must have good taste, but so do you. Rum and coke is a classic. As long as you don't use Malibu or Cruzan, we'll be fine," I said, popping another bite of zeppole in my mouth.

Her silence worried me, and I realized that might just be what she'd used to make her own drink.

I chortled. "I guess we all need to have flaws, hm?" I teased, leaning over to kiss the side of her head and take her hand. "I'm kidding; drink what makes you happy."

She seemed to go along with the teasing, not getting upset at me calling out her poor taste in liquor. "If it's alcoholic, it makes me happy," she said with a smile. "But now I want some zeppole. Should I try it plain or with the chocolate sauce?"

"Plain first," I said. "The chocolate is pretty powerful, and you should enjoy the flavor of the pastry and sugar first." I took a piece of zeppole off the platter and shook it a little to let the excess powdered sugar fall onto the tray. I brought it to Penny's lips, and she grinned at me before taking a bite. "So?"

Upon biting, her eyes nearly rolled into the back of her head in pleasure. I yearned to make her do that without the zeppole.

"Owen, this is *amazing*." She grinned. "I don't know how I'll live without it now." She took the zeppole square from my hands and took another bite, then tried dipping it in the chocolate sauce and was met with even more delight. "Oh, it's gotta have the chocolate sauce. But I see why you had me try it plain first."

"Exactly," I said with a smile, using my clean and sugar-free hand to push some of the hair that had escaped her half updo behind her ear. I let my hand linger on her cheek, and when she'd finished the zeppole, she turned into it and savored the caress. "Thank you for coming out with me tonight. I had an incredible time."

"I did too. I *am* having an incredible time ... who said the night was over yet?" She smiled.

And behind that smile, I knew just what she was insinuating.

As much as I'd wanted to take it slow with her, the sexual tension between us all evening could be cut with the dullest knife in her kitchen. And now, with the sugary treat sweetening up the evening, it was almost impossible to ignore that tension any longer.

Penny took the hand that had held her zeppoles and placed the tips of her fingers in her mouth, sucking lightly on them as she coyly met my glance in the corner of her eye. She knew exactly what she was doing to me, and I couldn't help but reciprocate.

Besides, how often was it that I had a night off from being Super Dad? I had to seize the opportunities that came to me. And in this instance, that opportunity was wearing a gorgeous dress and begging me to seize her as she sucked her fingers in front of me. I refused to disappoint.

Our lips met, and she stood, pulling me up by the hand to drag me into her bedroom.

# Chapter 25

PENNY

The path to my bedroom was filled with obstacles that we continually ran into as I wrapped my hands around Owen's neck, desperate for another touch, another kiss. Every second that our skin spent apart was another second I spent yearning for him.

When we found the door to my room, I placed my hand on the knob and turned it open, and the two of us nearly fell in together with a laugh. Owen grabbed me lightly by the small of my back, pressing his fingers into the dimples at the base of my spine, making me shiver.

The first time we'd had sex, it was rushed, drunken, and desperate for each other. Now, it was slow, filled with the anticipation and quiet delight we'd been teasing each other with over the last few days and weeks. Now the silence of gasps and moaning was interrupted by giggles, light breaths of delight, and kisses with smiling lips against each other.

Owen guided me to my bed, standing in front of me and taking the opportunity to ogle me a bit. I got bashful, turning my head, but he put his finger under my chin to bring me back to him, unraveling slowly under his touch. His hand found my cheek, then slipped down my shoulder to push the sleeve of my dress down, giving him room to kiss along my neck and collarbone. I moaned in response, almost against my will, but he smiled into my skin.

"I've been waiting a while to get to do this again," he said, and I turned my head to kiss his lips.

"Me too," I whispered against them, then placed my hands along his hips. I slid my fingers under the well-tailored waistband of his formal slacks, letting the fabric fall just to the curve of his incredible ass. I gave it a squeeze, and he chuckled.

"Squeeze all you want, darling," he said.

"Only if you promise to do the same," I replied.

Within minutes, we were almost completely naked, but our underwear remained as he crawled over me on the bed. I laid back, pressing my head into the pillow and arching my back to meet his chest. My breasts, suddenly free from the lacy fabric constraining them, were supple and my nipples sensitive, even more so when he placed his lips around them.

"God," I said, whimpering as he suckled on my breast, running his tongue over my nipple and just barely letting his teeth graze it. It drove me insane.

"Mm, Penny, how could I have forgotten how incredible your breasts are?" he asked, bringing his arms under my back to pull me closer to him as he straddled me from above. "I need to get more consistent reminders."

"I think that can be arranged," I said with a grin, and I instinctually pushed my groin against his. The cloth remaining between us was getting more frustrating by the second, and the fabric was becoming damp from my end.

"Someone's excited," he said, a hand slipping between my legs to feel the dampness.

"Of course, I am," I said, putting another hand on his ass and slipping it under the fabric of his boxer briefs. "Please, I want these off."

Even I was shocked at my boldness, but Owen seemed to find it appealing.

"If the lady requests." He sat up on his knees, giving me the opportunity to push myself further back up on the bed, and I admired his delicious body. He pushed the fabric down the rest of the way, bringing a leg up to slip himself out of them. I had forgotten how well-endowed he was, and I felt a lump in the back of my throat form out of anticipation.

"Please," I begged, squirming on the bed so much that I felt my soaking panties slip down over my behind underneath me. "Please, Owen."

"And so the lady receives," he said, pulling the panties down and over my legs as I stretched them out for him. He brought himself back over me and placed his cock on my pelvis, teasing along the entrance of my pussy as he let it sit on top of the folds, not diving between them yet. "Do you want me to use a condom?" he asked.

I considered it for a moment, and I knew if I wanted to, I could dig around my boxes and purses somewhere to find one. But I had hormonal birth control, and from what I knew of him, he wasn't having sex with anyone else. And all I wanted was the direct contract between us, so much that it drove me to the edge of my sanity.

"No, please. I want you in me, all of you. Please."

My eyes met his, and he held contact as he nodded, slipping his cock between my lips as he entered me slowly. Then, it was all at once.

This time, I *did* feel all of him. And it was *amazing*.

The sensation of feeling his pulse and twitch against me as he slid in and out, giving me a moment to adjust as we met all the way for the first time, drove me wild. My back arched against him, and we found a rhythm as he slipped inside me repeatedly. It was soft and gentle, but the speed picked up at some point, and I squeezed tight around him. That made him moan, and he found my lips again. We kissed deeply, tongues entwined, as his strides became stronger and stronger, harder and harder. Eventually, he was pounding into me, and my legs found his waist as I wrapped them tight around him, locking my ankles in place.

Owen broke away from my lips as he continued his thrusts to kiss along my neck, both of us panting into each other, longing to be closer, tighter, *deeper.*

It felt like ages of rocking against each other, moaning and whispering sweet nothings of affection into each other's ears. My fingers raked along his back, digging into his skin as he pressed further into me. With another thrust, Owen sat himself back on his knees and lifted my waist to him, giving him deep and full access to me as he pushed himself further and further, bringing me closer to the edge with each second.

I could feel he was close, too, based on how his cock twitched inside me and his brow furrowed, sweat dripping lightly down his hair and onto my chest. I grinned, playing with my breasts and nipples as he thrust. He seemed to like the visual, and it only made me smile wider to be pleasing him.

"Owen," I gasped, my head pressing into the pillow as far back as it would go. "Owen, I'm—"

"Yes, darling," he said, squeezing my hips tight as he pulled me close and ground me into him slow and hard. "Come for me. Come all over me."

"Ahh—" I whimpered, and within moments, I was coming undone, riding the wave of pleasure he rocked through me. I saw stars behind my eyes, and each of them echoed Owen's name and carried the same sparkle in his irises that I saw when I came to again, riddled with sweat and orgasmic lust.

"Can I—" he gasped on top of me, and I nodded, knowing exactly what he was asking.

"Yes, please, please," I groaned, already on the edge of finding my next orgasm.

At my begging, Owen lost control and sloppily pounded another thrust into me that came with a shooting deliciousness as his orgasm rocked through us both, and I came all over again.

Once we'd been spent, breathing hard and dripping with sweat, he collapsed next to me, his hand never leaving my skin, wanting that deep connection even still as he was no longer inside me. It was a comfort I didn't know I wanted, but now, I needed it. His breathing was the perfect noise to carry me into my dreams, where the night's activities only seemed to continue.

We passed out like that, holding each other, and the sun coming through my bedroom window the next morning gleamed on us, waking us from the slumber of the night before. I groaned, rolling onto my side to pull the curtain. I normally closed it before bed, along with doing the rest of my evening routine, but obviously, I was a little distracted last night. The distraction in question turned to me, wrapping an arm around my waist and pulling me into him. The feeling of his warm breath against my ear made me shiver, and I would have done anything to stay in bed next to him. By the way, his fingers and gripped my hips, he felt the same.

"It's much too bright out," he said, kissing along my jaw. "I think we need to stay here."

"Owen," I said with a giggle, rolling over into him and finding a new home in his arms, my lips against his chest. "We can't stay here all day. Don't you have work?"

"Yes," he groaned, pressing a hand to his forehead.

"When do you have to be in?" I asked. It was then I realized how little I knew about what he actually did, and I pondered it for a moment. "Where's your firm's office, anyway?"

His back stiffened, and I wondered if I had done something wrong by asking. I didn't think it was too invasive a question with where we were currently sitting. But as quickly as the fear in his face shone, it fell away.

"Nine," he said. "Usually eight, but people don't start complaining about my lack of presence until nine. Other than—" He brought his wrist up, still wearing his smart watch from the evening before. "God, so many messages ... Oh! A meeting at nine, and it's—"

I looked at my own phone on the side table, still low on charge from forgetting to plug it in last night. That was why a strict routine was helpful, even though I never stuck to any of them. At least I knew what they needed to be, whether or not I was successful in them.

"It's already eight-thirty," I said, sitting up and taking a sip from the water glass I've had at my bedside for at least two days.

"Shit," he groaned, following suit, and standing to slide on his boxers, which had fallen to the side of the bed. "I got a text from Mrs. Singh saying she got Lilly off to school, so she's fine, but ..." He sighed, walking back over to me and kneeling on the bed. "I have to head out to work. But I don't want you to think I'm willingly dipping out on you."

"You stayed all night," I said with a laugh. "And you're saying goodbye this morning, so you're doing much better than prior one-night stands."

184

"This isn't a one-night stand, Penny," he said and placed a hand on my cheek, rubbing my skin gently. "I had an incredible time last night."

I smiled. "I did too. One of the best dates I've been on in a while, happy ending or not," I said with a laugh. "It's okay you have to go. I have students today too, so I need to get up to start my day too."

"Good then, I'm glad I'm not the only one," Owen said with a smile, leaving me a light kiss on my cheek.

I relished in the touch for a moment before turning my head and kissing him back, playfully pulling him back on top of me on the bed. We both laughed, still naked, a joyous swirl of legs and arms around each other as we toppled toward the edge.

"Okay, okay," I said. "Go get your pants on before I drag you back in here."

"With an offer like that, I'm less inclined to get dressed." He grinned, wiggling his brows at me before he hopped off and pulled up his slacks. He dug for his shirt somewhere in the mess of sheets around us.

"Stop it!" I giggled. "Here," I said, handing him the shirt when I found it in the comforter. "It didn't get far."

"Thank you," he said.

I sat on the bed in awe, watching him get dressed. His body was utter perfection, and I wondered how he achieved such a figure without being at the gym every five minutes. I supposed having a child and doing all the running around himself was a hidden silver lining for his health and cardio.

"Are you going to stay in here all day then too?" he asked, smirking at my ogling.

"No, I just can't stop looking at you. You're gorgeous; it's not fair," I said.

"I'm a lawyer, sweetheart; I'm the first to say life isn't fair." Without another beat, he stepped out into the hall to get his things for work and make himself more presentable, I assumed.

"What firm are you at, anyway?" I asked, ever curious about the man I was continually finding my mind couldn't let go of.

"Oh," he started from out in the kitchen, and something about his tone felt off, "just a small one. My father used to own it, and now I step up to handle things. Hopefully, you'll never have to hear from us." He grinned. "Anyway, I really do have to get going. That meeting is important, and I'll be reprimanded if I'm not there on time." He returned to the bedroom, adjusting the tie he'd found on the chair.

"Okay," I said in the sultriest tone I could manage, getting out of the bed with only the sheet wrapped around me. He watched me, practically drooling with his jaw on the floor, as I strode to him with the sheet draped over my curves. I dropped it when standing directly in front of him and moved my hands to sit comfortably around his neck, twirling with little bits of his hair at the base of his spine. "Then you better get going, huh?"

Owen groaned from under my arms, wrapping his hands around my waist and pulling me into him. "Devil woman," he said, kissing me deeply before walking me back to the bed to sit. He gently pressed me down, not unlike an owner training his dog. Something about it got me off even more, and I smirked up at him. "I'll call you later. I promise."

"Good, because I'll be thinking of you all day," I said with a smile. I stood and walked to the back of my bedroom door, grabbing a robe to pull around myself. I often walked around the house in only that robe, at least until closer to the afternoon when the kids would be coming by.

He called out from the hall, where he was grabbing the last of his things, "Make sure to tell me all about it then," he said smiling. "Goodbye, Penny." He walked back into the bedroom to give me a last kiss.

"Bye, Owen," I said after smiling against his lips.

He walked out, and I heard the door close, but my mind remained in the blissful state of euphoria he'd left me in from our wonderful night together. If I had my way, I would remain there for the rest of my life.

# Chapter 26

OWEN

"Owen, there you are!" Lorenzo hollered as I made my way down the hall to the office. It was five past nine by the time I ran in, so he was already in meeting mode. "I delayed as much as I could, but you know how on top of things Adler can be. I told him we were having internet trouble. I hope you already pissed this morning; we have to go!"

"I know, I know, I'm sorry," I said, throwing my briefcase on the table as I strode into the conference room. "Randy, do you have any coffee going?" I asked, peeking my head out the door.

"Of course, Mr. Michaels," I heard a voice say, and within moments, there was a steaming mug in front of me. I couldn't wait to sip it, desperately craving the caffeine hit to get my mind on track from the daze I'd been in this morning. "Don't worry about it; we all get up on the wrong side every once in a while," Randy said when he dropped it off with a smile.

"Sure," I said, smirking. I'd gotten up on the right side alright; it was getting out of the bed that had been difficult.

"You ready?" Lorenzo asked, sitting next to me and getting the screen booted up. "Did you finish those reports? He's going to want to know why we haven't secured the Plumosa location yet."

"I know," I said, and while the repeated answer wasn't substantial, I didn't have the energy to focus on Lorenzo's pestering. Instead, I prepared myself for the pestering that would soon be coming through the computer projector screen. I took a big chug of my coffee, despite it being black and steaming hot, and I winced as it burned down my throat. It was worth it for the jolt of energy it sent through me.

Lorenzo raised an eyebrow at my desperation for coffee, undoubtedly combined with my unusual tardiness. "Just pull yourself together, O," he said, starting up the meeting.

On cue, Mr. Adler's face lit up the screen, joined by a mug covered in caricatured sloths. Adler grinned, clapping his hands together with enthusiasm. "My favorite team, how are you? Technical difficulties at the office?"

"Yes, I'm so sorry about that, Mr. Adler, we're having IT up here by this afternoon to double-check our wiring, but we should be good to go," Lorenzo said.

"How's the project going; did we manage to secure all our locations so we can break ground on development?" Adler asked.

Rather than taking the mantle on discussion, Lorenzo instead turned his head to me, awaiting my answer for Adler.

Adler seemed to notice the redirection and brought his eyes to me. "Owen, how are we doing?" he asked in clarification.

I nodded firmly, biting my bottom lip from within my mouth, where the nervous tick wouldn't be spotted. "Yes, sir, we're doing just fine. I did have some things I wanted to run by you, particularly regarding the location on Plumosa."

"Yes, did we manage to get an offer accepted by Ms. Lewis?" he asked.

"Not quite, sir," I said, swallowing hard. I brought my attention to my briefcase and was thankful I'd already prepped the files for today's meeting before my date last night. I'd known that this morning might be somewhat of a clusterfuck. And by golly, I'd been right. "I wanted to offer the idea of getting some of the locations on the other side of the planned development. It looks like there's an apartment complex there currently, on the other side of the freeway, and—"

"Another location?" Adler asked, clearly taken by surprise at the suggestion.

Lorenzo gave a nervous laugh, throwing a hand out to me. "Owen can come up with some crazy ideas, sir, but I assure you, we just need to make more compelling offers to Ms. Lewis. She's being a bit stubborn, and—"

I cut Lorenzo off, referring back to my files. "Mr. Adler, there's a good chance Ms. Lewis won't be willing to sell, no matter what we offer her. So what I'm offering *you*," I said, my tone shifting into more of a sales pitch than I'd intended, "is a chance at looking at even more development space by shifting the blueprints of the mall over to the other side of the freeway."

Adler was quiet for a moment, and I was terrified to meet his glance. Suddenly, I heard a chuckle and looking up, Adler smiled in a way that somehow felt both comforting and judgmental all at once. "Owen, I'm sure this all sounds like a great alternative plan, but I'm sure we can offer a higher price for the Plumosa residence. If we shifted plans, we're talking an extra few weeks of approval and reworking the blueprints with construction, plumbing, electric, the whole nine yards."

"He's just looking out for an emergency contingency plan, Mr. Adler," Lorenzo said, and he then took a deeper sip of his coffee from me. "We're all on the same page here; we're going to get the Plumosa location."

In some horribly fated plot to ruin all the secrets I'd been keeping under wraps where my personal and work life were colliding, I felt a buzzing in my pocket. I looked at my watch connected to my phone to read the message subject and check on the call—Penny's face lit up the screen. I panicked, covering my wrist with my files. I didn't know why she had to be calling now, but it would ruin everything I'd struggled to protect if it got out.

"Sir," I said, covering my tracks and sitting up taller, "I just want to make sure our options"

Lorenzo took over, speaking over me and sitting up further to bring himself closer to Adler and the camera. "We'll get the location, Mr. Adler. Within the month, we'll secure an offer for Ms. Lewis to make sure that the Plumosa residence is ready for demolition."

I raised my eyebrows at how willing he was to overstep, but Adler didn't seem to notice the discordance between us.

"Okay, boys," Adler said. "Owen, go ahead and send that report on the alternate location. I like the idea of a backup plan, so I'll look over the report, but I'm trusting you to do everything in your power to get this done. That's why you're the best; don't let me regret going with Tate Legal." Adler's eyes met Lorenzo, and he said, "Lorenzo, do keep Owen in line. Maybe he needs a little extra help in getting that spot; just make sure it happens."

I gritted my teeth and almost caught my tongue in the process of trying to avoid replying, knowing it would only dig my grave further. The meeting continued with talking about the budget for offers as well as the next steps following securing the location from Penny. Knowing what I knew about her now, the passion I held for the woman living at that residence, it was heartbreaking to hear them referring to her like a place on a map, even when they were only referencing the house.

"Ms. Lewis" was more than an object they could buy and sell at their discretion. Despite that, I held the very same tone only a few weeks ago.

After around twenty minutes of discussion, Adler hopped off the call with his typically cheery goodbyes, and Lorenzo shut down the monitor. The conference room was silent for a moment, and then he turned his head to me. "What the hell was that, Owen? We can't go into a meeting with Adler like that; we have to be on the same page. You're just going to throw out an alternate offer without even consulting me?"

"I'm sorry," I said with a sigh, taking another chug of the coffee. It had slightly cooled by now, but it still bubbled with warmth in my stomach once I swallowed it down. "I only just started drafting it over the weekend, and I was going to follow up with you. I just ran out of time." I went through the file and handed him the report I'd built on the Inertia Apartment Complex that sat on the opposite side of the freeway from Penny's location.

It'd been a bit of a scramble putting it together, but at this point, I needed to do as much work to ensure this wouldn't all blow up in my face. And now, my relationship with Penny sat on the line too, and I refused to lose her over it. Not after last night and realizing just how much I cared for her.

"I don't care, Owen; you can't blindside me like that in front of clients," he said, and to be honest, he was right. I'd pulled a shitty move.

"I know; I'm sorry, Lorenzo. That was wrong of me, but I promise ... just look into this as an option. I think it's—" I held out the paper to hand to him, and he nearly swiped it from my hands.

"Sure, whatever, I'll look at it today. I'm grabbing another coffee, then going out for a smoke," he said with a sigh, and I was frustrated with myself for letting it get this far. I worked well with Lorenzo; he was my friend, and I didn't want to disappoint him as that nor as a business partner.

As Lorenzo dug through his pockets looking for his cigarettes, he called out into the hall, "Randy, can we get another coffee in here while I'm out?"

My phone rang again, and I pulled it from my pocket to see Penny's face again, and my cheeks blanched.

"You okay? You seem pretty off this morning, partying too hard?" Lorenzo asked, finishing his first cup to allow for Randy to bring in the fresh one once it was ready. Lorenzo had a habit of leaving multiple mugs around, and poor Randy had to clean up the mess. The life of an unappreciated intern.

"It was just a long night. Sorry, I have to take this really quick," I said, and I picked up the phone, talking quietly. "Hey," I said, focused on not dropping any names.

Penny's voice rang through, and it made my heart soar just from the sound of it. She had me wrapped around her finger, and I didn't all that mind. "Hey, stranger. Sorry to call so soon, but I realized I was going to ask you some lawyer stuff last night that I forgot about. Do you have a minute?" she asked.

"Ah," I said, doing my best not to stumble through my words. "Sure, hold on." I moved out to the hall on the other side of the stairs, so when Lorenzo came through for his smoke break, he wouldn't hear me. I pulled the phone away from my ear, did a sigh of relief, and then brought it back. "What's going on?" I asked. I was optimistic—maybe it wasn't about the house, maybe she was suing someone, or working through legal fees of a parking ticket, or—

"These guys keep hounding me to buy my house. Is there anything I can do to get them off my back?" she said.

Damn.

I had to be violating every ethical boundary for both my relationship with Penny and my company, but I had dug my grave and now had to make myself comfortable in it to keep from being found out.

"Well," I said, "you have a few options. But really ..." I started, and then I swallowed hard, "I think you should at least consider the offer if it's sizable."

"What?" she asked, clearly stunned at my answer. "And just give into them?"

"No, not give in," I said, not wanting her to blow up at me. "I know that house means a lot to you, but if you take a deal where they're offering you a big amount for it, you can build a place yourself and completely customize it, make it a workable music studio, attach it to your living space and home. Don't you think that's something your grandmother might have wanted for you?"

I was treading water, and the waves were smashing against me, daring to take me under. At that moment, Lorenzo walked out of the office with his cigarette, giving me a wave as he strode toward the elevator.

"Maybe, but Owen, no," she said. "I don't want to sell the house. I don't see why they can't go somewhere else, and for what, a mall?" she scoffed, and I pressed my fingers to my nose.

After another deep breath with the phone on mute, while she was continuing her rant, I said, "At least consider it. But if not, there are ways you can get out of it. I ..." I started, then mentally groaned at the hoops I was jumping through to wiggle my way through the situation. "I can pull together some resources for you later, but I would really consider the offer, Penny."

She was quiet for a moment on the other line, and then I heard a grumble. At least she hadn't hung up on me for even suggesting it, so it could have gone worse. "Okay, I'll look into it. Thanks, Owen, just for letting me spew for a second. It's been really frustrating. I think one of them has been stalking my house, so next time I see him parked, I'm calling the cops."

"That's a good idea," I said, gritting my teeth and making a mental note to warn Lorenzo about watching his back for the cops and stop with the drive-bys. He was going to get us in trouble, which had seemed like my job up to now. "I have to get back to work, but I'm glad you called, okay?" I said with a smile that felt, for the most part, genuine. "I missed your voice."

"I did too," she said, and I heard her smiling too. "I'll talk to you later, Owen. Have a good day." She made a kissing noise, which made me laugh as we both hung up.

After the call ended, I exhaled deeply and looked out the window at the overcast sun. It blurred out the light through the clouds, and without a clear path, the rays shone down muted and gray. I huffed out a sigh, feeling like I, too, was missing the clarity the sun brought.

# Chapter 27

PENNY

Seamus came over for his lesson at around two o'clock, and Mrs. Morgenstern ended up staying the whole time. She often brought her little craft hobbies and sat patiently in the living room, listening to us play and bobbing her head to the music. Even while we were just warm-ups, she seemed to enjoy the ambiance it created.

After a few weeks of practice, Seamus had improved on his original goal songs, one of which was a piece by Mozart, and his fingers had started flying across the keys as he picked up the muscle memory and rhythm of the song. Upon completing it, his hands landed on the last chords with a thud of relief, and Mrs. Morgenstern burst into applause.

"Brava, sweetheart!" she cheered, her crochet needles falling to the floor with a clack in the process.

"Mom," he grumbled, looking down in embarrassment.

I nudged his shoulder with a grin. "She's proud of you, and you should be too," I said with a smile. "But Mrs. Morgenstern, I know you want to cheer for him, but I think holding off until after practice is done might be helpful," I said in my most calm and placating tone. "It's wonderful you want to applaud, but make sure this is a safe space for him to rehearse and explore the music."

"Of course," she said, fumbling around with her yarn and grabbing her needle from where it landed under the lip of the couch.

"Of course, I'm not even here." She jokingly lifted her crochet project—the start of what looked like a pair of gloves—over her face. It obviously didn't hide her, but it made Seamus smile.

"Alright, let's continue," I said, and we went through the song again, finding the places where he stumbled a little to clarify the technique. I also wanted him to learn not how to perform songs but how to play the piano and use it as a partner in creating beautiful music. *That* was the lesson I constantly tried to instill in my students, and I think I did an okay job.

We finished up around fifteen minutes later, and Mrs. Morgenstern waited until I gave her the cue with a nod to stand and applaud her son and his hard work. Seamus was done rehearsing at that point, so while he was still embarrassed, it faded into a smile soon enough.

"That was phenomenal, Seamus," she said, standing and putting her project back into her tote. "You're doing wonders here with Ms. Lewis."

"He's the one doing the hard work, I said, standing and helping him put away his sheet music.

"Thank you, Ms. Lewis; I'm so happy I finally got that progression change in the second-to-last stanza. I'd been working hard through that one, and you helped me get it!" He grinned. It wasn't often I saw a twelve-year-old boy express genuine excitement and gratitude, so I was thankful for it when it appeared.

Seamus got all his things packed up, and I chatted with Mrs. Morgenstern about his progress as I got a pot of water going in the kitchen.

"Thank you so much for your work today, Ms. Lewis," Mrs. Morgenstern said. "He's been improving so much, especially in his practice at home. Especially since you taught him how to play that Billy Joel song!" She grinned. "I love hearing that one around the house." Her arm reached out to Seamus to scrunch his hair, the curls bouncing up gently as she released it.

"Mom!" he said, shrugging her off and starting to walk out with his bag. He stopped to turn around and call back to me, "Thanks, Ms. Lewis."

"Keep practicing that chorus; once you get it, I think the rest will settle in!" I replied, waving a hand out. Once I helped Ms. Morgenstern out the door and waved goodbye, I reminded her to help Seamus keep studying that progression at home, even if he nailed it today, as the consistency was what made for a successful practice—I slipped inside to make some tea. I went for a favorite flavor, blackberry and cherry. It was non-caffeinated, which wasn't preferred, but I did my best to take it easy on my system when I wasn't on crunch time for a project or deadline. With just a touch of sugar and sometimes, if I was feeling adventurous, a dash of creamer made for afternoon perfection.

Today, I needed that perfection to keep myself calm. With my tea in hand, I moved over to the dining table, where the folder from the legal company sat. I'd avoided even opening it, not wanting to confront the idea of potentially selling the house just so some pencil-pushers could mow it down to make a shopping mall. Based on principle alone, that would have kept Grandma from supporting the sale. I knew Owen meant well when he mentioned it, but this was something I needed to handle and decide on my own. Though, I made a mental note to call Grace and ask her what she thought about the offer.

Upon opening the folder, I saw Tate Legal inscribed on the front in a fancy emboss. The unnecessary glamor of it all pushed me even further, but I started digging into the folder to see what kind of offer they were planning on making.

They were indeed planning on breaking down the land and using it to develop a mall along the freeway. To be honest, the town could do with a social location like that, especially as something to do around here other than hitting the bar or hanging out at the diner. Abilene wasn't the most exciting town, and you had to go at least two towns over to find anything more than a small department store. Their original offer sat at $400,000, which was a number I couldn't even begin to fathom. The secondary offer that came when Lorenzo stopped by to intimidate me upped it to $700k, which seemed astronomically insane. But Owen was right; in Abilene, I could use that money to more or less build a mansion, a home base that served me instead of one I was fitting myself into. I yearned to knock down a wall or two and build up a space for my own storage that didn't have wallpaper with cats printed on it, like the one in the front room closet. My grandmother had her eccentricities, but I often preferred those for the more private spaces that weren't always out for viewing. That said, the kooky designs were starting to grow on me, so it would be a mission to figure out what I'd change. Changing anything in this house felt like losing Grandma's spirit.

But despite how low my jaw had dropped at the mention of money for this house, flipping to the back of the offer folder had it on the ground.

At the top of the sheet sat information on the Tate Legal team, including their two heads. One was Lorenzo, the man I recognized who had stopped by and sat outside my house, staking me out. Something about him peeved me off, but not as much as the face next to him. It was a face I knew better than Lorenzo's, one I had grown to trust and see as a potential permanent fixture in my life.

With teeth shining bright and the light glinting in his eyes, Owen Michaels posed for his bio for the file, and my heart sank deep into my stomach.

Owen. He was working for this company the entire time.

He'd played dumb when I called him today, and he knew everything I'd been dealing with about this company going up my ass to buy me out. Hell, he *was* the company trying to buy me out.

I staggered to my feet, almost dropping my cup of tea as I took a sip to try and ground myself. I felt sick to my stomach, so I rushed off to the bathroom and emptied my gut of the small lunch of chicken soup I'd had before Seamus's lesson.

He'd lied to me. To my face. And I had believed him. He took the trust I'd placed so blindly in him and stomped all over it, making me regret ever meeting him.

I dug through the file, searching for contact information on their main office. It was under their bios, and it wasn't far at all. From being on the phone with him just a few hours earlier, I knew he was there. And he was going to hear from me.

Without another lesson for a few hours, I gathered up only the necessities, hopped in my car, and slammed on the gas toward the Tate Legal office. It was only about five minutes away, so the anger didn't have long to stew further. Thank God I didn't get pulled over, as, in my emotional state, I would probably be stated unfit to be driving. By the time I showed up at their building, I was seeing red and ready to punch a wall, but I would fight the urge to get assault charges today.

Swerving my car into a spot up front and shoving my foot into the parking break, I took a deep breath and stepped out, preparing myself for the storm ahead. I was glad I hadn't called to ensure he was there; I didn't want to give him the chance to duck out before I made a scene. And I would most definitely be making a scene.

The walk up to the building and the wait in the elevator both had me on edge, and each floor that clicked past was one more needle piled on my metaphorical camel's back. On the third floor, as listed on their address, I huffed once more and stepped out. The long hallway gave me time to find a stride, and when I yanked open the door for the office, I watched the receptionist at the front desk go from a kind greeting smile to fear when she saw the glare in my eyes.

"Where's Owen?" I asked, not offering any tonal chance for rejection.

"Ah," she stuttered, reaching for her phone. "Can I ask who is requesting? Do you have an appointment?"

"No, I don't have an appointment, but I need to see him. Now," I demanded.

"Penny?" I heard his voice call from down the hall. The office must not be very big, or I didn't know how loudly I was speaking. Either way, he stepped into view, and my anger toward him turned into a burning fury that could cut through glass.

The receptionist stood. "Mr. Michaels, I'm sorry, I—"

"You knew. The whole time, you knew, and you were trying to convince me to sell it," I accused.

His confusion turned to horrified understanding when he realized what I was saying. His eyebrows rose, and his pupils grew wide and dilated. Stepping forward, he put his hands out, looking like he needed to defend his safety. I must look more unhinged than I thought, but I didn't care.

"Penny, I can—" he started, but I cut him off.

"Don't you dare try to explain it. Because I'm pretty sure I understand everything," I said. I tried to fight them back, but I felt the sting of two tears peek through, blinking them away firmly. They betrayed me by falling, and I saw something in Owen soften. I hated it, with how explosive I was feeling. I didn't want his pity and comfort, not anymore.

Another two heads popped out of rooms along the hallway with how loud I was being, one of which I recognized as Lorenzo. Both looked ready to grab a bag of popcorn at the drama unfolding. The receptionist, on the other hand, looked terrified. Her hand was on the phone, seemingly ready to call the police. I wouldn't be here long enough to do so.

Owen shook his head, taking another step to reach out and touch me. I slapped his hand away. "Don't touch me. You lied to me, and you strung me along when I asked for your help on this. And you let that moron back there try to intimidate me into selling my grandmother's house when you know how much it means to me. How could you do that to me? How could you let me trust you like that, then rip it out from under me?" I felt tears in my eyes, and I cursed each one. I didn't want to show him that vulnerability now, especially in front of the rest of the company around us.

"Mr. Michaels, do you want me to call—" the receptionist said in a whisper.

I turned my head to her, calming my voice as much as possible. "Don't bother; I'm not going to hurt anyone. I'm just saying my piece, and none of you will ever see me again." When I turned back to Owen, the vitriol returned to my tone. "I am never selling to you or any other company. You're a piece of shit for what you did, and I never want to see your face," I spat at him. "I won't punish Lilly for this, she's a good kid and deserves a better father than you, so I'd prefer Darlene to bring her, but if you do, you better stay in the damn car."

I heard what sounded like a gasp of understanding from Lorenzo, and I assumed he was connecting the dots as to who I was to Owen.

"Penny—" His voice cracked as he said my name, and it broke another piece of my heart.

"No," I said. "No negotiation, save it for your legal bullshit. Goodbye, Owen." With that, I turned to the receptionist, whose name on the placard I now saw was Anne and gave her a gentle nod. "I'm sorry for causing a ruckus."

Without another word and leaving Owen standing there gawking at me, I walked out of the office and back toward the elevator. I stomped my way down the pavement, yanked my car door open, then huffed, gripping the wheel once again. I needed to get away from him, from this office, so I pulled out onto the main road, and as I took a breath and hoped I could move on from this awful day, I felt it. The pangs of hurt ripped through me, grieving the relationship I thought I would have had with this man who turned out to be a snake.

I couldn't hold back the sobs within me, so I pulled off again onto the side of the road and put the car into park. Then I took a deep breath, and I let it go. With my windows rolled up, droplets of rain fell onto the windshield, and I cried. I screamed, cried, whimpered, and hugged my chest. The tears flowed out of me like rain, threatening to keep me in its downpour.

# Chapter 28

OWEN

Following Penny's arrival and outburst, the tension in the office was heavy, and all eyes were on me. No one said anything about the situation to me, obviously realizing I didn't want to talk about it. Lorenzo brought up the conflict of interest it created and warned me about mixing work and pleasure. I didn't respond to him, staring silently out the window as he spoke. He seemed to get the message and left me alone for the rest of the day.

I tried calling Penny maybe five or six times throughout the day, but I wasn't sure what I was planning to achieve. She'd said her piece, and I knew she probably didn't want to hear from me, but that didn't stop me from trying repeatedly. She never picked up. I only left one with a message; the rest I clicked off before it went through. On that message, though, I did my best to hide the fact that I'd cried earlier and was now trying to hold myself together, asking calmly and placatingly if she would talk to me so I could explain my reasoning and apologize. I said, "I'm sorry," around forty times on a thirty-second message, but I had no idea if she'd ever listen to it.

After spending the rest of the day opening and closing the same document, taking phone calls and being barely able to hold a conversation, and enduring the judgment of an intern ten years my junior as he poured my coffee, I could say with ease that I'd done some reflecting. There wasn't a single excuse I could meaningfully make—I did this. From the conscious decision to keep the sale from Penny and come forward about the conflict of interest, I'd been sitting in wait of losing her the minute she found out. I knew what the house meant to her and what taking the side of someone trying to destroy it would mean to her.

I kept waiting on the relief of that recognition of responsibility, but the answer to lessen my pain never came.

The minute the clock struck four, I ducked out, not caring about it being earlier than normal. The office would survive the last hour without me, and no one seemed to complain when I hit the elevator. I even got what seemed to be a pitied look from Anne at the front desk, though I wasn't sure who she was pitying—Penny or me.

Once I was down in my car, I gripped the steering wheel tight, turning my knuckles white. The road was empty, surprisingly so, for a Tuesday afternoon. By the time I arrived at the house, I knew Lilly and Darlene would already be going about their afternoon, usually consisting of homework at the dining table. I had to prepare myself to be a Happy-Go-Lucky Dad for her after spending all day in a cycle of self-hatred and shame after what I had done and tried to hide. And then having that served to me on a platter in front of my coworkers. But in the end, Lilly's opinion of me mattered more than any of theirs.

Hers and now, Penny's.

Unlocking the door, I breathed, and Lilly rushed over to greet me, wrapping her arms firmly around my waist. It wasn't often I got these excited hellos as she grew older, and I cherished each one I got.

"Hey, Lillypad," I said, leaning to the side to set down my keys, and then I pulled her close. "How was school?"

"It was sucky," she replied, and I laughed, despite it feeling foreign right now. "What, it was!" She pulled off from the hug and crossed her arms.

Standing, I chuckled at her tone, at least thankful she hadn't dipped into using actual curse words yet. "So, what was so *sucky* about it?" I asked, overenunciating.

"Girls being cruel," I heard Darlene say in the other room. "I told her not to worry about what they think."

"Hi, Darlene," I said, waving to the table as I finished taking my coat and bag off my shoulder.

Lilly walked back to the table and sat in front of her homework next to Darlene. Her brows were furrowed as she crouched over a multiplication table sheet; it looked like double and triple digits this time. I looked at Darlene, who gave a gentle nod, and then Lilly explained.

"My class is doing a competition to get a lunch from Rally's, and to get it, you have to be the fastest at doing multiplying tables on the board," Lilly started, but Darlene interjected.

"And she was apparently doing great, so her teacher told me," she said.

I asked, "You spoke to the teacher?" Darlene had acted on my behalf with Lilly at her school before, but it had usually never been anything positive. I was heartbroken to be hearing about more problems.

Lilly ignored my question, then continued, "Stupid Eva and Charlotte kept making fun of me during my turn, and I started to cry, and they kept shouting at me, and the teacher got them in trouble."

"So those girls are in trouble, right?" I said, kicking into protective gear and lightly pressing my hands into the table.

206

Darlene put her hand out and said, "Yes, they're all in detention. But so is someone else." Her eyes turned to Lilly's head, which was still facing down on the paper. "Are you going to tell him?"

Without lifting her head, Lilly mumbled, "I threw the chalk stick at her, and it hit her in the face."

"You what?" I said, pulling up a chair to sit next to her. "Lilly, what were you thinking? You can't throw things at people; you know better than that."

"I just wanted them to stop laughing at me!" Lilly said, and I heard the lump forming in her throat.

"I know, honey, but you can hurt someone like that; that's not okay." I reached out and put my arm around her, but she didn't look up still. "Lillypad," I said, "look at me."

A sniffle, then she lifted up and met my glance for a moment before diverting to my chin. I could work with that.

"Lilly, those girls were wrong to do that. And you have every right to be frustrated and mad, but you can't let that make you get violent. They're going to be in trouble; let the teachers and principal handle them. You just focus on doing the best job you can, okay?" I said, one hand on her back and one reaching out for hers. At the last moment of my speech, she took it and tight.

She sighed deeply, and her voice was weak. I felt a teardrop or two on my hand, but thankfully, no snot. I wouldn't have minded. "I have a week; they have three days."

"Well, Lil, with you getting violent, I understand why. Sometimes we make mistakes, and we have to take responsibility for them. That's what being a good human being means." I leaned forward and kissed her head, and she finally took that as a cue to meet my eyes. "I love you, Lillypad."

"Love you, Dad," she said, sniffly and quiet. I couldn't even hear "Dad," but her quivering lips moved. She snuggled softly into my side, wrapping one arm around me.

Over her head, Darlene smiled softly. "We've been practicing the multiplication table sheets since we got home. She's going great."

"And I got the last sheet 100% right, and I finished it in a few minutes! And showed all my work!" Lilly exclaimed.

"I'm proud of you, honey," I said, standing. Why don't you finish this one while I talk to Darlene for a second about scheduling, and then I can help walk you through some too?" I kept my voice as calm as possible to keep her from getting worried, but I could tell she knew we would be talking about her and what had happened at school.

"Of course," Darlene said, standing with me and heading toward the hall. Lilly remained at the table, looking back at us a second before huffing in nervousness and turning her glance back to her sheet.

I followed Darlene, setting my hand gently on the doorframe to steady myself as I sighed and followed her into my bedroom for some privacy.

"Thank you for dealing with that today. You could have called too if it was too much or you thought I was needed," I told her, then sat on the edge of the bed, hands on my knees to grip for support. "She's never been violent before; that's a new one."

"I know, it's not like her," Darlene said, standing in front of me. "Her teacher was worried about her, but I said I'd talk to you at home. What can I do to help, Owen?" she asked.

I offered Darlene a weak smile. "Darlene, you already do the world to help both of us. This is something I need to take care of, I think, with her. She's been struggling a lot, and I think she's been feeling how tense I am with work."

208

"That is something to note," she said, but she didn't say it in an accusatory or judgmental way. "It also means you might need to get some outside help."

"I've been thinking of therapy for us both," I mentioned, and Darlene's head dipped up.

"Really?" she asked.

I nodded. "Yes. I've been acting in some ways that … that I just am not proud of. And I'm worried Lilly is seeing it, so I want to be better. For her."

"Just for her?" Darlene's smile was barely there, but I could see it in her eyes. And I knew exactly what she was referring to.

"And others," I clarified, thinking of Penny's beautiful eyes.

"You're a good dad, Owen. You care so much about Lilly."

"I wish being her dad was just about caring about her enough. All this work is exhausting," I said with a weak, tired laugh.

She joined me in it. "Yes, it is. But it's so rewarding, isn't it?"

I gave a light smile. "Yes. Yes, it is."

After trading off with Darlene and taking over at the table with Lilly for her multiplication tables, I was thankful to be home with my daughter after the day I'd had. As we went through each exercise, I was pretty sure Lilly got the message that something was amiss, including a few wayward glances when I said something and trailed off or redirected questions about how work went today.

An hour went by before she'd had enough of the dancing around, but it wasn't for the reason that preoccupied me. "Dad, I'm sorry about what happened at school today."

I was surprised by her mention of it again, bringing my focus back to her. "Thank you, honey, for apologizing. I want to work with you on how to get better at dealing with your emotions, but I'm not mad at you," I said, wanting to ensure she didn't worry about me holding this against her. As worried as I was about her, this would be a one-time deal as long as I kept working on communicating with her on how to help. It wasn't like her, and I would make sure it ended there.

"You're not?" she seemed genuinely concerned. "Then, Dad, what is wrong with you?" she asked. Always tactful, my daughter was.

"I'm fine," I said, shaking my head. "Just a long day."

"Why, what happened?" she asked, innocent and curious.

I looked down at her, wondering how I could begin to explain everything I'd done without her misunderstanding or viewing me differently as a father. I couldn't do that to her. So I went with the second-most honest answer, the half of the story.

"I'm trying to help a group of people buy a specific location, and the people at the location don't want to sell it to them." It was as vague as I could put it while still being enough to give the gist of what I was dealing with.

She listened slowly, nodding as I mentioned each description detail, trying to wrap her head around it. She knew I worked as a lawyer, but Lilly had yet to understand fully what I did in terms of legal work. In the end, she looked down at the table, piecing it all together. "Why are you helping the people that want to take away the person's land?"

"Well," I started, treading carefully. "That person's house is the best place for what they're trying to build. It's the last piece of the puzzle they need, and it's been my job to convince them to do the building there, which means making that person move houses."

"That's pretty sucky," she said, and I chuckled weakly.

"Yeah, it is," I sighed. "It's not fun to do, really, being in charge of selling someone's house when they don't want to move."

"Your job sucks, Dad."

I laughed, patting her back softly. "Alright, enough of the sucking. My job doesn't always …" I smirked at her and said, "frustrate me. But right now, it really is." I took a deep breath, looking at the table, remembering the look on Penny's face when she found out what I'd been trying to do.

Lilly got quiet for a moment, thinking the situation over. Then she turned her head up to me and said, "Why can't they build it somewhere else?" It was as if it were the easiest answer in the world. If only it were.

As I pondered her question, I heard a drizzle begin outside. A storm was forecast tonight, and it seemed its twinges began as a tree branch brushed up against the window when the wind picked up.

"I've been trying to convince them to," I said. *Albeit, not enough*, I thought to myself. "The house is in a really good spot for the traffic they need, and it's part of a plan to build a bigger thing. So they need the space."

"Have you seen the highway, Dad? All it is is space," Lilly remarked. And she wasn't wrong—the amount of space wasn't the problem. Placement of land and planning was. "Just tell them to scooch it over." She shrugged. "Seems silly to kick somebody out when there's so much other room."

And right there, my nine-year-old daughter planted the confidence in me to keep fighting this. Sure, she struggled with the legal nuance of renegotiating land allocation, but she had a good point—that no matter how I looked at the way Penny and her home were being treated, I came out feeling shameful. And it took the young girl I'd raised, wearing a sweater with frogs in scarves, to see it. Either way, I'd known deep down that continuing this project to get Penny to sell the house was a bad idea, and now it was time to fix it. I vowed to be the man my daughter would be proud of.

Without a second to consider another option, I stood from the table, picked up my cell from the counter, and dialed Lorenzo. Lilly watched me, her head swinging as I moved and paced, waiting for the phone to ring. Of all the times he'd called me at random occasions to discuss work, he'd take my call now.

"Dad?" she asked. "Did I say something wrong?"

"No, Lil, you were exactly right." I walked back over to the table and grabbed her head, playfully kissing the top six or seven times in succession, making her laugh. "You're right."

"Of course, I am," Lorenzo said as he picked up the phone. "But what about?"

"Hey, Lorenzo," I said, turning from Lilly toward the kitchen again as the storm raged outside. "We have to talk."

# Chapter 29

PENNY

Tina Turner belted from my bathroom as I swiped face mask lotion on my shirt on accident.

"Shit!" I yelled, lifting my cheek away from where it had covered the fabric in goopy, green solution. Frustrated, I went back to the bathroom to wash it off as more tears found my eyes. "Goddammit," I said with a sigh. I'd hoped the tears were over but getting frustrated just pushed me over the edge again.

Walking into the bathroom, I caught a look at my reflection in the mirror, covered in a face mask and sporting red, welled-up eyes. I looked ridiculous, and it only made me more upset. I frowned in the mirror, bending down to rinse my face.

My head bounced up when I heard thunder crack outside, and the roof was suddenly pelted with rain. It had hit quick, so I left my face dripping with water as I ran around the house to ensure all the windows were closed. The last thing I needed was a flood for the night, and the storm would probably only be getting worse. Stores around Abilene had been advertising generators and water bottles all week, but I had a good enough survival supply to get through this storm in the suitcase under my bed, which was full of emergency information, battery-operated electronics, clothes, and canned food.

No, I wasn't worried about my safety this evening. But I was worried about having to go through all this alone.

As if an angel appeared to me in prophecy, my phone rang. I checked the ID and saw Grace's goofy face light up the screen.

"Hey, Grace, are you okay?" I asked upon picking up.

"Yeah, just a little wet," she said on the other line, and I heard cars rushing by and the wind blowing around her.

"Are you out on the road in this?" I asked, listening to the rain pelt my window. "Are you safe?"

"I'm okay right now; the tow truck is on the way. My battery died on the freeway on the way to Topeka. I'm about 20 minutes out of Abilene, and he said he could give me a ride, but without the car … don't really have anywhere to go until I can replace it. Can I come over?" She sounded so exasperated and annoyed, but at least she's okay.

"Oh, my God, of course!" I said. "I had no idea you were even in the area. But keep me on the line until the truck gets there; I want to make sure you're safe in the storm. And get back in your car if you're on the freeway!"

I heard Grace do just that, slamming the door on the way there. "I know, thank you, Mom," she said with a huff. "Are you busy? I'm sorry if I was interrupting anything."

"No!" I said, putting my hand out as if she were in front of me, then thought myself silly for it. "I actually could really use the company tonight."

"Facemask kind of night?"

"Just washed it off."

"Perfect," Grace said, and I heard a smile in her reply. "I'll be over there soon, but tell me about your day to keep us talking."

"My day?" I laughed, flopping my head back on the couch. "I don't know where to start."

"Maybe at the beginning?"

214

I gave a little laugh at the simple way my sister put it, and I smiled weakly as I started unraveling my morning. I told her about the connection I made to Tate Legal and the scene I caused at the office. She was proud of me for standing up for myself, and then she said she bet I looked like a total badass. She wasn't wrong—I did feel like one. But even that didn't help soften the pain of losing trust in Owen.

A few minutes into the description, I heard the rumbles of a truck pulling up in the rain near her, and we hung up. She was at my door within the hour, and I reminded her to give the tow a tip for carting her to me amid a storm. After she got in, I helped dry her off and get her in clean clothes, an old sweatshirt, and leggings I had shoved in the back of my drawers. She had spare clothes here somewhere, but I'd had a feeling they were currently deep in the dirty laundry.

"God, it's nuts out there," she said, wringing out her hair in the towel. "I thought the wind would blow my head off when I got out to check the engine." She flopped on the couch, crossing her fuzzy-socked feet under her. "Thanks for the clothes and for letting me come over."

"Of course," I said, pouring a second cup of cocoa. As usual, mine had long gone cold, so I popped it in the microwave to warm it up again. "I'm just glad you're safe. When did you come into town?" I asked. "It's been a while since you've been here."

"Not really …" she said, biting her bottom lip with a smirk.

"Who is it now?" I laughed.

She raised her eyebrows. "You always think it's about somebody else. Maybe I had another shoot or wanted to go camping." She was playing dumb, and we both knew it.

"Who is it, Grace?"

Grace sighed, and her lips fell into a delighted smile. "Simone."

"That girl from the saloon shoot?" I said with a chuckle. "You're seeing models now? Isn't that a conflict of interest?"

She snorted a little. "Not as long as I don't abuse anyone and keep it professional on-set," she replied, twirling her toes underneath her. She's ... she's really amazing, Penny. I'm really into her."

Once my cocoa was warm again, I finished Grace's cup, then brought both over to the table and curled up next to her. "I'm glad you found someone you care about." I smiled, however weak it was. The thunder outside ripped, and the hammering of rain on the roof got stronger. The old me would have yearned for a partner to curl up next to on nights like these, but tonight, I didn't want anyone here but my sister.

Grace must have sensed my unease because she shifted to hug me from the side, wrapping her arms around me and squeezing tight. "So," she asked, pulling back, "are you gonna talk to me about how you're doing? I heard it over the phone too, but you look like someone ran over your heart with a bus."

"That's about right," I said with a sigh. "I don't want to drag you down."

"Listen, we've both been through hell, and I think we both know it's gonna be a long night. We might as well have some fun with it." She dug through her purse and yanked out a small metal tin—a flask. "Jack Daniels." Grace had been in the shortest engagement with her high school sweetheart and only made it two months before calling it off, but she'd already gone nuts with bridal décor at TJ Maxx, including the sparkly "Bride to Be" flask she was currently pouring from.

I raised my brows to her from where they'd been prior, focused on my dirty carpet floor that needed a deep vacuum. "Jesus, Grace ..." I laughed weakly. I didn't have the strength to ask for it, but I held out my mug, and she didn't disappoint. She gave it an ample pour, remaining a second longer after I gave a nod to stop. "You sure?" I asked.

"Yeah," she reassured me. "So get talking."

And I did. I talked for what felt like hours, though it was probably less than one. The tears started about ten minutes into it, and they didn't stop until I was a sniveling mess, using the cloth I'd brought over for the tea to wipe my nose and eyes. At some point, Grace gave me another ample pour when she saw my cup running low, then took a sip herself, shaking her head at the harshness of the strong liquor. She poured some in her own cocoa and then brought it to her lips and grinned at the smoky smell. I wasn't much of a whiskey girl, but Grace had been drinking the stuff straight since we went out together when she turned eighteen. I didn't remember most of that night, but Grace had held her own.

"And I think the worst part is that I was really starting to trust him, and he just rips it out from under me. Knowing what this house means to me." I shook my head, looking down at my hands, then taking another sip of my cocoa, noting its strength but getting buzzed enough not to care.

Grace sipped her own whiskey and cocoa, nodding with a scowl. "He's an asshole; he lied to your face about this for weeks."

"I know!" I said, groaning and taking another large gulp, feeling my cheeks redden as I pressed my cold hands to my face. "And now it's going to affect my teaching relationship with his daughter, who was doing so well with the consistency. I know if she breaks her routine, she's going to struggle to get back on track. It's just so ... UGH!" I hollered, throwing my head onto my pillow and screaming into it.

Grace's hand met my back and rubbed it gently. "Get it out," she said, setting down her mug to keep it from spilling. "Owen is a jerk, and you'll absolutely find someone better than him. Someone hotter than him. He's a lawyer, so probably not with more money, but the rest is still good too," and I laughed with her.

"God ..." I said with a sigh. "I just thought it was the real thing, you know? And ... I wasn't, like, thinking far into the future, but ..."

"Did you see yourself in a family with him?" Grace asked without a twinge of judgment in her voice.

"Yes. He and I just worked, and I really grew to care for Lilly, and Lilly really likes me; sometimes, I wonder if as more than just a teacher, and I think I was—" I ran out of air as I rambled, and then I sighed. "Is that crazy? This soon?"

"No, of course not." Grace gave me a wink. "I feel that way about Simone."

"Really?" I asked, glad my sister had started thinking more about her future.

"Yeah, but we're crazy. This, for you ... would be so normal. You know, the small town, the kid and house with a nice guy ..." Grace shrugged. "It has its appeal, and with how rocky everything has been for you, I think you really crave that stability."

I thought about a future life like that for me, one with a place to call home and people to call my family. "I do. I just wanted it with him." I felt the lump in my throat return as my eyes welled up lightly.

"Give him time. He's a man; they can be dumb. Maybe he'll come around. What if he apologizes? Do you think you could eventually work out and build up trust again?" Grace put her arm around my shoulder and pressed the other into the pillow on my lap.

I gave something between a nod and a shake of my head. "I appreciate the optimism, Gracie, I just … I don't know. It would take a while. I need some calm first."

At the mention of staying calm, a strong wind whipped along the windows, and we heard a crash come from my bedroom. Both of us immediately stood and ran toward the sound, dodging the empty tissue box I'd left crumpled on the floor in the hall and some of Grace's wet clothes.

When we entered, both of our jaws dropped to the floor. A tree had been blown down and knocked through my window, bringing down some of the wall with it. A cold and windy rain blew through the bedroom from the storm outside, and I felt the tears of overwhelm take over again.

"Okay, it looks stable now, so go get me as many towels as possible, Penny, and find some plastic tarps that Grandma kept out in the back yard, the ones we used for the fundraiser show," Grace said, for once taking over in adult-mode. She must have been able to tell how much I was struggling and then wanted to take the initiative to fix the situation. "Penny!"

"Towels and tarps, got it!" I said, running over to the cabinet to bring over a whole pile.

We stepped into the room together, avoiding the rain pounding through the side as much as possible. The tree—at least it was no more than five or six feet—had mostly fallen through the window and landed against the base of my bed. It made the mattress useless until we got someone in to take out the tree, but it minimized damage to my belongings. We brought over the towels one by one to ration them and got to work cleaning up the puddles as much as possible. As I kept cleaning and clearing out anything still in the path of the tree damage and rain coming through, Grace took the tarps and did her best to hang them along the area of the wall and down to sit against the tree, then she made a natural slide of it to make sure it didn't pool on the floor. It certainly wasn't perfect, but it was only to keep out a good chunk of water, and it would do that just fine.

I called 911 to ask about a removal, and the connector said that with the storm, techs would be going around for the next week, grabbing trees from windows just like mine. Sighing, I hung up and hoped the rain would let up soon.

Grace continued to pin up the tarp as much as possible, then joined me in collecting my things and bringing them out to the living room and the two other bedrooms. There was a solid amount of space to store things, but the fact that my bedroom was now going to be a construction zone was heart-wrenching.

At one point, I went outside to see how covered everything was from there and what the damage in the yard was like. Upon finding the fallen base of the tree, I noticed something weird along the stump: marks and cuts in the wood. I went over to the top half and realized the tree looked like it'd been chopped. During a storm, it's more expected to see a tree pulled up from the roots as the ground softened. But this one had snapped and broke at the base. Sure, it looked like the bark and layers had worn off over the years, but this tree had seen plenty of storms while remaining upright. Without an active hurricane or something stronger, it was surprising to see a storm had knocked it down. But I was too stressed by the cleaning to address it now. Instead, I took as much of a photo as I could manage with the rain pelting on us and the darkness shrouding most of the detail. Even so, the marks I thought were from an ax were visible, which was all I needed.

I went back inside, and after around two hours of cleaning, sorting, pinning, and drinking—I'd located a bottle of Sailor Jerry in the cabinet—we had done everything we could for the night, and we called it even, closing my bedroom door to put it out of mind.

"It had to be my bedroom and not the other two, huh?" I asked, taking a swig from the bottle. My distaste for liquor had long since faded, along with my sobriety this evening. "This sucks."

"Did you find anything outside?" Grace asked, sitting next to me on the couch, now housing five towels along the back frame. The rest of the wet towels were on every hangable surface in the bathroom and kitchen and on a small living room rack.

"Yeah, it was weird …" I said, remembering everything I'd wanted to update her on. "It looked … like the tree was chopped down."

"What?" she asked, shocked.

"There were chips in the wood around where the break was, ones that looked like they could've been made with an ax." I shook my head in disbelief and fear myself. "I don't know; I might be paranoid, but do you think someone would do that?"

"No sane person, at the least. Maybe it was just weak and got dinged with stuff over the years."

I raised an eyebrow, judging her suggestion.

"Okay, okay," she said, putting up her hands in defense. She reached for the Jerry, then took a swig, groaning after. "Ugh, I think I'm cutting myself off tonight. It might be from all that running around, but my stomach is rolling."

At that, the doorbell rang, and I curiously checked the clock, wondering who could be coming around at ten o'clock during a massive storm. Thinking it might be a neighbor checking in after seeing the tree, I opened the door without hesitation.

Owen stood in front of me, drenched, holding a wrapped bouquet of tulips and roses that were drooping and soggy.

"Owen?" I asked in disbelief, shocked I could speak at all.

"Hey, Penny," he said, and just hearing his voice again, this unexpectedly struck up a physical reaction in me. I couldn't quite tell if it was positive or negative yet, but it was definitely there.

Grace must have heard him because I turned my head to look at her, awestruck at the ridiculousness the night had turned into. She grabbed her flask, poured some of the Sailor Jerry in, set down the bottle, and then took a big gulp.

# Chapter 30

OWEN

I stood waiting outside her door, just barely protected under the overhang from the rain, wondering if I was making a mistake. Thunder clapped around me, and I only prayed she'd even heard the knock with how hard the wind and rain were pelting the house's walls. With Lilly in the car, I swallowed hard, wanting to keep my composure as much as possible. She had already watched me yell into a pillow back at the house in the middle of a call with Adler and Lorenzo, then again when she'd overheard the meeting and asked what had happened. I'd told her about Penny owning the house I was trying to help knock down for work and that I thought I could help them do something else, but that it was wrong not to tell Penny about it and then continue the deal. I was honest and candid, and she took it well. She had always seemed so mature, which scared me, but her forgiveness of me in that situation was shocking. Really, the only thing I'd left out was meeting Penny before at the bar.

After knocking a second time, I heard some shuffling vaguely behind the sound of the rain, and then the door opened. Penny stared at me, wide-eyed and gaping, though I didn't know if that was because she was surprised to see *me* or to see me in drenched clothing in the middle of a storm.

"Owen?" Penny asked.

I smiled. "Hi, Penny."

She turned back to look at someone in the living room, and I had the terrifying thought that she wasn't alone. Her head snapped back to me, and then she peeked her head outside and groaned. "It's raining really hard."

"Yeah. There's a storm," I said stupidly. I sputtered back to life, and when we both looked back at the car, Lilly waved back from the front seat. She was ever my cheerleader, even after the mistakes I'd made.

Clearing my throat, I turned back to Penny and said, "Can we come in? ... Is there someone already here?" I asked with trepidation.

She looked down, but I saw the corners of a smirk pull up her lips. "Yes, I'm ... I'm not alone, Owen."

"Oh, don't torture the guy; it's pouring out," I heard from inside.

Her sister. I sighed in relief.

"Grace is here, but yes, of course, both of you come inside," Penny said, waving out to Lilly past me. Her glance caught me when her arm brushed against my shoulder, and I swore we both relished in that moment of contact.

I went back out to the car, getting pelted again with rain, then held my jacket open for Lilly to huddle under as she clobbered out and darted up the stairs of the porch to dry land.

"Could we use a towel, Ms. Lewis? It was raining really hard," Lilly said in her sweetest voice. I'd told her I was going to Penny's house to apologize and try to win her back, and now she was overselling it just a bit.

"Of course," Penny said, turning to Grace. "Can you get some towels?"

I stepped in with Lilly and Penny, then took the towels from Grace once she had returned with them. Penny helped me dry off Lilly, but I took over to dry her hair a moment, rubbing the towel firmly into her scalp.

"Staahhp," Lilly whined with a laugh.

I left the towel flopped on her head like a wig, then returned to Penny, who sat on the edge of the couch currently being occupied by Grace. "I'm sorry for interrupting anything, and I appreciate you letting us in."

Penny was attentive to Lilly, who fluttered over to the couch next to Grace but ignored me with every fiber of her being. Even when she spoke directly to me, her eyes didn't meet mine. Like she couldn't bear to see me.

"So, what is this about, Owen?" Penny asked, staring right through me.

I turned to Grace and Lilly, having been hopeful I could have some privacy instead of an audience. But now was as good a time as any, and time was one thing not on my side.

"I just want you to know," Penny whispered, "if Lilly hadn't come with you, I would have sent you back out into the rain."

With a nod, I acknowledged her, having considered that when I brought Lilly along. "Thank you for letting me in, then. Penny, I know I have a lot to apologize for," I said. I didn't want to push it off any longer.

"Yes, you do."

"And I understand you're upset—"

Penny lightly gritted her teeth. "Yes. I am."

"Give him a chance," Lilly whined lightly from the couch.

I smiled softly. "I got this, Lil; thank you, honey." I made sure my tone was grateful and kind, so she would know how helpful she really was.

"Good job, kid," Grace whispered, and I watched them fist-bump out of the corner of my eye.

"Penny," I started again, "what I did, by not telling you about your grandmother's house and the development case, was wrong. I messed up, and it was horrible of me to do that to you. You deserve better than that, and I'm so sorry I lied to you."

I was sure to get the majority of the big points out in as much of one breath as I could muster but I still ran out of air toward the end. My eyes searched for Penny's the whole time, despite never meeting them. She stayed focused on anything but me: the floor, my shoes, what looked like the photos her sister had taken on the wall behind me. But at the last line, she looked up.

Once I had her contact, I utilized it firmly. "I'm sorry, Penny. Please, give me another chance." I said the words directly to her, and I could have sworn I saw something of the sparkle she once had when she looked at me.

Penny was quiet for a moment, and I watched her take in everything I said. Then she spoke. "You can't just come in here and pretend everything is fine when it's not, Owen. I'm not a client you can win over, and I won't turn over this house, especially not for you. So I don't know what your plan is there." Her hands flew up, and I nodded again, happy to address any of her questions.

"I ... I walked away from Tate Legal," I said slowly. It still hadn't sunk into her, but after the call with Lorenzo and Adler, I couldn't continue there. Not in good faith of who I wanted to be for my daughter and the people I loved. Because that pool was finally starting to grow.

"What do you mean you walked away?" Penny asked.

"Meaning I was on the phone this morning, trying to find a workaround for this project. And I said if we couldn't allow you to keep

226

your home and move forward, I would be quitting, effective immediately. And they couldn't find a solution. So ..." I trailed off, doing my best to make the reality of the situation sink in as I described it to her.

"I wasn't the man my daughter wanted me to be—that you wanted me to be—while I was there. And I need to be a man you two are proud of."

Courage sprang through me as I was vulnerable with Penny in front of Grace and Lilly, telling her just how much she truly meant to me. It was worth it for the promise of having her in my life.

My fingers clenched my sides nervously. "I wanted Lilly to be here because we usually come as a package deal. That and Darlene was busy this evening getting ready for her vacation," I said sheepishly, rubbing a hand through my hair. I felt like a schoolboy trying to impress his crush in front of the class. "But if you want me, us, to leave, I'll understand."

Penny watched me, seemingly analyzing my apology like a coded language. I only hoped I came across as genuine as I was truly feeling, but under pressure, I shifted to straighten my back and fix my posture.

To everyone's surprise, my daughter broke the silence between us all after more than ten seconds of empty space. "Please, Ms. Lewis. My dad just quit his job, which is, like, his whole life. He wants to try things over again." We all looked at her for a moment, and she continued, "He might be really sucky sometimes," and I reached a hand out to her.

"Watch it," I said in warning, but I was half-joking, and she understood.

"He only does the dumb stuff for work or to do the best he can. But please," Lilly said, giving her best puppy-dog eyes, "give him a chance."

I hadn't told her to do any of that—I hadn't really told her to do *anything*—but she took the liberty for the chance to perform.

As Lilly spoke, Grace looked at her with admiration, and Penny smiled lightly, holding her hands together just above her stomach. She was twisting them together, perhaps in anxiousness, but I couldn't be sure.

At long last, Penny spoke. "I don't want you to leave. If it's okay with you, Grace," she said, looking back to her sister before returning attention to me. "First of all, there's an awful storm outside, and I don't want you two getting stuck in it. Second," she sighed, looking to Grace again, "I may require your legal advice on what may have been a sabotaged fallen tree that is currently causing a storm to also occur in my bedroom."

"A tree fell on your house?" Lilly yelped, her head whipping around toward my room.

"What?" I asked, peering my head around the hall. "Is it in the back? I couldn't see it from the street; there's a tree in your bedroom?" I asked again, and she nodded. "And why do you think someone chopped it to fall on purpose?"

"I'm pretty sure I saw ax marks, but I can show you the tree and stump." She pulled her phone from her back pocket, scrolling through her photos to show me the most recent one. The darkness made seeing any detail next to impossible, but not completely so.

"Do you mind if I adjust it?" I asked.

"Yeah, do what you have to," she said, nodding.

I took the liberty of opening up the in-app photo editor, nothing too fancy. It was just enough to up the brightness and some of the contrast to see the shadows a little deeper. The colors lightened and clearly showed the divots that could have come from an ax. It also could have come from something whacking it along the side, like from a sharp car edge, but with the layout, she had back there, there was no way someone could get a vehicle going at that angle hard and fast enough. At some point in the recent past, an ax had been taken to that tree, and it looked like it broke through the wood enough to leave it vulnerable to the storm when before, it most likely would have been sturdy enough to take a beating.

She would absolutely have a case.

Lilly watched us with wild curiosity, not having expected all this from when I'd prepped her for what the evening might look like.

I nodded, using more professional tone than I normally would with Penny. I didn't want to overstep after only just having apologized a few minutes earlier. "Yes, I believe that could have legality on your side. Do you have any idea who might have chopped it?"

"None," Penny replied. "Why would someone try to chop down one of the trees in my yard?"

"How long has it had the marks, do you think?" I asked.

Penny shook her head as her cheeks lightly puffed up. "No clue, but it … it has to at least have been since the show back here. I put up signs and would have noticed them. Oh!" Her finger shot in the air. "Birdhouse!"

"Birdhouse?" Grace asked.

With a nod, Penny smiled. "Birdhouse. I put up a birdhouse out on the tree a few days ago. I took a pretty good look at it to find a good branch; I probably would have seen any chop-marks."

"Only a few days ..." I said. "Everyone in Abilene has known about the big storm since last week, at least. What if someone chopped at it to make it look like an accident, so it would fall from the weather?"

"Should have shaved down the side," Grace muttered from the couch. "Keeps 'em from noticing the chops. What?" she said in defense when we all turned to look at her.

"Grace, she's nine," Penny said about Lilly. "Don't say that shit in front of her." She nudged her sister on the side.

"Penny," I said, and her hands flew to her mouth.

Lilly laughed, and Penny just mouthed, "Sorry," but I waved her off.

"Anyway," I said. "You have a case here if you find out who chopped your tree. You can definitely get everything taken care of in terms of the house with insurance. Modern policies usually cover weather damage like this." I hesitated with a hitched breath, realizing I was pulling information I'd stored about the home for the file from work.

If Penny picked up on it, she didn't let me know.

She just nodded, taking in the information. "Yeah, it's got a policy; Grandma made sure I'd be taken care of with it," she added. She and Grace hugged on their sides, and I gave them the moment to get caught in the memory. I owed her that much.

It hit me like a flash in that moment of quiet contemplation. I turned to face Penny, eyes wide and beaming. "Penny, someone could be sabotaging your house to get you out of it. If it was damaged and cost money to repair and fix up again, even after a payout from insurance, it might drive you to want to sell. Anyone offering to buy lately?" I said leadingly, but we all knew the answer.

230

"Your company, did you …" Penny's hands found her mouth, and her eyes widened. "Did you tell someone to chop down a tree to sabotage my house?" she asked, standing from where she'd been perched against the arm of the couch. With the new space to discover the drama of the story, Lilly and Grace both leaned in.

I was galled she would even ask that, but this wasn't the conversation to ask how much of my character she questioned. "No, of course not. But …" I rubbed my cheek with one hand, picturing the first face that came to my mind. A gut reaction told me I was right, and I sighed. This could lead me into trouble if it didn't turn out to be true. "I know someone who might go to lengths most wouldn't to get you out of this house, so we … Tate," I corrected, "can arrange the sale."

"Lorenzo?" Penny asked, and I was put off that she had been thinking the same thing. How much had he intimidated her with his earlier visits? Whether I ever worked with Tate Legal again would be one thing, but I would be having a major conversation with Lorenzo on boundaries and harassment. "God, and he's been in my yard, chopping trees?" she asked, turning her head to face the back hall. "I don't know what I'm going to do, and I'm scared to be in this house now if people are sabotaging it. Thank God you came over when you did," she said to Grace, who nodded.

"I wouldn't exactly thank God, more like the storm."

"Either way," Penny said, then turned her eyes to me. "Please, Owen, help me."

She stared at me, and I knew she didn't forgive me, but she was backed into a corner and knew I was the one most equipped to help her. And it was true, with me at her side, I could find enough loopholes to make sure the place stayed in her hands. It would mean navigating Lorenzo and Adler from the other end and burning our bridges further.

"Penny, I'm going to help you take care of this. And … I'm helping you keep the house," I said. I hadn't exactly thought that through, but it felt right, so I didn't stop myself. "Whatever it takes."

# Chapter 31

Upon accepting Owen's offer to help, Grace and I—but mostly me—offered to have them stay and wait out the storm on the pullout, and Grace could stay in bed with me or take the blowup. Owen turned it down, mentioning how he'd driven in worse, however anxious it made me to have them leave with the storm pounding as hard as it was.

But at nine o'clock the next morning, he showed up again with Lilly, like the sun returning after the rain, and he was carrying donuts and coffee.

"Someone rang for a legal team?" he said with a smile.

Lilly, holding the bag of donuts, grinned. "I brought stuff to make posters!"

"Posters?" I asked, opening the door to let them in, and Lilly took the lead. "Of what?"

"For the fundraiser," Owen said as he walked in past me, following Lilly to the dining table.

"I got to stay home from school because of the storm!" Lilly said with delight.

"There was a flood; none of the busses could get in," Owen said, filling in the details. "Hello, Grace," he said to my sister, sitting on the couch on her phone.

"Owen," Grace replied, still as cold as ever to him. She could be so overprotective. But she opened her arms up to Lilly, who rushed over. "What's up, kid? long time no see!"

"I brought these for us all; give us a little morning comradery over coffee and pastries to get started," Owen said, opening up the bags and setting each coffee down on the table outside the carrier. "Is anyone lactose intolerant or who prefers oat milk?" he asked Grace and me.

"I usually prefer oat, actually," I said with a raised brow. "Grace chugs whipped cream like water, so she'll have whole." I reached for the oat milk. "Did you just get one just in case?"

"Maybe. I like to cover my bases," Owen said, and to my surprise, he winked. He was being bold with where we stood. But I didn't exactly want him to stop.

It was complicated.

"Like any good lawyer," I replied to him, taking a sip. "God, this is delicious, thank you," I said to Owen, opened the bag and reached for a crumble. "You got a great variety. Grace, do you want a maple? There's two."

"Oh, I call at least one," she said, then hopped up from the couch and met us at the table.

Lilly reached in after her, and the bag ended up ravenously emptied within minutes as Owen finally grabbed his own glazed bar.

"So," I began, chewing my donut and getting some cake crumble on my chin. "What exactly are we starting this morning that required such a feast?"

Owen nodded, reaching into a bag on his shoulder and setting a file on the table. "This is the information I have on the file they're building to get you to sell. This," he continued, pulling out his laptop and opening to a screen past the login that had already been referenced. "This is the website and form for filing a police report involving insurance on the tree that fell, and I have the numbers to call for the removal team I've helped others use." He turned to Lilly. "Lil?"

Lilly strode up to the table and set down markers, and unfolded large pieces of cardstock from a bag we'd brought with us. "These are posters we're going to make as a fundraiser to help with the repairs! And my dad said if we can get the community on your side," she said, seemingly reciting Owen's training word for word, "we can get the legal team to back off and let you keep your house!"

Owen nodded with a grin. "I know how Adler and Tate Legal work. If there's too much community hullabaloo, they'll be pushed to find another location or risk losing the entire project and their entire invested customer base in Abilene."

"That sounds like a long shot," Grace said, standing over Owen and looking at the website over his shoulder. "And wouldn't insurance pay for the whole thing?"

"Maybe, if we can prove it was Lorenzo and the Tate team. But they could also put up a fight in defense and keep you from being covered if they can argue it was an accident. In that case, you'll get the necessary repairs covered, but it'll still leave the house low in value, which is good for their team and bad for us," Owen explained.

All this legalese had my mind scrambled, and I shook my head to get it cleared. "And what about the fundraiser? What's that all about?"

"That is a contingency plan that will continue to work in our favor," he said. His continual use of the royal "we" had me teetering between annoyed and supported and cared for. I hadn't decided where I would sit in the end. "You already have a good amount of community approval. If we can spread the word that you're trying to save the place with something like another fundraiser concert, it'll get them involved. And the last thing Tate wants is a media circus before launching a new piece of real estate meant to bring the community together to spend money."

"I wouldn't call a mall a way to 'bring a community together,'" I said, placing my hands on my hips, then deciding for another sip of coffee instead.

"Sure, but that's how Adler sees it."

Grace walked between us, breaking up the planning energy with realistic grounding. "This is all well and good, but I'm going to ask the question here—why should we trust you with this? You've spent months trying to steal the house from her for the other team."

Owen looked at Grace and sighed, and I watched Lilly take his hand in support. "Because I want to help. I feel horrible about what I did, and there's nothing I can do to change the past. But I can do this."

"Grace, back off from the hounding," I said, putting my hands out. "We've got a big problem on our hands, and Owen is the only one who seems to have a plan to fix it. So ..." I said with a smile, taking the last bite of my donut. "Where do we start?"

\*\*\*

Lilly spent most of the day with Grace at the dining table, coming up with intricate and colorful designs for the posters. Most of them had variations of the phrase "Save Ms. Lewis's House" and "Choose Music Not Capitalism." That last one was from Grace, and she had to help Lilly spell the end of it. But they were covered in little stars and smiley faces, all in support of keeping my grandmother's house, and it meant the world to me.

Each poster had the details of the concert we'd scheduled to help promote awareness for the deal trying to go through and help with any needed repairs from the destruction of property. The concert would be in two weeks, which Owen said was just enough time before Tate Legal started moving forward with either a higher offer or a new location. But it would take them a lot to declare the initial plans involving my land as a wash, so they wouldn't go down without a fight.

Owen walked me through the online application for filing for the destruction of property and gave me notes on how to accuse Lorenzo with the information I had and the intimidation and stalking I'd experienced here at the house. He warned me about the potential repercussions of his involvement, but he would be dealing with that fallout, just like he would in the fallout of coming clean to me about everything.

That was what struck me the most; once I knew everything and I could see the place of desperation he was coming from when put in this tough situation, he became human to me again. He was no longer the monster I'd villainized in my head but a single dad who was doing what he could to keep his job and personal life afloat when they conflicted.

Plus, he'd actually quit. From what I'd heard from Lilly and Darlene about how much he threw himself into his company, that was no simple action.

"So it says that once the application is filed, we can call the service, and they'll be here within twenty-four hours to pull out the tree and repair the structural damage to the home. Anything like paint and design and things like that can be covered to an extent monetarily by the insurance company, but that payout comes after you make the charges and can take a while to process," Owen said with a sigh.

"So what you're saying is," I replied, "I'm on my own until it's done."

"No, you're not," Owen told me. "You have plenty of people around you who are making sure to help you in every way we can. And we're about to get a lot more people doing the same thing."

"I know," I said, and the overwhelm began to bubble in my stomach. "I just wish Grandma was still here for this house. I feel like an imposter, trying to care for it when she would take things by the horns without hesitation."

Grace must have heard my plight because I felt hands on my shoulders behind me. "Hey, she would have been proud of you. And hell, let's channel her a bit then. Take this shi—" she started but turned back to Lilly for a moment, who was absorbed in her poster coloring. "Take this *shit*," she whispered the word, "by the horns. Show that legal team they can't kick you out of your home."

"She's right," Owen said with a smile. "You have every ounce of your grandmother's strength inside you. Now it's time to show it."

With my sister on one side and Owen on the other, I did feel a little less alone. I forced a smile with what was left inside me, then pressed the submit button. "There. It's done."

"Great job," Owen said with a grin, and then he reached out to hug me.

I met him in it, pulling off Grace and finding comfort in his embrace. All other things aside, I'd missed being held by him, and having his arms around me felt right again.

We only hugged for a moment, then pulled back. Neither of us met each other's eyes, and I think it was clear we both felt something there. However much my mind fought against it, my heart didn't want it to stop.

Owen stood, brushing off his pants, looking nervous. "I'm going to go outside and take a look at the tree again so we can call the removal service."

"I'll come with you," I said before I could think it through. I turned around to face my sister. "Could you watch Lilly for a little bit?"

"Sure," she said with raised brows. "I'll holler if we need anything." She knew exactly what would happen if we went outside alone after a moment like that, so her not putting up a fight spoke to me as approval.

"I'll be outside if you need me, Lilly," Owen said to his daughter with a wave to the table. She gave a little grunt, focused on her project, and off he walked.

I went into the kitchen first for a glass of water, my mouth feeling desperate for hydration. The flip of jumping from being nearly in love with Owen, hating him deeply, trying to trust him again, and being unable to deny the butterflies that soared within me whenever we touched left me severely dehydrated. I only hoped he didn't notice.

Following him outside after gulping down the water, I made sure to grab my phone, so we could call for the removal. I was never one to deal with making a lot of phone calls well, so I appreciated having him there as an anchor for it, especially with the stress of having to deal with a fallen tree in my house.

When I arrived outside, he was inspecting the stump as his boots squelched in the damp mud from the rain last night. I stood next to him, peering at the stump with the ax marks I'd mentioned earlier, watching him run his fingers along the wood. It was slow and methodical as he moved, and I missed when he would look at and touch me like that.

"Yeah, you've definitely got the evidence here. Can I take pictures to send to you for the file?" he asked, absorbed in his task, even as I ogled him.

"Of course," I said. "Go ahead, whatever you need."

He took out his phone and took pictures from certain angles that seemed specifically revealing for the marks. Then he did the same on the other end of the tree, the one currently resting through my window. With the wind, more glass had fallen from the pane and around the yard, so I was careful to watch my step in my flimsy tennis shoes.

I walked over to the side currently covered in tarps, dripping wet from last night's storm, and sighed, thinking of all the work ahead of the team and me in fixing it back up to its former glory. I was so glad Grace and Owen were here; if I'd been on my own, I would have been so much more of a mess.

I lifted up one edge of the tarp, and water flowed out of the fold and onto the muddy grass below, where it met the cement from the back porch. "God, this is going to be a nightmare."

"But you won't be doing it alone," Owen said, and I felt him stand behind me. It wasn't in a way that felt cornering or frightening, and I had enough room to move away if I wanted the space from him.

Only I didn't.

Instead, I turned around to face him and reached out my hand to gently touch his. He had every chance to move it away or back off and stop himself before acting on an instinct that might be wrong.

Only he didn't.

It was only moments before I got closer and kissed him, needing the support of feeling him on me and around me to get through this horrible situation. And I was right—the minute his arms were around me, holding me and wanting me, everything else drifted away. Nothing felt like it mattered when I had him with me again, and his lips told me everything I needed to hear without a single word uttered.

His mouth opened and deepened our kiss, and soon my tongue slipped against his open mouth, and we stayed there together, hands running along clothed skin, surrounded by mud and broken glass and gravel.

After what seemed like forever, I pulled away, needing the time to breathe again. My head felt flooded with all the positive chemicals released by the kiss, and he must have sensed my tension because he gave me a tentative smile.

"Are you okay?" he asked. "Was that too much?"

I didn't want him to think I was uncomfortable with what we'd done, so I nodded quickly. "No, it … it was perfect." I smiled at him, pecking his lips again once, then twice.

"I'm glad," Owen said with a smile, placing his hands on my hips and pulling me into him. "I don't want you to think I'm going into this without thinking about what I did. I meant what I said. I want to earn your trust back, and I'm willing to work for it."

"You've definitely shown that much," I said, laughing. "Though I might recruit you some more once they pick up the tree. Grace and I are good at patching holes where needed, but we're not much for repairs. Would you know anyone?"

Owen grinned. "I know my way around construction tools; I might be able to give you a hand."

I put my arms around his neck, pulling him back down into me again. I whispered, "Good, I'll need your hands," quietly against his lips and felt the lightest moans go through him and into the kiss. We got lost in the moment again, and it wasn't until we heard a throat clear behind us that we realized how long we'd been gone and quiet.

"Did you two call the tree service?" Grace asked, her judgy brows higher than ever.

"Not yet," I said, pulling my hands from Owen and wiping my mouth a little. Thank goodness I hadn't been wearing lipstick, or it would be smeared all over us both. I looked at Owen, who was sheepishly smiling. "Owen was just about to help me make the call."

"Looks like you got distracted," Grace said, eying us up and down. "Listen, Lilly finished up a few of the signs, so I was going to take her on a walk to hang them around the block and downtown."

"Are you sure? I can go with her," Owen said, wanting to step up.

"No, I think … I think she and I will have a good time. Besides, it might get loud. You know, with the tree removal?" Grace smirked.

"Stop." I chuckled, smacking Grace's arm. "Really, Grace, are you sure?"

Grace nodded. "Yeah, she's a fun kid. More fun than being a third wheel to you two." She walked back around the corner. "I'll get us ready; you guys call the service and see when they're coming by. If they don't while we're out, I'm sure you guys will find another way to spend the time. Play some Parcheesi." I heard her snort as she walked inside.

Lilly's voice in the distance asked, "You have Parcheesi?"

"Nope," Grace replied. "Let's get out of here, kid."

# Chapter 32

As Lilly and Grace left, Penny and I smiled at her signs, all prepped to go, all covered in various decorations and music notes to accompany their message of support for Penny's home. My daughter's drive to help others warmed my heart deeply, and each day I grew prouder of her.

"Bye, honey—" I yelled to Lilly as she and Grace walked down the block with their posters in tow. "Are you sure she'll be okay?" I asked Penny. Lilly was nine, and she could hold her own, but it was still trusting my daughter's safety with someone who didn't trust me with a ten-foot pole. Granted, she had a good reason, but it didn't make me feel better.

"She'll be fine." Penny chuckled. "Grace can be overprotective sometimes as my sister, but she's great with kids, and Lilly adores her." She watched her sister walk Lilly down the block, then turned to me when they were out of view. "So, um … the tree service?"

"Right!" I said, taking my attention off the feeling I had standing next to her and back on task. "Let me get the number pulled up for you from the online application."

I turned my focus to the laptop again, opening it, unlocking it, then writing the number on the application on a piece of notepaper.

"Let's get it done," I said, handing Penny the piece of paper.

She nodded, typing the number into her phone and turning on the speaker before pressing the dial button.

After a few rings, a service operator picked up. "Markson's Tree Removal Service; how can I help you?"

With absolute poise, Penny explained the situation and her case information from the online application, immediately presenting she had a tree in her bedroom on Plumosa Avenue that needed removing. However apathetic she sounded, the woman was helpful enough and connected us to a team lead immediately. On that end, a manager mentioned they had a long list to get to after working through the storm, so it could be another couple of hours before they got a crew out. But Penny gave him her cell phone and mentioned she would be home all day and to just let her know if they needed anything else from her. They would be calling her when they were on the way.

"Thank you so much, Bill; you've been so helpful," she said with a smile, and I nodded in approval.

When she hung up, I squeezed her hands at her side. "So, they'll be here soon, and then you'll be one step closer to having your bedroom back."

"I really would like my bedroom back *now*," she said with a dramatic sigh, walking toward the tree currently occupying her wall space. "I can't believe he'd do something like this."

"I can," I said, giving a sigh of my own. "Lorenzo is a hopeless kiss-up and is willing to do just about anything to impress Tate, and Adler, by extension. I just didn't think he'd go to these kinds of lengths. I was wrong to trust him as my partner, even after these past few years of working together since Joseph took him on."

"It just makes me feel so ... violated," Penny said and crossed her hands over her chest, squeezing herself tightly. She looked like she was

245

holding herself together by her own sheer will and strength. I admired her deeply for how strong she was being in the midst of all this.

I walked up to her, putting my hands on hers and holding her at arms-length. "You're safe; I'll make sure of it. What if I stayed here to help make sure Lorenzo doesn't do anything stupid?"

Penny pouted, her shoulders hunching slightly. "That's a horrible idea, Owen. What about Lilly? And I ... I don't think I'm ready for sleepovers like that again yet."

My smile fell, though I tried my best to hide its shifting. She caught it, though, and she put her palm on my cheek, bringing my attention back to her eyes.

"I mean, we just have to work up to it, you know? Lots of steps before sleepovers, and most of them are lots of fun," she said with a wink. She pulled me into her, and we kissed deeply, this time, without my daughter or her sister walking in on us.

The privacy was indeed tantalizing, and I couldn't stop myself from putting my hands on her waist, squeezing her firmly along her love handles and at the base of her hips. "I missed you. So much," I mumbled into the kiss.

"We weren't even apart that long," she said, laughing into my lips. "But I did too." She turned her head back to the house, then at her phone that sat on the table near us. "The tree people will call before they get here."

"So will Grace and Lilly."

"Want to go inside?" Penny asked, and I nodded with a smile.

We could barely make it to the living room, and with Penny's bedroom off the list of options, the couch was the next best one. As we stumbled back inside, our hands explored each other, skin finding skin wherever possible. It had only been a few days since we'd touched each other, but with the emotional distance, days felt like months. I felt whole again, having her in my arms, unraveling beneath me.

***

As we announced the concert to the neighborhood and started talking about how we were fighting against a legal team to gain possession of the house, community support began to bubble. By Tuesday afternoon, two days after we put out the word, Penny had four students signed up to volunteer to perform and tons of tickets booked through the event page I'd helped her set up. She even had early donations coming in on the new Venmo page, every penny of which came of use when word of the insurance company came around.

"Yes, the tree was removed two days ago, but there's still a giant hole in my wall," Penny explained, then the person on the other line replied, and Penny fumed. "Only five hundred dollars?" she scoffed into the phone at the agent currently walking her through the insurance policy her grandmother had out on the house. "But the repair contractor said the cost would be in the thousand-dollar ballpark, and that's if the window isn't extra. How am I supposed to afford this repair?"

I rubbed her shoulders behind her, and Grace pulled up the policy pages again, gawking at the cockamamie scheme Ruthanne had gotten into upon signing for the house and insurance package. It barely covered any damages at all, but she got reimbursed for any "personal items" she could prove were damaged and $500 a year for home repairs that didn't roll over for any weather-related problems. They had preyed on a single mother who didn't know how to read the fine print.

"No, I think this is a ridiculous policy, and it's a wonder my grandmother didn't report you!" Silence for a moment, then, "I don't know, to the Better Business Bureau or something!" Another bout of silence, and then Penny laughed sardonically. "Yeah, I hope you have a good day too, *Suzette,*" she said, nearly spitting out the woman's name on the other line. Then she brought the phone down from her ear and slammed her finger on the "End" button. "Can you believe that?"

"Yes," I said grimly. "Insurance companies prey on vulnerable buyers all the time. What's most important is that's exactly why you're doing this fundraiser. To help fix the house." I walked to the front of the couch to stand between her legs and hold her face in my palms. "It's going to be okay, Penny. We're going to fix this."

"All of us are here with you," Grace said, leaning over from the paperwork.

If Lilly hadn't been at school, she would have been leaning her head on Penny's in support next to her.

With tears building in her eyes, Penny sighed deeply and nodded, hanging her head a little. "I'm so glad you guys are here. Both of you."

"We're happy to help," I said, kissing her head.

Grace pulled out her phone to look at her calendar, then said, "I do have to skip out to a shoot in Junction City, and the shop says my car should be good to go. But I'll be back in a few days, I think." She leaned in and nudged her sister on the shoulder. "I'm never far away."

The fundraiser slunk nearer and nearer, and all of us were on hyperdrive to advertise and get the word out about the concert so Penny could focus on teaching the six kids that had signed up, including Lilly. They only had four rehearsals to put together a song, and each had a solo to work on, so Penny needed all the focus she could muster. She was our quarterback, and all of us were hard at work clearing the field for her touchdown.

The day of the big event came with the house decorated in twinkle lights once again and crepe paper and balloons. Grace's shoot earlier that week had a ton of extra party supplies, so she took the liberty of "disposing of it" for her crew, which meant shoving it all into her car and carting it back to Abilene. Then she did the hard work of putting down the extra tarps I'd picked up to seal the base for the chairs from the grass that still retained water from the morning dew. One day, I would help Penny invest in a collapsible and removable stage for the yard.

Lilly and I had spent the day putting up those decorations until it was time for Lilly's dress rehearsal when I took over. As I hung lights and banners around the house and yard, I smiled at the sound of my daughter playing. She was doing a light version of "Your Song" by Elton John, one of my old favorites. Some of her notes came out a little clunky because she wasn't used to the flourishes and difficult transitions. But for her skill level, she did amazingly. I couldn't stop myself from clapping when she finished.

Lilly beamed from behind the piano. I could tell she was a little embarrassed, but she was still smiling from ear to ear in pride.

"Shh," Penny whispered behind her, and some other students giggled. Lilly didn't seem to take it hard, going back to her booklet to study some of her missed notes.

The rest of the practice went swimmingly, aside from one or two students needing to work on their transitions between notes.

Families and people wanting to support Penny and the house would be here in just a few minutes, and we had a guarantee of more people than the last concert they'd held back here. From the space cleared out by the tree (save two seats along the edge of the bare stump), we could comfortably seat another two rows with suitable views. Grace was already in the process of unfolding chairs and setting them out on the tarps, so once I was done with the last roll of crepe paper, I went out to help her.

"Looks like you came around to save the day, huh?" Grace said to me quietly as we unstacked chairs from against the wall where we'd pulled them from storage.

"I wouldn't say that."

"I would. Just makes me wonder what your motives are here," she said, plopping a chair down.

I picked up four chairs at once to bring to my row, and I wasn't sure if I was doing it to show off or get the job done faster. Either way, I grunted as I set them down, frustratingly out of shape.

"Grace," I started, taking one chair down. "What kind of motives *could* I have at this point? I quit my job, I've thrown myself into helping you and Penny organize this to save the house. I don't mean to be rude," I said, then set up the next two, "I want you to approve because you mean the world to Penny. But she's the only one I feel willing to grovel to. And I think we're doing okay. So can you ease up a bit?" I asked, setting the last chair down in a row and putting my hands on my hips.

Seemingly stunned by my candor, Grace stuck out her jaw a little and nodded. "Okay, fair, fair. She's just my sister. She's everything to me, and I remember what you put her through; I sat with her that night. So you had better do it right this time." Her threat was strong, but it came from a place of love, and it was something I could respect. If anyone did what I'd done to Penny to Lilly, I would snap and protect her in the same way. Family was family.

"I understand. And I promise to do everything in my power to keep proving my intentions are good to Penny," I said with a nod.

"Good." Grace smiled, clapping me with one hand like old frat brothers. But after a second, her eyes drifted to the front gate of the house. "Some people are early."

I turned and saw men in suits walking along the pavement toward the front walkway, and they hadn't spotted me yet. My stomach lurched, and I had the sudden urge to run and hide, though I knew I couldn't do that.

"Do you know them?" she asked, most likely curious over my obvious negative reaction.

I sighed and nodded, straightening up and pulling myself together. "Yes, unfortunately. Those are my prior employers."

I saw Adler walking next to a face that shocked me, Joseph Tate. He was rarely in town anymore, and I knew he'd been around due to the hullabaloo with Lorenzo being accused of damaging Penny's house. The media hadn't picked up on it yet, but I'd given him the heads up when Penny filed for the claim. He hadn't taken it well, and I was sure the appearance today would only further confirm that.

"I better go meet them out front before this causes a problem," I said, skirting through the back door and into the house, then meeting Penny at the front door. She'd heard the doorbell go off, and I beat her to the punch. "I'll get it," I said, and I gave her an eye that told her something was amiss.

"Who is it?" she whispered, looking up at me with worry.

"It's Adler and my old boss. I don't know what it's about, but I'll take care of it," I said. I didn't want to tell her out of fear of pulling her focus, but I was done with the lying and withholding. I kissed her cheek and waved her back to the kids. After hearing the truth from me, she was so distracted and focused on the performance that she listened, turning back to the pianos behind her. "Okay, everybody, let's all start

251

packing our things up and taking them outside!" she said, and the children started their breakdown.

I unlocked the door, pulled it open, and greeted Adler and Tate with a grin. I promised myself I would be honest and fair with the conversation but not bounce around the bush.

"Hello, gentlemen. Are you here for the performance? You're a bit early," I said, looking down at my watch. Even I was surprised at how passive-aggressive I could be when the opportunity called for it.

"Owen, we were hoping to find you here," Joseph said. "It's been a messy couple of days, and we've been wanting to sit down for a chat."

"And you couldn't send a text or call?" I asked, stepping outside and closing the door behind me.

"In-person is better for now, especially with where things are with Lorenzo. We don't need more proof of employee misconduct coming through," he said, Adler smirking at his side.

I scoffed. "I hardly committed employee misconduct," I said and crossed my arms over my chest, standing my ground.

"I would say it was a conflict of interest at the bare minimum," Adler said, and then he waved his hand at me. "None of this protective bear business; we're not here making threats."

Joseph nodded. "On the contrary. Owen, we want to offer you a new package."

"A new package?" I asked. "Joseph, I told you on the phone, I'm afraid if we can't—"

"Owen, we're willing to give you a $50,000 bonus if you can get this residential for us," Joseph said, all at once.

That was bigger than any bonus I'd ever seen at Tate Legal. My last ranged around twenty thousand, so I couldn't imagine the kind of pressure they must be getting to be putting that much investor money out on the line. Either way, I would have said Joseph was bluffing if he hadn't brought along Mr. Adler with him.

He took a turn addressing me, and between the two of them, I couldn't tell if I was being cornered or appeased. "I think it would be amiss to walk away from this generous offer, Owen."

"Mr. Adler, do you think I can have a moment with Joseph?" I asked.

Joseph looked surprised and Adler offended, but he stood aside and walked over to the entryway, looking at one of the programs Penny had set out for the concert. It featured information on the battle to repair and keep the house, and I know the description she put in wasn't kind to Adler and the team running the mall build. As I chatted with Joseph, I watched Adler's brow go up as he hit the right page.

"Why'd you ask Adler to step away?" Joseph asked.

I nodded at him. "Same reason you lost your stiffened stance. He's still your client, and I want him to respect you as a partner. The things I have to say are personal, and I don't want them to misconstrue his view of you."

"Thank you for that, then," he said. "How are you feeling about this deal, really, Owen? Between you and me?"

"Between you and me," I started, "I'm offended you would come to this event and ask. Mr. Tate," I said, using his last name to create some needed distance between us. "I care about Penny … Ms. Lewis. I care about this home. It was wrong of me to try and take it from her because I can't ethically stand behind my work anymore. For the sake of my daughter and Penny, I want to be a better man than that. And frankly," I said with a dark tone, "I can't faithfully work for a company that would do something like sabotaging a residential home to manipulate and coerce them into selling."

Joseph took everything I said with an empty-faced nod or two, ever the poker-faced lawyer. When I got to the accusation toward the end, his nod went deeper and slower, understanding the gravity of what I was saying.

Penny had made her report, and a few papers had picked up the story from her as well as run the advertisement for today's concert, so Joseph didn't want to make a scene in public. That said, he picked a public place for our conversation today. To avoid *me* making a scene. It was safer for both of us to handle this civilly and underhandedly, just like this business had always been run.

"Investigations are still being filed for Lorenzo," Joseph said, matter-of-factly.

"What is he on, paid sabbatical?" I scoffed. "You and I both know he won't get more than a slap on the wrist unless Penny decides to press charges, which you know she won't be able to afford with the repairs on the house. I'm willing to represent her to do so, but I don't want to do that to you. That said," I clenched my jaw firmly, "I will do it."

He didn't linger on my comment, instead moving forward with his eyes wandering around the entrance to the backyard that I'd been decorating all day with Grace.

"It's a nice little setup here. Too bad about the damage," he said, shoving his hands into his pockets. He was trying to appear casual, but it was a ploy we both understood. "That's a lot of work to do and pay for in a place like this."

"It's worth it," I said, and my words were biting. "You'd be surprised at how much the community is willing to give to help a member in need. That's what a community is supposed to do. Not bail each other out rather than hold them accountable for their actions."

"And what about you?" Joseph asked, making me turn.

"What about me?"

"What about your actions? Is Penny holding you accountable for what you've done and lying to her about it?"

For a man I'd once viewed as a secondary father to me, I was appalled with how far he was willing to go for this. His eyes never left mine, and we stared at each other in silence for a moment before I finally spoke up, back straight and hands in the lightest of fists at my side.

"I think you need to leave, Joseph," I said, cold.

Joseph chuckled, looking down at the ground, then back at me. "Owen, do you really think that's necessary?"

"Yes, I do."

He seemed to take that with dignity and nodded one last time. Then he reached in his coat pocket to grab his wallet and pull out a twenty-dollar bill. He handed me the bill and smiled, saying, "Best of luck on the repairs."

"I'll add this to the pile," I said, taking the money and gripping it tightly in my fist at my side. The amount was honestly insulting, if only because I knew he carried at least a hundred on his person at all times.

A few familiar faces strode up, and I quickly turned and greeted them with a smile, doing my best to be the supportive crew Penny needed today. "Welcome on in, you all; we're happy to have you! Seats right in the back, out through the living room to the yard," I directed, pointing them out.

As I did, I felt a bump on my hip, and Lilly appeared at my side with a wide smile that reached her eyes.

"What are you doing here; you're supposed to be getting ready!" I said, rubbing her head.

"I know. I just wanted to tell you that I saw you stand up to those guys from work, and you did really good," she said. "It looked hard."

My heart flooded with affection for my daughter, and I hugged her tight to my side. "It was, but it needed to happen. Thank you, honey. Now," I said, bumping her hip as she did me. "Get out there and get ready to play your heart out!"

I shooed her into the yard and went back out to the front gate, saying hello to patrons as I passed by. As I looked out, I saw Joseph at the sidewalk entrance, joined by Adler. I wondered if they'd seen me with Lilly, and I didn't go up to say goodbye or shake hands. Instead, I simply gave them one short wave and not a second more of my time and energy.

Pulling my attention from the two men walking away, Penny found me almost immediately, as if she'd sensed something from across the property in the backyard preparing the kids.

"Are you okay?" she asked. "Do you know them?"

I nodded and simply said, "Some old friends from work. They couldn't stay, unfortunately, but they made a donation." I offered up the now-crumpled twenty-dollar bill in my palm, and Penny raised one brow, taking it for the donation pot, and then she fluttered along, too distracted by the rest of the day's events to worry about things not immediately calling to her attention.

People continued to flood in through the house; many we recognized but quite a few we didn't. We ended up running out of seating, and a few concertgoers felt comfortable standing in the back.

Another face caught me in the crowd, one that had been missing from our lives for the past two weeks. Darlene's smiling face, notably more tan, beamed as she walked through the main doorway—we'd propped it open for the afternoon for the concert—and grabbed a program from the bowl. The minute she spotted me, her smile grew wide, and she did her elderly little shuffle up to wrap me in a tight hug. At her size, it was almost comical, but I'd missed her so much that I didn't care.

"What are you doing back? I thought you would be out of town until the end of the month?" I asked, pulling back from the hug. She had left the morning of the big storm; it was a wonder she'd skipped out before the weather took a toll for the worst.

"I was, but I got word about the concert from Lilly when she called me last week, and I couldn't miss it for the world," she said, and she meant it with every fiber of her being.

"You flew back early from Europe for a backyard fundraiser concert?" I chuckled.

"My daughter is still there and enjoying the time with her husband instead; he met us out there around Tuesday, and I've been a third wheel ever since. Needed the excuse to come home," she said with a grin, and I knew she was leading me with that. "Now, what's this I hear about the house being sold and tree damage?" she asked wide-eyed.

Before we could say another word to each other, Penny yelled out from the yard, "Thank you, everyone, we're about to begin!"

# Chapter 33

PENNY

My mind went from bogglingly frantic to focused as I brought myself to the stage and my attention to the kids surrounding me. Surrounded by pianos, from my view out to the audience, it was a charming echo of the concert from just a few months back. Only this time, there was more at stake than just an extra piano or lessons for a scholarship student. I'd also got a sturdier stage setup thanks to Grace and some of her latest shoot's generous platform rentals and an extra few rows of seats to go with the standing room at the back.

"Ladies and gentlemen, I can't thank you enough for joining us here today. And it's incredible to see just how many of you are here and how far some of you have come just to see our show." I smiled brightly, waving my hands toward the students. "This support you've shown means the world to my students and me, and I'm sure they can't wait for you to hear what they can do!"

I swallowed hard, knowing I hadn't scripted the rest, but I pressed on in my passion. "This home you're all in, that once belonged to my grandmother and now serves as both my home and music school, is being threatened. After the damage done to my property in an effort to get me to sell to a real estate company that wants to demolish my family home, a tree knocked through my wall and window during the big storm a few weeks ago." I waved my hand to the side of the house still covered with tarps and temporary boarded walls left behind after the tree removal.

258

"I create music from this home. This home grounded me when I had nowhere to go growing up, and it served as a regrouping station after my grandmother, Ruthanne Desmond, passed away last year. That can't just be sold away. So please, continue to make donations, as those are what make the repairs on this home possible to keep up the value and avoid selling."

I felt tears well in my eyes against my will, and I watched Owen give me a little shaken fist of support from the front row with a grin. He was so supportive and excited for me that I couldn't help letting that excitement inspire me.

"Now, enough of all the droopy backstory—let's get this show on the road!"

***

The crowd filling the little backyard and the squished space between the back door and the house erupted in applause as Lilly finished her solo instrumental Elton John cover. She stood from her piano bench to the front of the piano, then took a tiny curtsy. She'd done an incredible job on her piano performance, even with the few keys pressed in addition to their proper chords and placements. She had sold it as part of the performance, embodying Sir Elton by pointing at the audience and jamming along with one hand, even as notes were wrongly hit.

The audience had clearly eaten it up, and she strode off the stage toward her seat along the side with pride.

Two more students went with solos fitting their talent level—Caroline did a very traditional piece by Chopin, targeting every note and move perfectly, while a new student I'd brought on named Lindsay did a slightly dolled-up version of chopsticks that cycled four times. For her first performance ever, the girl did lovely.

At the group number, all the students got up on stage and took their positions at the pianos, and we revealed the final song—an instrumental version of "Don't Stop Me Now" by Freddie Mercury, with all of the students singing along. Older pianists, like Seamus and Caroline, helped hold the melody and accompaniment while younger students sang the chorus. Lilly did both, playing the parts she could and singing the majority of the way through with the other kids.

The audience waved and clapped with each chorus, and by the end, everyone was standing, cheering on the players. The song ended with applause that left the students grinning from ear to ear.

The crowd finally settled down again, and I took the stage one more time. "Thank you all so much for being with us today. It warms my heart to know so many people are willing to support me and all the incredible students I have up here on stage with me today. It's been an honor teaching you, and for most of you, I'll see you at your next lesson!" I said, then waved my hand in the air. "Our donation bin is sitting at the table in the back; feel free to drop anything you're comfortable with before you leave!"

***

Once the crowd fully dispersed through the front of the house, I helped guide them all along to the donation bin, collecting anything anyone was willing to give. We also had a Venmo QR-code printed on the box, and I'd seen a few people get out their phones to scan it. I hadn't checked my phone for any transfers, but I kept my fingers crossed.

Each audience member was abuzz with pride for their students, and pretty much everyone donated at least something. I'd chatted with Owen beforehand about the closeup plan, so he helped clear everyone out so I could run the numbers while he, Lilly, and Grace all started cleanup. I would be joining them soon, but I was too anxious to see how much we had brought in to make a dent in the repairs.

The bills took the longest to go through because so many paid in smaller bills like ones and fives. The counting seemed endless, going single after single, but I got through it all after about an hour, including the funds sent over via Venmo.

By the time I had gotten it all, a sigh found its way to my chest. It added up to about four hundred and fifty dollars. Granted, that would help get us much closer to our goal for repair, but it was still relatively minimal.

That said, the support we got for the concert, including photos taken that I would be posting on social media, made it all worthwhile. The real point of the event was to get the community aware of the need to save the house, and today, they'd done that and more.

Still feeling anxious about needing to pay the bills, however, my head sank into my hands at the table, and I closed my eyes to try and shut it all out.

"Penny?" Lilly asked, and I perked my head up to look at her.

"Hey, Lil," I said. She'd taken to start calling me by my first name instead of Ms. Lewis, and I wasn't sure if that had started with how close we'd grown in class—I was usually strict about students and parents calling me Ms. Lewis for professionalism's sake—or from the relationship I'd built with her and her father. "What can I do for you, kiddo?" I asked her.

"I …" Lilly seemed quiet and stammered as she began, "I messed up the last chorus on my song, where it vamps up. Would you help me work on it again? I want to practice it right at home."

I couldn't tell if Lilly realized I was not doing well with coming to terms with the money or if she truly just wanted the help now because we'd finished the concert, and it was still fresh in her mind.

"Sure, Lilly," I said, and I stood and walked to her piano as Owen looked on and continued breaking down with Grace. "I'll help you guys in a second, okay?" I cleared with them, and they both nodded, waving me on to time with Lilly.

Once we were sitting at the piano, Lilly's fingers set on the keys, positioning themselves properly to start the song.

I smiled. "Good, you've got great muscle memory. Okay, why don't you jump to the part you struggled with, and we can work through it?" I asked, taking a seat next to her.

For the next half hour, I did more or less of a private lesson with Lilly to the sound of wood being undrilled and tarps being rolled and folded. Lilly followed along, dancing along the keys and showing just how much she'd improved in her focus and dexterity alone in the past few months of working with her. And now, with her movement in the final chorus, nailing each one she had missed, she glowed.

The sounds of deconstruction around us quietened, and Grace and Owen wandered over to listen to Lilly play. Owen found my side, and his arm almost wrapped around me instinctually from the way it fell back down again. While still listening to Lilly's song, I quickly brought my hand to pull his arm back, and he squeezed my shoulder firmly when he did. I smiled.

She breathed deeply on the last chord progression, keeping her formal back position up. Then she turned her head to look at us all with a grin so wide that each cheek puffed up with delight.

We all applauded her deeply, I hugged her from the side, and she wrapped her arms around my waist and hugged me back. Owen pulled the two of us in from behind, followed by Grace, creating a tight wrap of the four of us that made Lilly and me both pant for lack of air as we all laughed.

Grace squeezed firmly around the inner three of us, and Lilly squealed.

"I! Can't! Get air! Dying!" she panted out with each dramatic breath, and we all loosened up as the giggles and smiles continued.

"Kid, you're amazing, you know that?" Grace said.

"Yeah, duh. Ms. Lewis is the best teacher! Do you know how much easier it would have been to learn piano before with her as a teacher?" she asked, grinning at me. "Thank you. Ms. Lewis."

"You can call me Penny if you want, Lilly," I said.

Lilly stuck out her tongue, making us chuckle. "Ew, no way. It's so weird calling adults by their real names. Maybe you can have a nickname sometime!" she said.

While one or two came to mind immediately, Owen squeezed my shoulder again. "We can figure it out," he said with a laugh.

"Yeah," I said with a smile, taking a deep breath as I grounded myself with the chosen family around me. "We can figure it out."

# Chapter 34

OWEN

After helping Penny and Grace clean up the rest of the house and yard from the performance, I brought Lilly home, and we made cups of hot cocoa on the stove. Lilly pulled up Pirates of the Caribbean: Dead Man's Chest—the second and, she would argue, the best one—and I made some popcorn for us both to share in a giant bowl with homemade garlic butter.

In the aftermath of quitting my position at Tate Legal, while one part of my life had fallen into disarray, two others had been highlighted, and that outweighed the bad. After losing Fiona, I'd had the foresight to ensure putting aside as much of my salary as we could manage to have a good chunk saved up for an emergency, so we had the budget to sit on our laurels for a while. It came with more days like these, spending the priceless hours of Lilly's youth with her and enjoying that time while I could. And I didn't want to miss another moment. When she played the piano earlier with Penny and Grace, it struck me just how much I missed the sound of Fiona playing music, and hearing her again through Lilly, my heart felt her again, in a way that was different yet familiar.

I pulled Lilly into my lap, cuddling her to my chest like a sack of potatoes the way I had when she was smaller. She reached down to the floor, leaning tentatively over my leg with an audible groan, and grabbed a fluffy blue blanket in one hand. In the other, she held Lucia, her stuffed pig.

Right as we got comfortable on the couch, the bowl in Lilly's lap, the doorbell rang.

Looking at the clock, I wondered who it would be at this hour, but I leaned to Lilly and said, "I'll be right back," and she sat up so I could rise to go and check on it.

My eye peered through the peephole. Outside, Darlene stood in her coat, and a scarf wrapped tightly around her neck and a hat with poms on her head.

"Darlene?" I asked, opening the door and standing aside so she could come in. She did, huffing all the way in the cold. "What are you doing; it's pretty cold out!

"Oh, I'm out for my night walk," she said, pulling the scarf through and letting it rest on the collar of her coat as she opened the buttons. "I'm sorry to burst in; I hope I'm not interrupting." She looked past me at Lilly, who smiled and waved broadly.

"We're watching Pirates of the Caribbean!" she yelled from the couch, and Darlene smiled at the reply. Lilly was probably too comfortable under her cushy blanket to want to move.

I turned back to Darlene. "Is everything okay?"

"Yes. No, and yes," she admitted, then shook her head. "Let me start over. I made a connection this evening to something, and I wanted to talk to you about it before I brought it up to Penny."

"Oh?" I walked with her into the kitchen to discuss privately, and I saw Lilly's head peer around the corner as we went, but she didn't follow. "What's the matter?" I asked Darlene.

She looked up at me and took a breath, then began, "The damage to Penny's house. It was a tree falling, right? She says she thinks someone chopped at it to get it to fall so she would sell."

"Yes," I said with a nod. "Why do you ask?"

"Because I saw something."

"What did you see, Darlene?" I asked.

She swallowed hard, and even without the context, I could sense the gravity of the situation. "I saw someone in her yard the night before the storm. I thought it was you, but I also saw a green car I didn't recognize down the block while walking. I think it could have been that Lorenzo from your work."

Of course, it hadn't been me outside; that had been the night of my date with Penny, and we were inside asleep by then. But someone else could have matched my description late at night.

Darlene was reporting things I'd already considered, as Lorenzo was under investigation. But what *did* matter was Darlene as an eyewitness, having spotted his car in the driveway and someone in Penny's yard near the tree the night before the storm that blew it in through the window. All it would take was a few well-timed chops to weaken the trunk and make it much more likely to fall with the wind the next night.

But he'd been spotted.

"I didn't want to go to Penny with this information until I was sure it was right. But he had a similar hair color to you, dark, and he was wearing a dark long-sleeved shirt and dark jeans," Darlene said.

It wasn't much, but it was enough detail to build a solid case against Lorenzo.

And so I asked, "Would you be willing to testify if we sued them?"

Darlene scoffed. "Of course, I would! Do you know how many of those legal shows I watch, and you think I'd miss a chance to be on the stand with how quiet my life is?" she said, and we both laughed heartily. "I like that Penny; she's a great woman. She's good for all of us, you and Lilly included. I want to do what I can to help. And if that means going into a court, that's what it means!"

"Who's going to court?" Lilly yelled from the other room.

"No one, Lil; I'll be there in a second!" I yelled back.

Darlene looked down at the floor before meeting me again. "Did you talk to Penny about the deal?"

I nodded.

"Good. Now you can start winning her back. Because you don't want to lose her, I'll tell you that right now," she said, giving me the "I'm-wiser-than-you" pursed-lip she was an expert at.

I sighed and nodded, knowing how true her words were in my core. Then she walked back out toward the door. "I'll see you later, honey; great job today!" she yelled to Lilly.

Lilly, to my surprise, came running up to hug Darlene and met her in the doorway, smiling wide as her socked toes twirled on the hardwood. "Thank you for coming today, Darlene; I'm so happy you were there."

Darlene seemed a bit surprised at Lilly's fervor, but she hugged her back close. "Me too. You get some rest. Good night, and good night, Owen!" she said, walking back outside to the sidewalk with a wave.

I met her with a wave of my own, then locked the door and saw Lilly had readjusted on the couch with Lucia and her blanket.

"Ready?"

I went to the kitchen to grab the salt, and then I smiled.

"Yeah, we're ready, kid."

268

Then I went back out to the couch and scootched her over with my hip to her shoulder, and she laughed as she adjusted.

\*\*\*

The next morning, I took Lilly to school and then came back home and made myself an omelet with the leftovers from her lunch fixings to enjoy with a cup of coffee. After I'd taken my time, I called Joseph Tate.

His phone rang five times before he picked up, which was abnormal for a call in the mid-morning. When he did pick up the call, he displayed the same distrust and disregard he'd shown me yesterday at the fundraiser.

"Hello, Owen, I'm glad you called," Joseph said. "Did you rethink our conversation yesterday?"

I mentally scoffed but stayed audibly stable. I didn't want him to know my emotional reaction to anything he said. "No, I'm firm on that. I called because I wanted to let you know that we've got someone as an eyewitness to Lorenzo chopping the tree in Penny's yard the night before the storm. We're prepared to move forward with a lawsuit against Tate Legal.

I got everything out in one breath, partially because I was afraid I would leave something important out. As someone who worked for him, I knew how he worked, and I knew his responses to situational emergencies and work fires like this. So I knew what his answer would be—he would do what was necessary to keep it out of court. And now, I was using that information to our advantage.

Joseph sighed on the other line, then broke the silence. "I'm really disappointed with how this turned out, Owen."

"I am too, Joseph. I know Lorenzo didn't act alone. He wouldn't have gone as far to the destruction of property without being pushed by you, would he?" I asked, and the momentary quiet told me everything I needed to know.

"You've been like a second father to me for a long time," I said.

270

"And as such, you're willing to go to this length to throw us to the sharks? Outside of the costs of a lawsuit like that, we're already cutting into costs for the relocation from Plumosa. You've proven that to be a wash, haven't you?" Joseph asked.

I chuckled. "We're not looking to wipe you, however much you might deserve it with that destruction of property act. Penny just wants to repair and keep the house." I knew I hadn't had the conversation with Penny about how much she would have wanted to get from suing Tate Legal, but I'd meant what I said—he was like a father to me. And at some length, I did give him slack for the poor business decisions he made. But now, I had other people holding me accountable. So I had to hold him accountable too.

"That's all she wants?" Joseph asks. "For a lawsuit case like this, you could have gone for much more."

"Penny and that house are worth more than that," I said, and Joseph was quiet for another beat.

He cleared his throat, then said, "Owen, you're a good lawyer. A good man, and I respect you for wanting to be a better one for your family."

"Thank you, sir," I said, and I meant it.

"I do want to follow up with you on the details, but I think we'd be willing to settle out of court. We can look at repair fees to cover once the investigation is concluded, following the formal submission of written testimony to Tate Legal on the misconduct of Lorenzo Jamison." Joseph sighed again, giving out a small groan. "We'll be letting him go then. He was willing to take the fall."

"And Tate Legal goes on?" I asked, genuinely curious about where Joseph stood.

"We always do.

271

\*\*\*

After getting off my call with Joseph, I knew it was time to tell Penny where everything stood. I knew she had a lesson today at eleven, so I waited until after lunch to stop by her place. The flowers outside had been drowned during the storm, but it had been a few weeks since, and they now bloomed and sprouted in greater numbers alongside the grass. It was a symbol of hope, and I took it as a good sign when I knocked on her door.

She must have heard or seen me before opening the door because when she did, she enthusiastically greeted me with a hug and arms wrapped around my neck. I breathed her in, pulling her close to my chest. No matter what happened, her support—with Lilly's—was what got me through. I was so happy she'd decided to give me another chance, and in the past two weeks, I'd done the work to show her I meant business.

"Hey, you," she said, pulling back to meet my lips in a kiss. "What are you doing here?"

"I had some news," I said, and I pushed some of her hair behind her ear with my fingertip, holding the other side of her face with my free palm. "I wanted to deliver it in person. That, and I have an astonishing amount of free time now, and I missed you …" I said with a shrug.

To my surprise, Penny stepped back from the doorway and yanked me in by my collar, tugging me back to her lips. She kissed me deeply, and it was more energy than I was expecting at this hour.

"I haven't even told you the good news yet, and you can't keep your hands off me," I said with a laugh. My own hands found her waist, and I squeezed any skin I could get. "I'm not complaining, don't get me wrong."

"Now the news is good?" she asked with a smile. "Then spill the beans!"

I laughed, then leaned forward and kissed her forehead. "I know I didn't talk about it with you first, which I will apologize for, but I talked to Joseph over at Tate Legal, because we have an eyewitness account of Lorenzo sabotaging the tree in your yard. And it was enough to sue. So I brought the table to him."

"You told him we're suing?" she said, somewhat surprised. "Are you sure we should?"

"No, we won't need to," I said with a smile. "I told him the stakes and that you want the house repaired and protected. He's willing to settle to those terms out of court."

Her surprise turned to shock, and I swore I saw her jaw drop to the floor. "He's willing to settle? You mean I get to keep the house?"

I gave two long and slow nods then kissed her on the head again with glee. "The house is yours. They're readjusting, and they're going to help pay for repairs."

Penny was silent for a moment, letting the information sink in. But when it did, it was like a bomb went off inside her and she grinned wide, jumping up and down a few times before kissing me again. I laughed into the kiss, pecking her again and again as her lips kept finding my skin and traveled down my cheek and neck in celebration.

I met her excitement with fingers running up her back and arms, causing her to shiver in my arms when I touched the right spots. My hands slipped under the flannel she had on to feel the sensitive skin at the base of her spine, right along the curve of her bottom. My fingers rested there, and she smiled into a kiss when I squeezed it teasingly.

"Let's lock the door," she said, and I nodded with a chuckle. She stepped back and twisted the lock, then brought her primal attention back to me. Lips found skin, and soon, clothing found the floor as we stumbled through the house together, barely able to keep our hands off each other as our anticipation grew.

"Do you have any lessons for a bit?" I asked between breaths, panting lightly as she unbuttoned my shirt one by one.

"No, I'm free. And Grace is out on a shoot for a few days before she drops back in again. Close the window," she said with a grin, and I obliged. Without the bedroom—she'd been sleeping on the couch until the repairs were done, and Grace's stuff was still mostly in hers—we would have to get a bit creative. But once again, there wasn't a soul complaining.

Once all the blinds were closed, she had my button-up off, and my jeans had found the ground moments later. She swirled around me in her panties and bra, and it was enough to make me salivate as I worked to get my hands all over her. In the excitement of it all, she pushed me down on the couch and sat on top of me, straddling my waist and squeezing her thighs firmly around me. It made my boxer briefs feel like a prison beneath her, and she could tell by the look of her grin. Her lips found me again, and she pulled away for a moment, letting her palms rest on each side of my cheeks, making me look at her.

"I love you, Owen," she said, as clear as day. And it sounded like a melody I had longed to hear.

I grinned widely, squeezing her hips in my palms. "I love you too, Penny. I love you," I said again, and I said it over and over again as I kissed along her jawbone and down her chest until my hands yanked down the strap of her bra and freed her breasts from beneath the fabric.

Having been teased with all the heavy petting of the last few minutes, her nipples were already pretty firm, and they only stiffened further when my tongue found them, sucking lightly on each before letting my teeth gently graze along the skin.

"God," she whimpered in my arms, and I couldn't resist how the sound alone fueled me, the melody humming in my ear with each moan she made.

She scooted up on my lap so I could pull down my briefs, and she didn't waste a moment before taking me in her mouth and folding herself down to lick and suck at me. My head pushed back on the couch cushion, and my waist instinctually pushed up toward her, needing and wanting her more, more.

With one swift move, she lifted herself off for a second to yank down her panties, and they dropped to the floor as she shook her hips to get them down. Penny straddled me again, this time sitting down on me fully and taking me inside her.

I kissed her as she did, and we moaned into each other, panting with each thrust I made. She dripped onto me, wet from the amount of teasing and kissing we'd already done since I'd arrived.

"I love you, Penny," I repeated as she bounced herself up and down on my cock, squeezing tight around me and letting me stroke into her. It felt like a heaven I never knew existed, even with all the other times we'd gotten frisky. Now it felt like needing, wanting, more than anything I had ever desired in my life. At this moment, all I wanted and needed was her.

She felt me stiffen further as I grew closer and closer to the edge, and she moaned at the sensation of my twitching. Because I needed her to feel the satisfaction I had, I grinned against her lips, and my thumb found her clit. As I continued pumping in and out of her, slowly, then quickly, then slowly again, the bed of my thumb rolled over her swollen clit, and she whimpered with each touch.

After going slow for a moment, I sped up, and she met me with it, bouncing on me hard as we made love, whispering sweet nothings of affection into each other's ears.

"Owen, I, ahh—" she moaned, and I nodded, moving my thumb faster.

"Do it for me, love. Cum all over me, let me feel all of you," I said, and I kissed along her neck, continuing to rub her clit as I thrust hard into her, so close to my own precipice.

Once she was squeezing tight around me, coming undone, I relished in the sound of her peak, her moans becoming a yell at the last minute as she orgasmed, and I followed only moments after. Her sensitive entrance made my orgasm that much deeper, and I pushed my hips into her as it rolled through me, forcing my eyes into the back of my skull with pleasure as I held her around the waist, hugging her to me.

Our sweat-stained bodies dripped on each other, and the smiles we shared told me the feeling was mutual. My lips kissed her drenched forehead, and we laughed at how wet our entire bodies had become with the exertion. Even so, neither of us moved, wanting to stay in that moment of bliss for as long as the world would allow.

After what seemed like hours—that was most likely only minutes—she sat up and off of me, then stretched down to regain strength in her legs and practice standing. She wobbled for a bit, and I laughed as I reached out to catch her.

"Watch it there," I said with a chuckle. "You've had quite the workout."

"Best one of my life." She grinned, leaning forward to kiss me again. "It was amazing. And it was even more amazing because it was with you," she said, and then she plopped on the couch next to me.

I opened my arm to her, and despite how sweaty we both still were, we basked in the joy of the closeness, breathing hard to find regulation again. After some time, I smiled down at her and kissed her head.

"You really love me?" I asked.

"I do. I wasn't just saying that. And then saying it again, and again, and again," she giggled, nuzzling into my side. "I love you, Owen Michaels."

I smiled softly, closing my eyes and squeezing her into me. "I love you too, Penny Lewis."

# Epilog

*One year later*

PENNY

Listening to the rain pound on the roof, I walked out to the living room, checking to make sure I'd closed the windows and doors to avoid a leak. Then I slipped back to my bedroom and sat on the corner of my bed, breathing in excitement for the news I'd just discovered.

I looked out the window, remembering when a tree had blown through it, bursting through the wall like paper in the middle of the last big storm. It had been repaired around six months ago after the paperwork was through from the investigation with Lorenzo and the settlement with Tate Legal was complete.

The company had reimbursed me fully for all repairs for the window and storm damage, so I could put the donations received from the fundraiser concert toward building my music school, including doing alterations on the house to create a designated rehearsal and performance space out in the yard that could be utilized during bad weather. Grace had helped me design the structure and base, and she and Owen had taken it up as a passion project over the last few months. It still needed a few coats of paint, and we still needed to install the collapsible chair risers, but it was coming together nicely.

I was alerted to my tea in the kitchen by a whistling, so I rushed over and turned off the kettle, pouring from the spout into my prepared cup of chamomile tea. I had only taken two sips when the doorbell rang, and I was delighted at who I knew would be there waiting.

"Well, hello there, missy!" I said to Lilly as she waved when I opened the door. She had gone through a growth spurt this year and was now at about eye level with me. It wasn't saying much, but Owen seemed to hate it.

"Hi, Penny!" she said, running in to hug me as her backpack swung from side to side, and her lunchbox knocked me on the hip.

Owen strode in behind her, looking smart as always in a suit for work. "Good afternoon, love," he said, following Lilly in and kissing me as he entered. His hand slipped around my waist, and he pulled me in close, so when Lilly turned around, she playfully gagged.

"Gross, guys!" she said, hopping into the kitchen to grab an afterschool snack.

"Oh, stop being so dramatic," I said with a laugh, and I pecked Owen on the cheek one more time, then lingered in his ear. "I have something to show you when we have a chance," I whispered against him, and then I pulled back with a smile, so he would know it was good news.

"Okay," he said and nodded.

As we walked inside and the two of them got settled from a long day out, I went into the kitchen and yelled out, "Anyone want some tea? Water is still hot."

The two of them shouted at the same time, but luckily, the same flavor. "Citrus, please!" they both said, nearly in unison. We'd found a new citrus tea at the market a few weeks back, and both Owen and Lilly

280

couldn't get enough of it. It wasn't as much to my taste, but I enjoyed it now and again.

I grabbed two more cups and pulled down their favorite tea bags, placing one in each cup. Then I took what was left of the water and split it between them, which worked out well as Lilly drank from a smaller mug.

I walked back out to the living room with a cup in each hand and placed them on the table. Lilly was already on the couch, her nose thrust into her phone that Owen had gotten her a few months back. I thought it was a bad idea, but as she'd grown in her social confidence, so had her engagement calendar. Lilly having her own phone, even at ten years old, gave him the peace of mind that she was safe, and I couldn't blame him for that.

I stepped over to Owen, who sat at the desk I had set for him in the living room when he and Lilly moved in more full-time. It had been about three months since the move-in, and while it was a bit tighter with them both here, we had quickly found a rhythm of comfort with the close quarters. Since I owned the house and land, it also made for a lot of opportunities to expand and redesign the structure should we decide we needed more space. Lilly had taken my grandmother's old bedroom while Owen and I were in an updated version of my room, and we used Grace's old room as storage for the music school and for her to stay when she came through town. With how much demand she was in, that wasn't all that often anymore, so it was mostly for free space.

Owen's desk sat against the back window, letting the sun shine in along his face, making his eyes sparkle. I stood behind him and wrapped my arms around his shoulder, joining him in that sunlight and delighting in its warmth.

"You have a good day at the office?" I asked. Owen had started his own legal company a few months ago, and while it was still in its infancy, I could tell how happy he was to be working for himself for once.

"Oh, yeah. I just signed on the pro-bono case for the quarter, a single mother is trying to keep her house from being repossessed, and a few things are sitting with the bank keeping it in flux. It's a whole case; I don't need to go into it." He laughed.

"I like when you talk about things you're passionate about," I said. "Especially with your new pro-bono cases. I'm proud of you for them."

"Thank you, love," he said, then pulled my chin down for a kiss. "You wanted to chat, right?" I nodded in reply, and he turned to Lilly on the couch. "Lil, we're gonna go talk in our room for a bit, okay?" I asked. That sweet girl barely lifted her head, but she gave us the most award-winning grin without letting her eyes leave her phone screen.

Owen stood, and I took his hand to pull him into the bedroom with me. Once we were out of view from Lilly at the doorframe, I did a little yank. He stumbled with a chuckle as I caught him and wrapped my arms around his neck, meeting him in a kiss.

"We can't do much," he said, raising an eyebrow. "Lilly is still awake, and—"

"Not that," I said, deepening the kiss as I spoke against his mouth. "I just want to kiss you before I tell you this news."

"Okay," he said, and something in his voice sounded tentative. I didn't blame him, as I was being relatively quiet about where this was going, but only because I knew there was no way to give hints without dropping the entire bomb at once. It was a bomb we'd talked about on a few occasions but hadn't particularly planned for this early, but something told me he would be delighted.

And when I handed him the test with two little lines coming down the middle of the center, I knew I was right.

Owen's smile was brighter than I'd ever seen it, and he brought the test close to his eyes to see it clearly. Once he remembered I'd peed on it, though, he made a little grimace. I laughed at the action.

"You really are?" he asked, turning to me and setting the test on the bed next to us.

I nodded firmly. "I still need to get an official checkup test, but I'm late. And that's the second one I've taken," I said. "How … is this okay?"

Owen's face brightened, and he wrapped his arms around me, lifting me in a deep hug. I laughed as I held him tight, afraid to let go out of fear of falling.

"Owen, put me down!" I giggled.

"I'm just excited!" Owen said delightedly, kissing my cheeks over and over again. "Penny, this is amazing news. Yeah, it's a little sooner than we thought, but … I think we can do this. If you want this, then I want this," he said, and with how locked his eyes were on mine, I knew he was genuine.

"What are you excited about?" we heard out in the hall, and I looked up at him for reassurance.

Owen nodded, and we both smiled as I peeped my head into the doorway to wave Lilly inside as I sat on the edge of the bed. Owen sat next to me, and he pulled Lilly toward us, having her perch on the corner of his lap.

"We have some news that you might want to know, Lilly. Can we share it with you?" he asked, rubbing her shoulder lovingly.

She nodded quickly, already excited about having some kind of intel. "What's going on?" she asked, looking between us for a hint but coming up empty.

Owen looked at me and nodded, signaling me to say it. He was right; it was something I wanted to tell Lilly myself. Our relationship had blossomed, and though I constantly worried she thought I was taking over for her mother, I hoped she knew just how much I cared about her and wanted to be here for her.

"Well, Lilly," I started, putting a hand on hers where it rested in her lap. "We're still going to wait to hear from the doctor, but I think I could be pregnant. We might be having a baby." I offered a hopeful smile, unsure of how she'd take it.

In somewhere between surprise and expectation, she grinned wildly, elated at the idea. "You're pregnant?" she asked, then looked to Owen. "I'm gonna have a little sister or brother? Are you serious?" Lilly's voice grew higher with every exclamation, and both Owen and I laughed at her positive reaction.

"Yeah, we are," Owen said, hugging Lilly tight. "What do you think? Do you want to be a big sister?"

"More than anything ever!" she yelped, hopping off his lap. "When Riley from school got a baby sister, she got to take care of her all the time, and she puts her little sister in these cute little hats, and we're going to take so many selfies together, and we can—"

"Okay, Lilly," Owen said with a laugh, watching her spin around in her excitement for the new family member who would be joining us in just under a year. "It's going to be a while before the baby's born. Penny's got a long pregnancy ahead of her. Are you going to be able to help out?"

Lilly nodded furiously, then darted to me and hugged me tight, squeezing firmly until her eyes widened. Then she eased the hug and moved her head down to my stomach, where she gave it a sweet little smile. "I'm gonna be the best big sister ever." She gasped, raising a finger in the air. "I have to start practicing a song for when she's born!" she said, then darted out of the room, most likely to her piano in her bedroom.

"You have a while still, Lilly!" Owen hollered after her, then he chuckled and waved her off, returning his attention to me. "You okay?"

My soft smile radiated through my body, and I nodded, leaning my head on his shoulder. "Yeah. I'm perfect," I said, and I kissed his cheek.

# THE END

Made in the USA
Monee, IL
24 October 2022

16521079R00157